MOONSTONE SECRETS

Book II, Seattle Trilogy

A Contemporary Christian novel

DAWN V. CAHILL

"That if thou shalt confess with thy mouth the Lord Jesus,
and shalt believe in thine heart that God hath raised him
from the dead, thou shalt be saved. For with the heart man
believeth unto
righteousness; and with the mouth confession is made unto
salvation."
Romans 10:9-10, KJV

Moonstone Secrets
Copyright © 2017 Dawn V. Cahill

Cover design by: Dineen Miller
Edited by Brilliant Cut Editing
Formatting by Rik - Wild Seas Formatting

Published By Spring Mountain Publishing
Gladstone, OR.

ISBN 978-0-9974521-5-0

To my sons – My joy and my inspiration

You rock!

Other books by Dawn V. Cahill

SEATTLE TRILOGY

WHEN LYRIC MET LIMERICK - PREQUEL
SAPPHIRE SECRETS – BOOK I

GOLDEN STATE TRILOGY

PAINT THE STORM – BOOK I

Chapter One

Everyone knows killer whales don't eat people, DeeDee McCreary's boyfriend assured her.

"But have you ever wondered why?" Nick Rush leaned on the rail, his eyes as blue as the sea around them. The ferry, stinking of diesel, rumbled as it cruised across the Puget Sound orca habitat. The cool, fierce morning wind lifted DeeDee's hair and tickled it across her face.

She shrugged, a task made difficult by the two sweaters bunched under her black parka. "Not really."

Nick grinned. "It's because we're not tasty enough for them."

"Seriously?"

"Seriously." He closed his eyes. "Dun—dun, dun—dun—"

DeeDee laughed as he crooned the classic rock song "To The Last Whale".

Opening his eyes, he smiled and brushed the hair out of her face with gloved fingers. "That was kind of cheesy, wasn't it? Sorry. I blame the scenery. It's casting a spell on me." Beyond the railing, seawater rushed by. Behind them, the green Washington shoreline shrank with each passing mile. In the distance, Orcas Island rose out of the water like its namesake, the orca whale.

She snuggled closer. "I'm in the mood for cheesy songs."

Nick could jump on the rail and do cartwheels for all she cared. The prospect of meeting his Canadian family for the first time put her in a magnanimous mood.

He cupped her face and planted a long kiss on her, and she leaned in, not caring if the other passengers watched. An icy gust blasted her. He must have felt her shiver, because he eased away. "Are you cold?"

She nodded, her teeth clattering, and tightened her hood.

"Come on." He clasped her gloved hand. "Let's go to the café and get something warm to drink."

They climbed a metal staircase, their steps echoing, to the enclosed upper deck where tinny Christmas songs played over the sound system. The warmth enveloped her, soaking into her cold bones like the electric blanket on her bed. They chose prepackaged sandwiches from the cooler and hot cocoa from the dispenser and walked them to the cafeteria register. "Twelve twenty-nine," the smiling clerk singsonged, and Nick handed her his card.

As the ocean rolled by, DeeDee recalled her mood-dampening conversation with Grandma this morning. An unexpected tremor surged through her, prickling her skin under the snug parka. As though goose bumps sprouted on her arms but had nowhere to go.

Grandma's premonition about this trip must be getting to her.

She shifted to the frowning clerk, who was swiping Nick's card hard enough to snap it in two.

"Declined," she announced, a bit less friendly.

Nick's curse drew DeeDee's gaze to his glowering face. "No way."

As the prickles gave way to hot waves of alarm, she glanced over her shoulder. The woman behind her glared back and tapped her foot.

"Try it again," he instructed.

"I've already run it twice." The clerk's terse tone

matched her face. "It declined both times."

He uttered another oath. "I'll try my Visa."

The card blurred through the machine. "Declined."

"What the—"

DeeDee stepped up. "Here, let me get it."

Nick clenched his jaw. Sure, it hurt his pride for his girlfriend to buy his treat. But the hostile line behind them grew longer by the minute. She sensed, more than saw, eyes watching their every move, feet tapping in exasperation.

The card went through. They took their wares to a bench near the windows. Nick's face turned darker, more forbidding, as if storm clouds gathered inside him. He retrieved his tablet from his backpack.

DeeDee, a finger of dread squeezing her heart, paced as she sipped her cocoa, focused on the sea undulating in the ferry's wake while Nick searched his banking sites. She wrestled free from the parka and tossed it to the bench. She should have heeded Grandma's warning. "I have a bad feeling about your trip to Canada," she'd said. "Can't you put it off for a few days?"

But she'd shrugged it off.

Behind her, a sound like a wail burst from Nick's mouth. She whirled. His mouth hung open, his forehead a canvas of creases.

"My account's been hacked."

She gasped. "Oh, Nick. I can't believe it. What are you going to do?"

"Look at this."

She sat and fingered the gold heart around her neck, the one he'd given her for her twenty-eighth birthday. He angled the tablet toward her. "Someone wired money out of both my savings and my checking and left me with a grand total of seventeen cents." Swear words spewed from his mouth.

Her jaw dropped. "Can you tell where the wires came

from?"

"Royal Bank of Canada, Toronto."

"Do you know anyone in Toronto?"

He shook his head. "The RBC's headquarters is in Toronto. Someone got ahold of my routing number and did it all remotely. No need anymore to walk into a bank and rob it at gunpoint."

True, bank holdups did seem to be declining. No doubt, crooks preferred high-tech methods now.

"Sorry," she whispered. "I know this is upsetting for you." She simply didn't know what to say. How to comfort him. She knew women who groveled apologies to their men for every little infraction. But she'd never been one of them.

If only she'd listened to Grandma.

He didn't reply as he logged onto his credit card site. More bad news. "Surprise. My Visa's maxed out."

"Oh no!"

"Oh yes. Most of these purchases were made in Vancouver over the last week. Sheesh! The person spent five grand at Rockstar Guitar. That's a lot of guitars."

She swallowed hard, not trusting herself to speak.

"A thousand at Hudson's Bay. Another couple grand at Nordstrom. Several purchases from Amazon and eBay."

She leaned on his shoulder, peering at the screen, and then gasped. "Whoever it was bought something from Moonstone Truffles, Ltd."

"Oh, that was me."

"It was?" You'd think he wouldn't want to support his ex-wife's business.

"Yes, I ordered Christmas gifts."

"Oh." Better not go there. "Do you have fraud protection?"

She shrank away from the are-you-crazy look he leveled on her.

"Of course, I do. What do you take me for, an idiot?"

She wouldn't apologize this time. Instead, she dredged up the strength she knew was there. "Nick, come on. I'm not your enemy."

His shoulders sagged. "I know, babe. Sorry for the outburst. This is beyond baffling. I've never been careless with my personal information. Guess I should've checked my balances every day instead of assuming they were okay."

She bit back a groan. The ferry was still more than an hour from Friday Harbor, where they would transfer to a Victoria-bound vessel. How long before Nick could pay his way again? She hadn't planned to pay for both of them. Not that she was hard up for money. The dance school she and Livy owned was finally bringing in a decent income. But her generous, old-fashioned man had promised to pick up the tab for this trip.

"I hope we don't have to stay with my parents," Nick muttered.

DeeDee tried to comfort him with shoulder pats. "It's okay. I don't mind."

"I do." He scowled. His religious parents had prohibited them from sharing a bed while staying under their roof. So Nick had booked a hotel room.

She broached a suggestion she already knew the answer to. "I can pay for the room."

"No." His flat tone discouraged argument. "I have other family members who aren't so straitlaced. I'll make sure we stay together."

Even after nine months of dating, DeeDee hadn't yet seen Nick's dark side. Until now. His normally cheerful countenance remained shadowed and brooding. Tense, prickly silence wrapped around them like an old tweed jacket.

Pressure built at the base of her skull, radiating through her head. *Oh no. Not a migraine. Please, not now.* If only Livy were here. Her very presence would chase away the headache.

She peeked once at his screen. He'd logged onto his fraud protection site. She dug in her purse for her pain meds, the ache accumulating by the second. The minutes dragged. The island-studded sea no longer welcomed them on a joyful adventure. Instead, it stretched out forever, a stark, empty blue wasteland.

✤✤✤

Nick seethed, sucked in deep breaths. He couldn't let DeeDee see him so upset. He hadn't been this angry since his ex-wife's son "misplaced" his Fender bass—a euphemism for "stole."

But this…far more serious than a stolen instrument. When he got his hands on the culprit, that person was going to get hurt. His stomach soured, and ice chilled him from the inside out. The more he thought about it, the faster and harder his breath came.

What a way to start a much-anticipated vacation. As if the hacked bank account weren't bad enough, his ex-wife's e-mail from last week had run through his mind so many times, he could recite it aloud.

> Hello, Nick. You're probably wondering why I'd contact you after all these years. Well, I found out something interesting, something you will want to know about. But I warn you it could shake things up a little. Can we get together while you're here? Please?
>
> PS – In case you're wondering why I'd discuss this with you instead of my husband, let's just say it's not the sort of news he would want to know.

Uneasiness prickled his spine. What sort of news could Pam discuss with an ex-husband, but not with her current one?

This better not be related to that long-ago day when he'd made the worst decision of his life. He could almost hear Grandpa's booming voice echoing from beyond the grave—"Be sure your sins will find you out!" And Gracie's bitter accusations just before she walked out of his life pounded him until he wanted to wrest a pair of earbuds in his ears to drown out her outraged voice.

But maybe Pam was referring to something else. Baffled curiosity had coaxed him to agree at the time, but now he wasn't so sure.

He'd meet her on Monday, told her to text him to arrange a time and place. Now for the tricky part: figuring out how to tell DeeDee.

Chapter Two

Livy paused at the doorway of the upscale restaurant, admiring the distant play of jagged Olympic Mountains against orange sky. Even a lifelong Seattleite like herself never tired of it. Few scenes on earth could top a Seattle sunset for beauty and romance.

Scott grasped her elbow, steering her into the interior, dim except for the setting sun's apricot rays through the glass wall. "Bring back memories?" he murmured beside her, evoking recollections of their first date right here at Heathman By the Bay. Had it really been three months ago? Last night when he'd suggested a return trip, she'd cocked her head at him.

"Really?" she said. "What's the occasion?"

He only grinned. "The occasion is, I want to take my beautiful lady to a nice dinner."

What a dear man. She'd readily agreed, and here they were. She skimmed the empty tables, all dressed up for dinner in their flawless white tablecloths, poised and ready to serve equally well-dressed guests. "Looks like we're the first ones here. I guess most people aren't ready for dinner at four o'clock."

"I didn't want us to miss the sunset. Especially on such a clear day." A rare occurrence for a December day in rainy Seattle.

The maître d' led them to a table for two next to the floor-to-ceiling window, returning in minutes with a bottle of Veuve Cliquot champagne and two leather-bound menus.

Here, at the edge of this restaurant perched mere blocks up the hill from the water, Livy could almost be basking on an open-air deck. Particularly when sitting beside the invisible wall. She couldn't resist tapping the glass pane, just to make sure it was really there.

Pulling her gaze away from the Bremerton ferry glowing in the setting sun, Livy took a sip. "Champagne? What's up, honey? This smells like a celebration."

Scott merely smiled. "It's our three-month anniversary."

"That was so last week, silly."

His smile widened. "Okay, our three-month-and-one-week anniversary."

She cast him the smile she knew got to him. Sure enough, his eyes sparked, accompanied by an off-kilter grin, the one he used only on her. He looked especially handsome in his dark dress shirt, the same shade of green as twilight-shrouded Alki Point off in the distance.

She repeated the words she'd uttered on their first date. "You're such a romantic, Mr. Lorenzo."

He clasped her hands in both of his warm, large ones. His eyes, their green enhanced by the shirt's deep hue, caressed her face as his fingers sent tingles up her arm. "You bring out the romantic in me."

Behind her, a commotion ensued, and she turned. Ten feet away, two men and two women arranged Queen Anne chairs and music stands in a semicircle. A woman in a long red dress with spaghetti straps hauled a shiny cello, while a woman in blue clutched a golden-brown double bass. One tuxedoed man held a violin, the other a viola.

"Oh look, a string quartet. I don't think they were here last time. Were they?"

Scott's eyes gleamed. He shook his head. "Do you like classical strings?"

She nodded. "You know me. If it's music, I like it." Just

because she had Declan Decker for a father didn't mean she couldn't appreciate all sorts of music. Lucky for her and DeeDee, their rocker father had insisted on classical music training for them throughout their years at private school. "A string quartet. It suits this place, doesn't it?"

A waiter stopped at their table to take their orders, pulling her attention back to the menu. Eventually, she opted for herb-crusted Alaskan halibut, and Scott ordered crab cakes. The quartet warmed up as they waited for their food. The peaceful setting, combined with the splendid view, seeped in and quieted their voices to near whispers.

The red sky had darkened to burnt sienna by the time their dinners arrived. The waiter touched the miniature lamp on the table, and light pooled onto the triangulated napkins and bounced off the silverware. Soft strains from the string quartet serenaded them. And still, no other guests showed.

When the four musicians took a break, they passed by her and Scott. He nodded to them, sporting a broad grin as though they were long-lost friends. Five minutes later, berry cobbler a la mode arrived in sync with the musicians' return. The violinist gave Scott another nod.

She scrunched her face. "Do you know that guy?"

"What guy?"

"The one who nodded at you."

He shook his head, the corners of his mouth twitching. Something was going on. He'd better let her in on it soon, or she'd burst. She scooped a bite of ice-cream-soaked cobbler. "Mmm, this is delicious." But he didn't seem to hear. He was studying something behind her, and she whirled to see the violinist approaching. The other three musicians observed from their seats, amused smiles curving their faces as though they were in on a joke.

The violinist bowed, then broke into a familiar pop tune. One she'd heard umpteen times. Always in one particular context.

Which meant Scott was going to…

She swiveled to him, feeling her mouth drop open, but he merely grinned. Then he was fumbling in his pocket, and all the while, the violinist kept playing Bruno Mars's "Marry You." And Scott was holding something. A little box. And then he was kneeling at her feet and opening the box.

A sparkling diamond ring, studded with sapphires, proclaimed his message loud and clear.

Her jaw ached from gaping.

"Livy," he was saying. His intense green eyes latched to hers—eyes that never failed to thrill her. "I've loved you since the day you showed up at my door like a gift from God. And my love for you only grows stronger every day." He swept the ring under her disbelieving gaze. "Will you be my wife?"

Scott had planned all this…the empty restaurant, the romantic serenade. He'd really outdone himself. The violinist, all smiles, gave her an encouraging nod. "Say yes," he mouthed as he worked the bow over the strings.

Sheer joy bubbled out in laughter. "Yes, Scott!" She threw her arms around his neck. "Yes, I'll marry you!"

He pulled her to her feet and into a tight embrace, dropping happy kisses all over her face and hair and murmuring endearments.

The musicians stopped playing. Thick, waiting silence fell over the room. She wriggled out of Scott's arms long enough to see the quartet, the maître d', and the waiter all sporting identical sappy grins. The maître d' clapped. Then the others joined in applause.

"Congratulations!"

"Best wishes to the happy couple!"

Champagne flowed, and by the time they left the restaurant, Livy's cheeks hurt, as though they'd done a hundred pushups, from all the smiling.

Chapter Three

After all the negatives she'd faced, at least DeeDee aborted the headache threat before the ferry shuddered to a stop in Sidney, British Columbia. She'd downed medication and now lay in the car while they crept through customs.

"Feeling better?" Nick asked after the customs agent examined their passports, inquired of their destination, and then waved them through.

"Yeah." She eased the seat up. "My head stopped swimming."

"Good. Maybe this day can be salvaged after all." He'd filed a claim with his fraud protection service, reputed for its skill in recovering stolen funds.

DeeDee grasped onto the hope he held out. This weekend couldn't possibly get any worse.

"Welcome to the Island." Nick's smile hadn't quite returned when he drove his Alfa Romeo onto Canadian soil, but at least, he looked slightly less scary. "We'll need to keep our driving to a minimum so the gas in the tank will last us for the week."

"Aren't you glad now you bought your Christmas presents early?"

He nodded and kept his eyes on the road. His closed-off body language screamed he didn't want to discuss the theft. Too bad she couldn't find the words to give him hope, assure him this was merely a temporary setback.

But how long of a temporary setback? Days? Or months? The uncertainty scraped her nerves like an emery board on fingernails.

"Where are you taking us first?"

"My sister, Renee's. She texted me a little bit ago and invited us to dinner tonight. The whole clan will be there."

"Even your stepson?"

"No, not tonight. You'll get to meet Leon tomorrow."

Couldn't he try a little harder not to sound so terse? She tried to ignore the flutters in her stomach over meeting his entire family. They'd probably be scrutinizing her, judging her either worthy or unworthy of their beloved boy.

"Do you think Renee would let me see her figure-skating videos?"

"Probably so, although they're almost twenty years old. Last time she competed was during the Bush Administration."

"Does she still skate?"

"No, now she teaches kids." He glanced at her. "Like you. Something the two of you have in common."

"I'm looking forward to getting to know her better."

Stately homes lined well-tended streets. Except for its decidedly non-shabby look, it could easily pass for any seaside town in Washington. Nick swung the wheel left onto a busy boulevard. "You must be a bit nervous about meeting them, eh?" he said as if he'd seen into her heart.

DeeDee flinched at the smile he pasted on. His I'm-in-a-bad-mood-but-I'm-not-going-to-talk-about-it smile.

Fine. Whatever would get his mind off his troubles.

"To be honest, yeah. I am. A little."

He flicked a quick glance in the rearview mirror. "They'll love you."

"Are you sure? I'm not exactly the Goody Two Shoes your parents were hoping for."

The car in front slowed, and Nick braked, reaching over to squeeze her hand. "You're sweet and beautiful. What's not to love?"

The traffic started moving, and Nick proceeded forward. A warm surge welled up in her heart. Nobody but Nick would ever label her as sweet. If that wasn't true love…

A red light neared—the reason for the congestion. He braked again, and she ventured a question. "Are you going to tell them what happened?"

"Probably not." He shrugged. "What can they do about it, eh?" He pointed out the windshield. "Look. Up ahead is Victoria International Airport. And over there," he gestured to the left, "is the site of my first band's first gig ever."

DeeDee's gaze followed his pointing finger. The Quaking Aspen said the sign outside the nightclub. "Very cool. How old were you?"

"Fifteen. Too young to know what I was doing. They thought I was nineteen. I kept messing up. Lucky for me, I didn't get fired."

"And look at you now, twenty years later—a highly sought-out studio musician. A master on the bass guitar."

A smile, genuine this time, broke through the bleakness on his face. He flipped his signal and moved into the left lane. "Quaking Aspen is still one of my favorite hangouts. If not for my cleaned-out bank account, I'd take you there for drinks and dancing."

"We could still go. We don't have to spend a lot."

"Maybe. I might be able to sweet-talk the owner into giving us free drinks. Leon's father owns it. He and I go way back."

He swerved to avoid a speeding sports car that threatened to broadside them, then cursed. "Wow. I'd forgotten how crazy some of these drivers can get."

DeeDee's phone pulsed, and a text from Livy, filled with emoticons, flashed. *Scott gave me the most gorgeous engagement ring!!!* She'd attached a photo, and DeeDee gave a little whistle at the exquisite diamond surrounded by a starburst of tiny sapphires, and a sapphire-studded band.

Nick glanced at her. "What are you so excited about?"

"Scott proposed to Livy."

"Congratulations to them."

DeeDee narrowed her eyes on him. His flat tone hid what he was thinking. His impassive face looked straight ahead. Did he think she was trying to finagle a proposal? They'd been dating six months longer than Livy and Scott, yet he hadn't once mentioned marriage.

Come to think of it, a double wedding with her sister would be fun to plan. *If* she could finagle a proposal out of Nick. And *if* he got his money back. Until then, marriage would be off his radar. Not even a blip on the screen.

෴෴෴

DeeDee rocked from one foot to the other on the steps of a two-story stucco home, her purse strap suddenly too long, her hair blowing obnoxiously. Were her stretch boots and jeggings too casual for a meet-the-family dinner? Why hadn't she worn her conservative black skirt? She stilled when the door opened, and Nick's sister Renee greeted them with hugs, her dark blonde hair brushing DeeDee's cheek like silk. They'd met briefly last summer when Renee and her husband, Gavin, passed through Seattle. Renee's expressive blue eyes, so like Nick's, echoed the welcoming smile on her mouth.

"Come in, come in!" Chattering, she beckoned them into the living room, artfully cluttered with flashy metallic accessories—chrome table bowls, brass wall sculptures, bronze vases. Trophies proudly lined the mantle, and DeeDee promised herself a closer look later. As Renee led them to the home's east wing and spare room, DeeDee breathed deep the aroma of roasting meat, her stomach responding with a painful twinge. Lengthening her steps to keep up with Renee's brisk stride, she couldn't help admiring the other woman's lithe build so common among figure skaters and dancers.

She and Nick deposited their belongings in the creamy guest room, the luggage sinking into the plush comforter patterned in geometric grays and blacks as if it were attempting to stay gender-neutral. Then Nick left to find Gavin. DeeDee dropped onto the bed and wasted no time calling Livy. They shared a couple of excited squeals before DeeDee said, "So tell me everything!"

As Livy related the proposal story, DeeDee swallowed hard, fingers twisting up the striped pillow sham. Something was choking the excitement from her heart. She'd once been interested in Scott herself, but he'd never reciprocated. Instead, he'd focused his interest on her kinder, gentler twin, even though she and Livy looked exactly alike.

"He told me later he hired the string quartet to serenade me."

Unlike herself, Livy had landed a marriage-minded man. Nick claimed to love her but seemed completely unconcerned about their future. And marriage had been the furthest thing from her mind. Until Livy beat her to it.

"He reached in his pocket and took out a little velvet box…"

Even alone in the room, she forced herself to smile, hoping to chase away the ugly sensation gripping her spirit like talons. She hadn't felt jealous of her sister in years.

"And then, you know what he said?"

She sighed and offered the obligatory answer. "No, what?"

"He said he's loved me ever since the day I showed up on his doorstep like a gift from God. Isn't that romantic?"

"I think he was secretly in love with you even before

that. Anyway, go on."

Livy heaved a dreamy sigh. "Then he knelt down, opened the box, and asked me to be his wife."

"What did you say?"

"I just sat there stunned for a minute. The ring took my breath away. Then the violinist winked and nodded at me, and I threw my arms around Scott and said yes!"

The talons twisted her heart, robbing her of a reply. What was wrong with her, that she couldn't even be happy for her twin?

"I'm going to be Mrs. Olivia September McCreary Lorenzo!"

She forced out the words. "Congratulations, future Mrs. Lorenzo."

"What about you? When are you going to become Mrs. Diana Sapphire Rush?"

DeeDee grit her teeth. "After this morning, it doesn't look promising." And the story of Nick's hacked account poured out of her.

"What terrible timing. Someone must have been desperate for Christmas money."

"Nick canceled our hotel room. We're staying with his sister. Who, by the way, looks like his female counterpart."

"A female Sting?" They shared a laugh, both of them remembering how DeeDee charmed Nick with the first words she'd uttered to him, telling him he looked like the rocker.

After a quick knock, Nick poked his head in. "Everybody's here."

She motioned that she'd be right there. "Gotta go, Livs. Time to meet the family."

❧❧❧

Livy leaned against Scott while he led her around her

sunroom in the easiest dance ever, the Texas two-step. Or rather, he tried to.

"You're getting there."

Although she appreciated his encouragement, she wasn't fooled. This limp of hers was dashing her dream to dance with her husband at their wedding.

When he stopped and steadied her, tears stung her eyes. She blinked them away. "The lead isn't supposed to have to keep grabbing the follow to keep her upright."

"I don't mind. We could do a slow dance if you prefer." He pulled her to him and stroked her head. His breath whispered against her hair. "I'd hold you tight. Just like this."

No doubt, he would. She rested her head on his shoulder and breathed in his familiar scent, a comforting mixture of Axe aftershave and Fresh Linen detergent. "I'd love to slow-dance with you, babe. But I'm determined to dance the Cupid Shuffle at our wedding."

"Attagirl." He held out his arm, linking hers in the two-step frame. *Quick-quick, slow, slow...*

Once again, her knee buckled on the fourth count. "Argh! That was more like quick-quick, slow, ouch."

"We have time to practice. I'm betting you'll be back to normal by our wedding day. Don't you think?"

In her frame of mind, she didn't.

"What if I'm not?" she whispered against his shoulder.

After a short pause, his voice rang with assurance. "Between the two of us, we'll come up with something. We'll just pray real hard. Okay?"

Chapter Four

Nick had warned her he came from a family of devout churchgoers. But she still wasn't prepared for the pre-dinner prayer.

A reverent hush fell over the table when Nick's dad invited them to join him in thanking the Lord for the food. Even Nick closed his eyes while Mr. Rush droned out a prayer of gratitude to his God. She couldn't bring herself to close her eyes. What was the point? Nick's mom moved her mouth while her husband prayed, but DeeDee couldn't tell what she was saying. Renee's husband, Gavin Maxwell, stared at his plate, his face somber. When her gaze reached their teenage son, Gabe, she caught him watching her and squelched a sudden urge to giggle. Laughter during prayer would not go over well.

Good thing Nick hadn't caught the religious bug.

Brenda, Nick's mom, smiled across the table at DeeDee after her husband said amen. "Nick tells me you own a dance school in Seattle." She spoke with the same warm, lilting tones as her daughter.

DeeDee nodded as she savored the ham Renee had roasted. With Christmas just days away, the tall apple-cinnamon candle centered on the table inside a holly wreath provided a festive feel.

"My twin, Livy, and I named it Saffire School Of Dance. Most of our students are younger than thirteen."

Renee spooned mashed potatoes onto her plate. "What type of dance do you teach?"

"Pretty much everything."

Nick chuckled and pulled her tight against him. "The night I met her, she told me she taught everything but the Macarena."

That got a hearty laugh, but the tense lines in Nick's face betrayed his effort to behave like his usual suave self. He didn't want his family to know about his shambled finances.

The conversation lulled, and DeeDee braced herself. Any second now, someone was going to ask her about her father. Nick had told them her father was famed rock singer Declan Decker, but warned them not to quiz her, especially Gavin, who'd been a FireAnts fan many years ago. But Nick, as if he'd read her mind, steered the conversation to his upcoming gigs. Like a crackling fire and a fuzzy robe, his effort to stick with safe topics warmed her.

Until she noticed Gavin's dark eyes studying her, as though he were searching for Declan Decker in her face. She wrested her gaze away to discourage him from asking questions. Especially questions about Dad's song "Double Trouble". She'd scream if anyone asked her ever again if she and Livy were the inspiration for his '90s-era hit song. How could they be? The song was about a narcissistic lover.

When the meal ended, she let herself relax. No one had put her on the spot. Renee and Gavin cleared away the dishes, and Nick excused himself, explaining that his dad wanted a chat. From the look on his face, he dreaded it. "I think I know what he wants to talk about."

"What?"

He arced his finger between them. "You and me."

She widened her eyes and squeezed his leg. "Is that good or bad?"

He placed his hand over hers and squeezed back. "I'll let you know."

She followed the others into the kitchen. Brenda and

Renee stood busy at the sink, while Gavin and Gabe put away the leftovers.

She laid a hand on Renee's arm. "That was a delicious meal. Thank you so much."

Renee responded with a wet-handed hug. "We loved having you."

"I loved seeing you again. But now I need to use your bathroom. Can you direct me?"

"Sure." Renee pointed down the hall. "Take a left, then a right."

She strode along the hall, searching for the correct door in the dimly-lit passage. When voices rumbled behind a partially opened door to her left, she stopped.

"...make an honest woman out of her," Mr. Rush was saying.

Her breath caught, and a finger of guilt for eavesdropping needled her. But she stayed rooted in place.

"That's such a passé concept." Nick's steady tone sounded forced, laced with barely-veiled irritation.

"Passé or not, it's the decent thing to do. I assume she wants children someday?"

Something rustled, and Nick's heavy huff weighed on her from where she stood. "Are we through?" he said in a surprisingly calm, light tone.

She fled to the bathroom and enclosed herself in it. She'd never given much thought to children. She got enough exposure through teaching dance. But suddenly, the question became important. What if baby hunger hit her unexpectedly, as some of her friends had experienced? She might marry Nick only to find out he was adamantly opposed to child rearing. But why, after all these years, did it even matter?

When Nick returned to the living room, she searched his face. He sat next to her and took her hand.

"What did he want to talk about?"

Standing, he pulled her to her feet. "Come on, grab your coat. Let's take a walk." Once she'd bundled up, he led her out the door and around back to a landscaped yard crisscrossed with gravel paths lit by tall electric lanterns. Clouds turned the full moon into a hazy white beacon.

Nick lowered his head as he always did when deep in thought. "Dad doesn't approve of us sharing a bed. He was just reminding me of it. In the end, I told him he's entitled to his opinion."

Not a mention of the M-word. Or the C-word, either. She sought his gaze, but his eyes, barely visible in the lamplight, hid in the shadows casting sharp angles over his features, turning him into a caricature.

"That was all?"

He shrugged. "Pretty much."

She drooped, annoyed by his lack of forthrightness. He hadn't exactly lied, just omitted details he didn't want to discuss.

The gravel crunched under their feet as they wandered along the paths, puffs of misty breath leading the way. After they returned to the house, he asked Renee to put on the DVD of her final skating performance, then steered DeeDee to the black vinyl sofa. "You'll love this, sweetheart." He tucked her under his arm, his breath warming her cold ear. "She and her partner, Joaquin, won the Canadian Amateur Ice Dance competition."

DeeDee raised her brows. "I'm impressed."

Renee flashed her a quick smile, as if she were afraid to appear overly proud. "Sometimes I miss performing." The half-smile flickered as she worked the remote. "But it was time to stop. My body was starting to protest in too many ways."

Renee curled up against her husband on the sofa while

the family watched her flawless performance. Brenda edged forward, her mouth slightly ajar. "I still cringe every time I watch him lift her, then drop her onto one foot, even though I know she will land it perfectly."

Gavin nodded. "I like the way he wraps her around his waist like she's a rag doll." He looked at his wife as though he'd like to do the same.

DeeDee grinned. If she and Nick had a future, she hoped that, after so many years together, he'd still look at her the way Gavin looked at Renee.

As Renee jumped and twirled all over the ice, DeeDee ignored the growing ache in her head that supplanted the ache in her heart. She marveled over Renee's ability to glide on one leg with her free leg in attitude for such long stretches. Every other type of dance required both legs.

When the teenage image of Renee and her lanky partner took their bows, she applauded. "Very nice job."

She and Renee talked dance moves and choreography until Gavin, gazing at his wife, interjected, "We met at an ice rink, in fact. I'd go early just to watch her skate. Did that for two months before I got up the nerve to introduce myself."

Renee's eyes softened as she returned his look. "Yes, Gavin plays hockey. Gabe, too."

"I'm not a pro, but I love a good match with my pals."

Nick's dad punched the air. "Speaking of hockey, how about those Canucks?"

DeeDee tuned out the animated male voices discussing a sport she had no interest in and focused on the TV, where the third-place couple glided to the ice. The ballroom influence pervaded the choreography, yet on ice, it translated to a different sort of beauty, a fast and fluid river of motion racing over rocks and bubbling with exuberant energy.

When the headache peaked, she excused herself, ignoring the worried looks, then hurried to the bedroom and plopped face up on the bed.

◈◈◈

With encouragement from Nick, DeeDee laid her head in his lap as he massaged it until the pain meds kicked in.

"It's just stress," she told him as his fingers probed firm circles on her scalp. "What a terrible day. Mmm, that feels good." She moved his hands to her temples.

Nick worked his fingers around her ears. "You're the lucky recipient of my years of experience. Pam used to get migraines fairly regularly. I got pretty good at knowing where to rub."

DeeDee stiffened at the rare mention of Pam. Nick's hands slowed, as though he just realized he'd spoken aloud.

A hard, tense moment pulsed between them, in sync with her throbbing head.

"Sorry, I didn't mean to bring up my ex."

"No worries." Best not to let it ruin the moment. "Speaking of which," she sighed the pain out, "will you take me to her chocolate shop tomorrow?"

"We'll see," he said in his usual abrupt, all-business tone whenever she quizzed him about Pam.

Visions of glossy smooth nuggets made DeeDee's mouth water. "I'm dying to try the White Russian truffle. The website describes it as 'Genuine Kahlua merges with rich Belgian chocolate. A little bite of heaven.'"

Nick's hands sped up. "Well..." He cleared his throat. "I may have to give you a rain check."

"You don't have to see your ex. I just want a taste of luxury."

"She doesn't spend much time there anyway. She pays her assistant well to run the place and just rakes in the profits."

"What a nice life." DeeDee tilted her head toward his.

"I have to hand it to you. Unlike some men I've dated, you rarely talk about your former marriage. Sometimes I can't help wondering why."

"What's to tell? We married. She cheated on me. We divorced."

"She cheated on you? I didn't know that."

"She cheated on both of her husbands." A bitter edge bit through his tone. "And on her current one, too."

Ha. A tramp. "Does he know? Um, wait a minute…How would *you* know?"

As she lifted her gaze to Nick's face, he clamped his mouth tight. "Never mind. I've said too much. It's all in the past, dead and buried."

Then why are you still talking about it? The question hovered on her lips.

"But at least I was always faithful to her."

She screwed up her courage and forced out the question. "Since we're on the subject of your exes," she sighed at the release of pain dissipating through Nick's skillful, methodical fingers, "can you tell me what happened between you and Gracie?" She braced herself, wishing she could ask if Gracie had cheated, too.

A ten-second pause. Then he pulled his hands away. "She was a rebound relationship. She helped me through my divorce. That's pretty much it."

"The day you and I met, Dad said you'd just ended a long-term engagement."

"Not an engagement. A relationship that served its purpose. We both knew when it was time to move on."

He gave a tiny, almost unnoticeable glance at the closed door. Was he hoping for an escape route?

Then he exhaled, his smile light, airy. "Feeling better now?"

"Yes, thanks to your strategic fingers."

"Maybe we should wait to visit Leon. He can be a real headache." False heartiness rang in his tone. His I'm-changing-the-subject-now voice.

She chuckled. "No, I want to meet him. He can't be all that bad if you raised him."

Chapter Five

"Believe it or not, Leon is only four years younger than you," Nick told her as he drove into his stepson's driveway.

"Pam must have been real young when he was born."

"Not that young. Twenty or so."

She did the math, so Pam had been six years older than Nick. Something else about his former marriage she hadn't known.

Did he prefer older women?

They strolled hand-in-hand to the shabby ranch's wood porch. "Careful." Nick grasped her hand tighter. "The steps are wet." He knocked on a door marred by deep scratches, as though it had been out in the elements too long. Like the house itself, its old white paint job now more of a faded gray, its lawn sporting more weeds than grass.

The door burst open, and Leon thrust out a hand to DeeDee even before Nick made introductions. "You the girlfriend? Glad to meet you. I'm Leon." His rapid-fire speech slurred his words as his inky black eyes danced. Clearly Pam's son, his Aleutian heritage showed in his black hair, partially covered by a striped beanie. Lifting an energy drink to his mouth, he took two quick swigs like a hyperactive mime.

Somewhere in the house, dogs barked. A high yip and a low ruff echoed in a syncopated rhythm. The men exchanged backslapping hugs, and Leon led them into a living room containing only a black vinyl couch and a big-screen TV showing a soccer game. Piles of mail and video game components littered the carpet.

Nick glanced around as if looking for something. "No Christmas tree this year?"

Leon shook his head. "Not yet. We're going tree-hunting soon."

"Who's we?"

"Me and Jazzy."

"Jazzy?"

"Yeah. Which reminds me. Got big news."

Nick's eyes widened. "Good or bad?"

"Judge for yourself. You're lookin' at a newly-married man."

His jaw dropped. "Serious? You and Jazzy…?"

Uncontrollable grin. "Yep."

Nick visibly jolted. "When?"

DeeDee wanted to bop Nick on his oblong head. They were talking as though she wasn't even there. Who on earth was Jazzy?

As if in answer, a pajama-clad young woman wandered in from the hallway, yawning and rubbing her eyes. Nick swung his gaze to her, recognition flashing in his eyes.

"Hey, Jazzy. Good to see you."

The petite young woman squinted, then focused bleary eyes on him. "Hi, Nick." She yawned again and swept golden-brown hair off her face, then pinned DeeDee with a look. "You must be Nick's girlfriend." She stuck out her hand. "I'm Jasmine."

"Hi, I'm DeeDee." She shook the thin, cool hand. "You must be the new wife."

Jazzy grinned, showing flawless teeth. "Mm hmm. We got married last week."

"I get the feeling it was a big surprise to everyone."

A smile lit up her eyes. "Kinda spur of the moment."

Leon picked up a remote and switched off the TV.

"Wanna go get some coffee?"

Jasmine pointed to herself. "Like this, you jokester? Now that we're married, you're gonna start dragging me out in my PJs?"

Leon crinkled his face. "Uh, I was talking to Nick."

She made a face back, then grabbed a black leather biker jacket from a coat rack near the door, shooting an accusing look at Nick as though he planned to pilfer it. "Welcome home, Nick, you stud. Now, let me go get decent."

She scurried back the way she came. Leon stared after her, shaking his head, then repeated his offer.

Nick's jaw tightened, and his eyes turned weary. "I'll pass this time."

"Never known you to turn down coffee." Leon rapped the remote against the Red Bull can. The metallic beats shuddered over her spine until DeeDee wanted to grind her teeth. "C'mon, I'll buy. It's just coffee." He eyed DeeDee with a glint as if confident he could win her over. Then he dredged a key ring out of his pocket, sending a square of folded paper to the floor. Oblivious, he chattered on. "Let me buy you a double-double. Ever tried Latte Choco-Latte?"

Jazzy teetered back in on high heels, her hair brushed, her thin body clad in a shiny leather jacket-and-pants combo, which must have cost several hundred dollars.

"Jazzy, I love your outfit." DeeDee scanned the sparsely-furnished space, unsure how the woman could afford such an outfit, compared to their home's modest contents. "It looks like a Rebecca Taylor."

Jazzy swept her hair away from her face, revealing a missing button on the jacket cuff. Ah ha. It must have been drastically reduced. Made sense now.

"Oh, it's not mine. I'm borrowing it."

Yes, indeed, she'd misjudged the young woman. "I almost bought one myself at Nordstrom just last week." But she'd opted for a red Michael Kors.

Leon opened the front door, gesturing them outside. Nick stayed where he was. "I'll meet you outside. Just need to use your bathroom."

Leon nodded to Jazzy and DeeDee. "After you, ladies."

They emerged into the chilly morning. Leon squatted before Nick's Alfa Romeo and whistled. "He got a new ride. Sweet!"

Nick materialized beside them, rattling keys. "How about I drive?"

"Sweet!" Leon repeated. "How much did that baby cost you?"

Nick shot him an irritated look. "More than it should have."

DeeDee piled into the front seat. Leon and Jazzy clambered in back. Nick glanced behind him as he pulled into traffic. "How's the job at Moonstone going?"

"Same ol', same ol," he drawled like a lazy teenager. "I'm still Leon the Peon."

"Your mom isn't letting you climb the ladder?"

"When I pass Chocolate Making 101." A half-snort. "Kidding. She says I have to prove myself first."

"You'll get there. How's your dad?"

"Same-oh, same-oh. He just bought himself a new fishing boat. A 2004 Glastron."

Light rain spattered on the windshield. Obviously, these three shared a history she knew nothing about. She gazed out the window for a glimpse of the ocean. Until she heard her name.

"You gonna marry this loser someday?"

She whirled to see Leon grinning at her. *What a rude thing to say.* "I don't know," she snapped.

Leon's grin wavered. "Hey, just giving old stepdad here a hard time."

She allowed herself a small chuckle, but Nick glowered. She couldn't decide if she liked Leon, or if his high-octane energy got on her nerves. Maybe a little of both.

He and Jazzy Jasmine belonged together.

At the coffee shop, so many people came up to greet Nick that she gathered he was somewhat of a local celebrity. Having played with so many well-known bands, he was their hometown hero. He introduced her to each and every one, not once mentioning her father.

Jazzy, to her right, grinned at her. "You didn't know you had such a popular boyfriend, did you?"

DeeDee smiled back at the younger woman, feeling as though Jazzy had vicariously paid her a compliment. "I've always known he was special."

"Special. That's our Nick." She flipped her hair over her shoulder. "My rock-star-wannabe husband has always looked up to Nick. He'd *be* Nick if he could."

"Is Leon in a band?"

Jazzy snorted. "He is, but it isn't doing well. If he could master the guitar, he could go far. But…" She rolled her eyes and put her mouth close to DeeDee's ear. "Don't tell him I said this. I don't think he's naturally musically inclined."

"Ah."

Jazzy's gaze lingered on DeeDee's face. "Your makeup looks nice. Very professional. Who does your face?"

"Oh, thank you. I do my own."

"Really? You're good. Have you ever thought about cosmetology as a career?"

"No way. I have no desire to get up close and personal with other people's pores."

Jazzy grinned. "It's not so bad. I just finished cosmetology school. Hoping to set up my own practice soon."

DeeDee eyed the young woman's cosmetic-free face.

For the handful of makeup artists she knew, their own faces served as their favorite canvases. Maybe Jazzy just hadn't wanted to take the time this morning. "I'd like to see what you can do. Do you have photos? A portfolio?"

"Sure. I'd love to show you. Facebook friend me, and you can see everything I've done."

The afternoon passed in a pleasant buzz. By the time they headed home, a chilly downpour mixed with ice pellets pummeled the road. En route to Leon's house, the car skidded on a slick patch. Nick wrestled to straighten the steering wheel, but the right fender scraped someone's mailbox anyway.

Jazzy screamed. The car lurched to a halt, sending DeeDee's head to bounce off the window.

"Mmpph!" Her teeth chomped down hard on her tongue. Nick bounded out of the car to inspect the damage, but his feet slipped out from under him. When he landed on the pavement, the string of curses from his mouth matched DeeDee's in intensity.

As Leon groaned, she opened her door and edged onto the gravel shoulder, surges of pain shooting through her head and tongue. Her sturdy leather boots gripped the pavement, but frozen rain blew sideways and lashed her cheek. Gritting her teeth, she shuffled around the car to Nick's side. Grimacing, he grabbed her outstretched hand. She clung to the side mirror as he hoisted himself to his feet. "Are you all right, my love?"

He put weight on his left foot. "Ow!"

DeeDee gasped. "How bad is it?"

"Hurts pretty bad." His face twisted. "Murphy's Law strikes again."

Through the open door, Leon sounded a false note of cheer. "When it rains, it pours."

And she sharpened her tone. "We don't need a cliché

fest right now. Let's get you to an emergency room."

☙☙☙

At the hospital, X-rays showed a sprain in Nick's ankle, and the doctor wrapped it and encouraged him to stay off his feet for a few days. DeeDee swallowed Tylenol and lingered in the waiting room with a bag of ice on her head. As long as she didn't move, the pain stayed away.

Leon drove them back to the Maxwells'. Then Gavin drove Leon and Jazzy home. Nick said very little until they both plopped their weary, hurting bodies onto the bed.

"I'm starting to wonder if it was a mistake to come here." He stared at the ceiling, his mouth in a hard slit. "As soon as we stepped onto the ferry, it's been one bad thing after another."

"Are you saying you want to cut our trip short and head home?"

"Maybe we should since this trip seems to be cursed."

DeeDee didn't dare reply, unsure how to respond to this unfamiliar stranger who had taken over her boyfriend's body, mind, and soul. But when he reached for her and pulled her head into his chest, murmuring an apology, the steadfast thump of his heart, the familiar musky scent of him, reassured her he was still the man she fell in love with.

"Thank God, I have you." His whisper tickled her cheek.

Wow. Nick Rush, the epitome of cool, needed her. If only she could stretch out this rare but priceless moment for the rest of the trip. Or rather, for the rest of her life.

☙☙☙

DeeDee paced in the guest room, her fingers rubbing the gold heart around her neck as if they could absorb Nick's love through osmosis. Her steps grew more agitated. He'd been out in his car way too long. He must be freezing. He'd told her he needed to make a phone call and to wait for him inside. Who was he talking to, anyway? Should she go out there and urge him in?

She peeked through the drapes again, her gaze on the car hunkered in the driveway. Hoping to see better, she turned off the light, then cracked open the window. Icy air surged in. The thud of a slamming car door reverberated through the screen. Nick limped up the walk, a crutch under one arm, his phone to his ear.

She ducked down.

"Only one way to know. If the stuff's there, I'll text you the photos." He paused, and she ventured a peek. He leaned against a front-porch pillar. "You will? Okay, e-mail me the directions, and I'll see you there."

See who where? And when? But Nick was entering the house, so she scurried to close the window and flip the lights back on. By the time he entered the room, she'd settled cross-legged on the bed, engrossed in her tablet.

She cast him her best nonchalant smile. "Who were you talking to?"

He shrugged, avoiding her gaze. "An old friend."

"Oh." She gave the screen a casual swipe, not really seeing it. Nick sat on the bed's edge, hoisted his right leg to his knee, and removed his single shoe.

She squeezed his knee, needing to draw him out. "You probably feel like staying home tomorrow, right?"

She watched him closely as he fumbled to reply. "Not really. I've got a few ideas."

"Like what?" She injected a dose of enthusiasm into her tone.

He dug his hand into his pocket. "Well, obviously it's got to be free." His head drooped as the keys in his hand clanked out a nervous rhythm. "Don't worry. We'll think of something."

Chapter Six

After a fitful night's sleep, DeeDee came awake slowly. She vaguely remembered Nick getting up a couple of times during the night, doing who knew what. But she'd fallen back into a restless sleep before getting a chance to ask what he was up to.

The bedside clock blinked at her—8:53. She reached for Nick, but her hand fell onto the empty mattress.

Where was he? Surely not off on his clandestine rendezvous already.

She stared at the Nick-shaped indentation on the sheet, the throbbing knot above her right temple reawakening memories of last night's accident. The tender spot on her tongue pulsed.

She gasped out a breath. Today was going to be a Tylenol-and-ice-pack day. She groped for the painkillers on the table, her water bottle beside them, and managed to down two capsules. After she donned her robe, she went to look for Nick. Since it was Monday morning, Gavin had already left for work and Gabe for school.

The pungent aroma of brewing coffee pulled her toward the kitchen. Renee sat at the table sipping coffee and perusing her tablet.

She looked up quickly when DeeDee walked in and just as quickly slid her gaze away. "Good morning." She half-stood, her eyes on her tablet, then sat back down. "Want some coffee?"

Why was she acting so strange? At DeeDee's agreement,

Renee got to her feet again and retrieved a coffee mug then filled it with steaming brew fresh from the pot.

"Cream? Sugar?"

"Black." DeeDee held the cup and took a minuscule sip, tilting her head to the side to keep the coffee away from the sore spot on her tongue. "Mmm, this is good. Thank you. Where's Nick?"

Renee's gaze spun toward the front door. "He left."

"Left when?"

"He wanted me to give you his apologies and tell you there was something he needed to do, and he'd be back tonight." Renee finally looked at her with those compassionate blue eyes. "He told me to keep you company today and not to worry about him."

DeeDee tightened her grip on the mug. "How long ago was that?"

"About half an hour."

She sat across from Renee. "I wonder what was so urgent. He can hardly walk."

Renee shook her head. "I gave him a piece of my mind for taking off and leaving you, so he said he'd text or call you."

"The doctor told him to stay off his feet." A knot formed in her chest. Why wouldn't Nick just be honest? "Did he give you any clue as to what he was doing?"

"Not a one."

"Did he seem upset?"

"Not really. Just seemed to be in a hurry." Her wide blue eyes prodded DeeDee. "Are the two of you doing okay?"

"Oh sure, we're fine," she hastened to say. "But it's not like him to be all mysterious."

"He said he just didn't want us making a big deal out of it."

DeeDee bristled at the veiled rebuke. She was anything

but a drama queen. "Well, if he's being secretive, I can't help but worry. I assume he took his car?"

"He did, despite my protests. He reminded me his right foot works just fine."

"What was he wearing?"

"Warm jacket, gloves, hiking boots."

"Hiking boots? Even with his ankle bound up?"

Renee nodded. "They're the low-cut kind."

"I can't imagine him being able to hike anywhere. This is getting stranger and stranger." DeeDee stood. "I'm going to check my phone. Maybe he already texted me." She spun toward the guest room.

But he hadn't texted her. Her hands trembled as she composed a message. *Hey, my love, Renee said you left. What are you up to today? Or is it a surprise??*

She hoped she'd struck the right casual, lighthearted tone. She gripped the phone and paced for a moment, her face stiff as she peered out the window at the dry, gray morning. How unusual for Nick to take off without telling her his plans.

She glanced again at the phone's empty screen. Then she swiveled toward the bathroom to shower and get ready for a girls' day out.

སྲིསྲིསྲི

The sign for the Chemainus city limits neared, and Nick slowed the rented U-Haul to the lower speed limit. West, near Mt. Sicker, hovered a heavy layer of cloud cover. His destination lay at the base of the shrouded peak. He needed to arrive before his scoundrel of a stepson beat him to it.

He'd bet his townhouse those illicit credit card purchases were hidden away in Pam's late grandfather's empty house. Yet Leon had been as casual as ever yesterday. Hadn't flinched when he'd opened the door and seen Nick standing there. All surprised innocence. What an actor. The guy ought to be ashamed of himself. Thankfully, Pam had agreed to make the roughly hour-long drive north to meet him so he could check out his suspicions, show her the evidence, and hear her earthshaking news.

But what if she tried...no, he wouldn't let himself make the same mistake with her again. He vowed he'd never do to DeeDee what he'd done to Gracie. Would he ever rid himself of the guilt from that day?

Speaking of guilt and DeeDee...Renee had looked properly horrified when he announced his departure this morning, as well she should. He hadn't thought this through enough, hadn't considered how DeeDee would feel, and now it was too late. He needed to send his ladylove an apologetic text and hope she'd forgive him tonight. Especially if he could impress her with a mission accomplished. She'd understand...Wouldn't she?

In the wee morning hours, while DeeDee slept, he'd slipped his tablet onto his lap and checked his e-mail for the third time, hoping for an update from his fraud-protection service. Instead, a bold message from DomaineMusic informed him a royalty check had been auto-deposited into his account. His jaw dropped, and the tight knot lodged in his stomach since yesterday loosened. He hadn't expected that one until next week. He wouldn't have to beg Renee for a loan after all. Lucky for him, he was still pulling in royalties from all the bands he'd recorded with. If not for this morning's two-grand payment, he wouldn't have a way to make this excursion.

His mother would call it God's Providence. But Mom worshiped a loving God...so different from Grandpa's conscience-hammering God. No wonder he'd been so confused growing up. Which God was the true one?

He had to admit today's payment was a little too

convenient. But God wouldn't care about a black sheep like Nick Rush. He'd chosen years ago that if he had to give up music to please his parents' God, then he'd take music. Today, he served the god of music.

His phone buzzed so he took it from his jacket pocket. It finally showed all five bars. And a text DeeDee sent two hours ago. She'd sent a second, more urgent-toned one about forty-five minutes ago.

He read them and frowned. She must be frantic.

Hi, love, he replied. *Sorry. Something urgent came up. Will tell you all about it tonight. Should be home by ten. Enjoy your day. Love you.*

Next, he messaged Pam. *On my way. See you soon?*

And it wouldn't hurt to send a request to the heavens, just in case his mother's God happened to be listening.

Gazing upward at the industrial-gray sky, he prayed a prayer he'd been taught as a child. *God, I don't deserve Your favor. But please, keep me safe and guide my steps.*

కొకొకొ

In the Maxwells' guest room, DeeDee scanned Nick's belongings to determine what he might have taken with him. The corner where he'd set his backpack was empty. And his tablet was gone.

He'd been so evasive last night. Out of character. She allowed herself a moment to contemplate a dreaded possibility: that he'd left to meet up with another woman.

Scoffing, she rejected the idea. Nick had never given her reason to doubt his fidelity. Glancing into the open closet, she nudged her booted toe against his clothes from yesterday, strewn in a heap on the floor. Hoping to find a clue, she knelt and rummaged through his pockets and shook out a few loose coins—Canadian loonies and American quarters and nickels. Some American dollar bills. A confirmation receipt from BC Ferries. She held it closer, puzzling over the date—last Wednesday, two days before she and Nick left Seattle. She looked at the ceiling. Nick hadn't been anywhere near British Columbia on Wednesday, much less a ferry. He'd been with her most of the day. So where had this came from?

Perhaps the other pockets held more clues. Setting the paper down, she dug around again. Nothing. Hands pushing against her knees, she straightened. His robe draped crookedly over a chair. Something stuck out of the pocket. She reached in, removed a folded paper. Almost reluctant to see the inside, she opened a printout from Google maps. A road called Black Bear Lane snaked the length of the paper, while a crooked line branching off to the left led to a handwritten square labeled HERE in block letters. She tilted her head. A series of digits, starting with forty-eight, was written at the junction of the two lines, in Nick's angular hand.

So this is what he'd been up to last night. But what did the numbers mean?

She retrieved her tablet and searched Google maps for Black Bear Lane. Colorado had about five Black Bear Lanes. But so did British Columbia.

She sighed. She had no way to know which Black Bear Lane Nick was headed to.

She picked up the receipt and the map and took them to Renee, who raised bewildered eyes. "I have no idea where Nick was going. Or why he would have a BC Ferry receipt from last week."

"I know this sounds farfetched, but did he by chance borrow any money?"

"Nick borrow money? He's been known to loan us money, but never vice-versa."

"I—" DeeDee stopped herself from giving anything

else away.

Renee placed her hand on DeeDee's arm, her eyes soft. "Why don't we go sightseeing? It'll get your mind off things. Nick's a big boy. I'm sure he'll be home tonight as he said."

Chapter Seven

By the time Nick reached Chemainus proper, his eyes drooped and his stomach protested. He found a side street and parallel-parked the nine-foot cargo van, a trickier feat than parking his aerodynamic little Alfa Romeo. His mouth watered in anticipation as he strode toward hippie-friendly Willow Street and Willow Leaf Café, which served the best Belgian waffles west of the Rockies.

Visualizing a thick slab topped with dense burgundy compote and an abundant pile of cardamom whipped cream, he quickened his pace, since he had twenty minutes until the café closed at one.

Even though he wasn't well known here, still he pulled his Seattle Mariners baseball cap lower over his eyes. He aimed to stroll casually inside without limping and hoped no one got a clear look at his face, then get on with the plan before anyone at home figured out what he was up to.

He found a table next to the windows looking out on colorful Willow Street, then ordered coffee and the heavenly waffles from a twig of a waitress named Mary. She returned with his hot brew and eyed his backpack. "It's not exactly a good time of year to go hiking. Are you here for sightseeing?"

He nodded and picked up the steaming cup, making it clear he wasn't here for chitchat.

She got the message and retreated, and he took out his tablet and checked his e-mail. AntiFraud, Inc. had responded to his claim. The quick response, combined with the coffee, lifted his spirits. The company promised they would trace the wire's origin and inform his bank of the fraudulent transaction. They assured him they would make every reasonable effort to identify the perpetrator or perpetrators.

He pondered on his conversation this morning. Over coffee at Starbucks, he'd placed a call to Rockstar Guitar. A few leading questions…dropped hints…and he got the answers he needed.

"Hi," he'd said when a chirpy young male voice answered. "I made a purchase last Wednesday and want to return one of the items."

"Sure. Just bring it in with the receipt."

"Well, that's the problem. I can't find the receipt. But I do have the transaction number and the date of purchase. Would that help?"

A long hesitation. "Our policy is to allow returns only with a receipt."

"You don't have an invoice for transaction number 47583?" He peered at his credit card statement on the screen. "It came to five thousand forty-three dollars, and it was shipped to…uh…" Acting on his hunch, he finished, "Chemainus, BC."

Clacking keys on the other end, a couple of "hmms" later, then, "I found it." The young man's voice came out substantially less chirpy. "A Korg piano, an amp, and a synthesizer."

The pieces were clinking into place. "Correct," Nick managed and swallowed. "I'll find the receipt."

"Can I help you with anything else?"

"No. No, thank you."

"Have a good day."

Nick hung up, shaken to the core. But even more determined to nail the perp.

⁊⁊⁊

Renee backed the car to the street. "Have you ever visited our city?"

"A few times." DeeDee nodded. "But not for about ten years."

The cloudy daylight lent Renee's thin hair a sheen like soft mink. "I want to show you the castle, then we can go hang out at the Empress Hotel. I promise you an unforgettable experience."

Renee lived on a crescent-shaped street that sloped down to a busy boulevard. Many of the homes they passed had curved, wrought-iron balconies on the upper-story windows and tidy yards with well-kept exteriors.

"Before you head back home," Renee said, "you've got to see the Magic of Christmas at Butchart Gardens. It's breathtaking. They put up some amazing light displays. They have carolers, entertainment, the works. Even an ice-skating rink. I used to skate there every Christmas."

Despite Renee's efforts to distract her, DeeDee kept peeking at her phone. But Nick remained incommunicado. As they came around a bend and up a slight hill, she caught her first glimpse of the imposing Craigdarroch Castle. Far across a lawn of purest emerald green, statuesque stone chimneys and graceful turrets rose from a steep red roof. Ornate, wrought-iron balconies hugged aged granite walls.

"Wicked cool," she breathed.

Renee grinned. "I know, right? That was my reaction, too, when I first saw it as a kid. Wait till you see the inside."

They ascended wide concrete steps to the columned front porch and paid admission. Once inside, a smiling young tour guide introduced himself as Noah, beckoning them into a cavernous entryway and past a Titanic-worthy staircase. She'd seen some high-end homes in her lifetime, but never a staircase so massive it shouted for attention from every carving of its twin pillars.

Awestruck, she followed through room after room of velvet furnishings, intricate moldings, ancient portraits. All the polished wood paneling inhibited the light from permeating the silent rooms. It was as though, once the residents left, the mansion had fallen asleep fully dressed. She tried hard to focus on Noah's animated narrative. His passion for the castle and his job radiated in every enthusiastic inflection.

I'd love to live someplace like this. With Nick.

Instead of getting her mind off Nick, the place flaunted reminders of his absence around every corner and up each skinny staircase. Every magnificent room suggested how much she longed to experience it with him. He'd love the game room and its enormous billiard table. She could almost hear him mutter, "How did they get that huge thing up *those* stairs?"

"And here we are at the Dance Hall," Noah announced.

DeeDee's ears perked up. How had they gotten to the fourth floor already? She wandered inside, losing herself in the ornate woodwork, velvet draperies, stained-glass windows. She stopped and closed her eyes. The voices around her faded as she imagined long-ago society couples waltzing around the room. She shivered when an air current brushed her skin, as though ancient ghosts still danced nearby.

If she and Nick had lived here a hundred years ago, no doubt they...

"DeeDee?" Renee's voice jolted her out of her daydream. When she opened her eyes, the rest of the group stood over by the tall south-facing windows. "You've got to see this view."

The city spread out below, blanketed with various shades of green, the ice-blue water peeking out from the distance. "On a clear day," Noah was saying, "you can see the Olympic Mountains. Unfortunately, today the clouds obscure them." He cast them a hopeful grin. "So consider it motivation to come back and visit us on a clear day to feast your eyes on this amazing view."

She followed Renee and Noah back to the corridor where she checked her phone again. Nothing. She sighed, the forlorn noise seeming to fill the atmosphere with a mournful tune.

Renee frowned at her, stopping to let the other three tourists go on ahead. "Still haven't heard from Nick?"

"No, not since this morning." She put her phone away, hoping her voice didn't wobble. "What if he's with someone else?"

Renee's frown turned to wide-eyed surprise. "Do you really think he'd bring you here to meet his family if he were trysting with someone? I can tell he's very much into you. You have no reason to worry."

"I won't stop worrying until he's back safe and sound with a plausible explanation for why he left with no warning. And how he—" She had nearly slipped and divulged the theft Nick hadn't shared with his family yet.

"How he what?"

"How he—is managing with his injured ankle."

Renee nodded, seeming satisfied. The rest of the tour passed in a blur, and afterward, they browsed in the gift shop where DeeDee stocked up on souvenirs. Renee drove them downtown, past the vast Parliament Buildings. DeeDee gaped. "This reminds me of Buckingham Palace."

"You've been to London?"

"Yes, when Livy and I toured with Nils Nelsson's band. Free The Defendants. We rarely stayed anywhere long enough to do any decent sightseeing."

"What a life."

DeeDee reminisced aloud on her life as a backup singer

and dancer while Renee drove to the Empress Hotel. The world-famous structure sat resplendent in its ivy-covered glory as if it were transplanted directly from Oxford University. They indulged in some pampering at the spa, and English-style tea and crumpets. One o'clock became two, then three. Darkness would fall soon.

On the hotel's front lawn, they stopped to admire the Christmas-themed ice pavilion, all decked out with fairy lights and swag curtains. Soft clomping hoofbeats struck the pavement beyond them, the Christmassy jingle of a harness urging the trolley onward. Meanwhile, inside the living postcard, ice-skaters glided to nostalgic holiday tunes, vintage clothing the only embellishment missing.

DeeDee nudged Renee. "Are you wishing you could be out there?"

"Not really." Renee's head moved in a slow arc, following the skaters. "But I enjoy trying to guess which little kid will grow up to be a pro. You can tell the ones who have potential just by the way they carry themselves." She gestured to a little girl of about four. "See how that little one in red moves with confidence? She'll be good someday. Because she believes she will be. As opposed to the girl in white next to her. She makes a face every time she falls. She's angry at herself for not being perfect right now. I'm guessing she'll get tired of expending so much effort with so little payoff, and move onto something else."

"Unless she has parents who're putting pressure on her."

"In that case, I feel sorry for her."

"Yeah, Livy and I get our share of Dance Moms at our studio. I hate to see kids forced to dance because their parents are living vicariously through them."

"Skate Moms exist, too. But luckily my mom wasn't one of them."

As they walked to the car, horse-drawn carriages ambled by, their lanterns casting a warm glow into the misty day while Renee regaled her with stories from her ice dancing years—the grueling training, the demanding competitions. DeeDee nodded along, every word resonating, and shared with her new friend her own love/hate history with dance.

"Were you and Nick close growing up?" They whizzed along a speeding highway, following a double-decker bus north toward Sidney. Renee wanted to show her the beach where Gavin proposed to her.

"As kids, we were. But we grew apart once I got married and moved to Vancouver. When we finally moved back here, Nick and Pam were divorcing."

"What do you think of his stepson?"

"Leon Jr.? I've only met him a few times. During that season of Nick's life, we lived across the strait, but it might have been the ocean for all the times we saw him and his new family."

"He's the most hyper twenty-three-year-old I've ever met. I bet he was a Ritalin kid."

Renee laughed, a surprisingly robust sound coming out of such a frail-looking frame. "He takes after his mom. Pam's this skinny ex-model who really rocks the exotic look. Leon looks just like her."

"I know. I've seen photos." Little surprise, Nick chose a drop-dead gorgeous woman to marry. Pam reminded DeeDee of the pop singer Bjork. Or rather, Bjork's tall, beautiful sister—if she had one. A woman who made DeeDee feel quite ordinary. And so did Gracie, with her waist-length strawberry blonde hair and legs as long as the Space Needle...

"Nick has always dated beautiful women."

Of course, he had. DeeDee stared out the window, unsure if Renee was including her. A low-flying jet, on approach to the airport, filled the horizon. To her right, the seascape blurred as tears pressed against her eyes.

Renee glanced over. "And you're as beautiful as any of them, even more so."

"Thanks," she croaked, swiping a finger under her eyes. The silence lengthened. She swallowed and searched her mind for a safe subject until a familiar sight invaded her view.

"Oh, hey." She pointed to the right. "Nick showed me that place on Saturday, the site of his first gig."

"The Quaking Aspen—amazing burgers." Renee slowed as though she considered turning in. "Do you want to try one?"

"Well, I'm not hungry yet. How about on the way back?"

"Okay." Renee nodded and kept going.

"Did you know Leon's father owns it?"

"I didn't."

"How does Nick know him?"

"I believe they played in a band together. Back when Leon Sr. was still married to Pam."

"Seems Nick's played in a band with everybody and their mother. No wonder he's quite the celebrity here." She forced out a laugh, hoping Renee didn't hear it strain.

Chapter Eight

Nick climbed into the rented cargo van and set out down River Road toward Highway 1 and Mt. Sicker. The temperature had dropped about ten degrees while he ate, and now the cold bit through his gloves and into his fingers. The cabin—five hundred feet above sea level—would be even colder. Ice and snow would only make his job more difficult on an injured ankle.

He pulled into a shabby real estate office parking lot, where weeds sprouted through the pavement cracks, and checked the weather on his tablet, something he should have done an hour ago. The forecast showed possible light snow flurries later in the day. He tensed all over.

"God," he muttered. "I really hope You're up there listening. I could use some divine help right now. If You could hold off the snow until tomorrow, I'd be forever grateful."

Feeling a shiver coming on, he fiddled with the heater settings until a surge of lukewarm air blew on him. Overhead, the sheet of deepening gray hung forebodingly, a dark quilt heavy with moisture. A bolt of anxiety left him shaken, and he nearly turned the vehicle around.

Maybe he should just inform law enforcement of his suspicions, let them deal with it.

But no. This was between him and Junior. Plus, he needed to return it all and get his money back.

Had Pam arrived yet? Maybe she was sitting there now, waiting for him. Yet she hadn't responded to his previous message. Nonetheless, he tried again. *I'm about 15 minutes from the cabin. Whereabouts are you?*

๙๙๙

By the time Nick reached the cabin, ice pellets bounced off the van hood and windshield. So far, they hadn't stuck to the road. The towering firs sheltered the ground like flailing umbrellas. Tall as skyscrapers, they blocked the already dim daylight. Even in summer, the Douglas firs kept the property in a perpetual state of cool, murky dusk.

He heard Jack barking as soon as the tires crunched gravel. Surely, Pam's parents hadn't left the Rottweiler here after her grandpa passed last year? Granted, Jack kept a sinister watch for intruders. Still, even vicious dogs needed companionship.

He wasn't sure if his racing heart meant fear or excitement. Either way, he needed to calm himself, so he stopped the van, letting it idle, and took out his two-six of Crown Royal whiskey. Two shots of liquid courage relaxed his heart rate without impairing his senses.

He checked the time again. Where had the day gone? This far north, the sun set around four o'clock this time of year, leaving him only a precious few daylight hours.

He put the gearshift in drive and crept up the thirty-degree incline he'd last driven ten years ago. Snarling, barking Jack bounded along inside the chain-link fence. To his relief, brambles and broom bushes hadn't swallowed the dirt-and-gravel driveway, and shoulders relaxing, he followed it north to the rear of the cabin and parked in front of the rickety carport.

No other cars. Why hadn't Pam made it yet? Or communicated her timetable with him. He'd have to start without her.

First stop—the storage room behind the carport, a

52

perfect hiding spot for stolen goods. His boots crunched a path through the pine needles to the structure's backside, where he found the door unlocked. Ah ha. Letting out a whistle, he scanned the grounds for signs of recent visitors, then stopped. Were those fresh tire tracks running parallel to his? Pam must have come and gone. But why? He wasn't quite sure how to react, whether to hope for her return or be angry she'd left him in the lurch.

Jack's barks intensified, each blast ending in a yelp. Nick opened the storage door, fumbling for a light switch, finding none. Once his eyes adjusted to the dimness, he scanned the four bare concrete walls. No recent purchases. Only old boxes and rusted tools.

And a gun rack, with several firearms, the chains loosened. He gave a low whistle. This place had been unoccupied for months. Who could have broken in here and stolen a gun?

Or perhaps the explanation was simpler than that. This had Leon written all over it. No surprise he would "borrow" a gun for hunting, then conveniently forget to lock up. His stepson's attention deficit at times turned him into a walking disaster.

He filed it away in his mind as something to confront Leon with later and focused anew on the rifles. He might need a gun if the dog tried to stop him from entering the house. Much as he hated to shoot a dog, he'd do it if he had to.

He grabbed a rifle off the rack and checked the chambers. Not loaded. Maybe the carport or the shed held the ammo.

He found an unlocked cabinet in the carport containing ammo. He ground his teeth. The guy who kept an eye on the place should take better care to make sure everything was legal. Anyone could waltz in here and grab a gun. He'd just done so himself.

After loading the bullets, he carried the rifle back outside. Jack had bounded to the fence at the half-acre property's far north end, pawing the ground and growling. Nick peered through the dimness to see what caught Jack's attention, but could only discern what looked like slender, downed tree trunks beyond the shed.

A rabbit or something similar must have distracted the dog. Unless someone was hiding back there... He raised the gun, debating whether to investigate or get on with his task. A deep gloom settled over the grounds, and a prickle down his spine left him shaken. He didn't remember the place feeling quite so spooky.

Nothing moved over there. He wished Jack would stop barking so he could listen for telltale sounds of movement.

As he crept along the fence, an idea hit him. Returning to the van, Nick reached into the box of leftovers from the restaurant and pulled out a half-eaten sausage link. He'd bet his Fender bass that Jack loved sausage.

Breathing another quick prayer, he eased out. Jack had returned to his former spot next to the fence, and his obnoxiously loud barks grated on Nick's nerves. "Here, boy!" He launched the sausage over the fence, and Jack pounced on it. When he finished chewing, he eyed Nick and gruffed out a couple of half-hearted barks.

Nick broke off another piece of sausage and threw it. Fortunately, he'd brought several links with him. He and Jack would be the best of friends when he was through.

After four sausage pieces, Jack stood at the fence wagging, whining for another helping. Nick donned a thick gardening glove he'd brought in case Jack decided to bite and eased open the gate. Breaking off another piece of sausage, he knelt and let Jack sniff it, then threw it hard.

Jack bounded away, and Nick limped across the yard,

holding the gun in the shed's direction. Jack munched contentedly, and Nick stopped, straining his eyes and ears for signs of someone hiding in the shed or behind it.

All he heard was light wind sighing through the evergreens. An animal must have spooked Jack, not a human.

Kicking pinecones from his path, he approached the back porch and propped the gun, hoping the spare key was where Pam said it was. Under the eave directly above the porch light. Yes, there it was.

Hearing a growl, he spun around. Jack stood motionless, staring at him. Nick repeated the sausage trick, and Jack took off.

He reached again for the nail, and the sharp teeth of a key pricked his fingers. His heart leaped as he plucked the key into his hand. Turning the doorknob quiet as he could, he peeked inside and held his breath. The deserted kitchen yawned before him, and the empty silence sent another chill across his shoulders.

Only the ancient-forest-and-wet-moss smell of the place greeted him when he stepped inside. Squinting, he tried to discern the interior in the cloudy daylight. He limped through the kitchen to the front room, where he froze. Boxes stacked against the walls. Drum set components cluttered the floor.

Leon had set up this place to house a band. Propped against the wall was a brand-new, still-in-the-box Korg piano. Over in the west corner, a Peavey amp.

He swallowed hard. Emotions raged. Anger at his stepson mingled with gratitude to God and relief over having his suspicions proved correct. But he dreaded the enormity of the task ahead. He needed to get all this loaded in the U-Haul and out of here before dark, a grueling task even for a healthy man. Pam had promised that, if he was right about

Leon storing the stuff here, she'd stay and help him load it. So where was she? She still hadn't replied to his last two messages. If she didn't get here soon, they'd be here after dark.

Exhaling, he lifted his phone and started snapping photos.

Chapter Nine

Renee was right. The cheeseburger DeeDee ordered at the Quaking Aspen was the tastiest she'd ever had. A smoky flavor infused the meat. White and yellow cheese dripped from the sides. Slabs of fries in a savory gravy and curds, which Renee called "poutine," and a couple of dense, dark beers completed the meal. The occasional roar of jets accompanied their conversation.

"I can't wait to tell Nick I ate here tonight." The place reminded DeeDee of a hunting lodge. Lots of heavy, dark wood. Thick beams crisscrossing the ceiling. Deer and moose heads perched on the walls. On the stage, a drum set promised a live band later in the evening. She tried to visualize a teenaged Nick on this same stage, but could only come up with a blond Justin Bieber caricature.

She finished off her beer, which pushed the tension out of her like a hot shower, leaving her with a sudden urge to giggle. Catching the eye of the young waitress who hovered nearby, DeeDee waved her over.

"Another beer, please?"

"Certainly." The blonde woman's nametag, Devon, flashed silver in the low lighting as she pranced over. "Ever eaten here before?"

"Never." The beer loosened DeeDee's tongue. "This is my first time, and this is the best burger—ever. I wish we had something this good in Seattle."

"You're from Seattle?"

DeeDee nodded, introduced herself and Renee, then

said, "My boyfriend played a gig here twenty years ago, and he knows the owner."

The waitress's eyes lit. "He knows Senior?"

"Who?"

"Leon Brown Sr. He owns the place. Around here, he and his son are known as Senior and Junior." She shifted the tray to her other hip. "I'll let him know you're here. What's your boyfriend's name?"

"Nick Rush."

"Nick is your boyfriend?" The words came out as squeaky as a teenager talking to her crush. Devon's curls bounced, and a tress slid over her eyes as she grinned. "Wow, you lucky woman." Renee snickered as Devon eyed DeeDee up and down. "Senior will be thrilled that you're here."

"I'd love to meet an old friend of Nick's."

"You should have brought him."

"I would've, but he left on some mysterious mission. Some place called Black Bear Lane. Do you have any idea where it is?"

Devon scrunched her face and repeated the name, enunciating each syllable. "It sounds a bit familiar, though I'm not sure why."

"He's supposed to be back tonight. I'll see if I can drag him here tomorrow."

"You do that. I'd best go get your beer now."

She left, returning in minutes with a full mug, trailed by a forty-something gentleman with a headful of thick auburn curls. "This is Senior," she announced. "Senior, meet Nick Rush's girlfriend."

The man thrust out a hand, his smile revealing stained teeth. "Well, well! So nice to meet you!" His casual polo shirt and jeans didn't hint to his businessman status.

DeeDee, the beer and the food making her feel friendlier by the minute, moved over and patted the seat she'd vacated. "Hey, come talk to me about Nick. Were you here when he played his first gig at age fifteen?"

Senior sat, leaning his elbows on the table, his hands clasped together. "My father owned this place at the time. I remember it well. I acquired it about ten years ago when he passed away."

"I don't recall if Nick ever mentioned you."

"He sure talks about you. Nothing but good, I might add."

Warmth filled her. "Really? When did you last talk to him?"

"The day after you Americans celebrate Thanksgiving. Five of us guys got together for a weekend in the bush."

"I remember. Your male-bonding weekend."

Senior smiled. "We hiked, drank beer, got high." His eyes turned merry. "Sang 'Kumbayah' around the campfire. The usual things men do when the women aren't around."

"You so did not sing 'Kumbayah' around the campfire."

He chuckled, leaning back and bracing an arm across the booth behind him. "Kidding. I would've loved to see him today. Devon said he's on some mission."

"All I know is, he went to a place called Black Bear Lane. And he doesn't even hunt."

His face went taut. "He told you he was going there?"

"No, I found a map. Why? Do you know the place?"

"I do." A crease appeared between his brows.

"What? You have to tell me."

"Why would he go there?"

"How would I know?" she screeched, her voice rising toward hysteria. The man's secretive attitude was freaking her out. He even had Renee's undivided attention. "What do you know about the place? And where is it?"

Sitting stiffly forward, Senior laced his fingers together and studied them while he spoke. "This may not be what you want to hear." He turned a wary gaze on her. "His ex-wife owns a house there."

She sprang to her feet, her heart thudding. "Renee, let's go. I need to call that man."

⚘⚘⚘

Nick paused, straightened to his full height, and rubbed his back after the second trip to the U-Haul. This was going to take longer than he anticipated. And he was down to his last sausage link.

Apparently, something had delayed Pam. He gritted his teeth and stuffed the swear words he longed to fling at her. She could've at least let him know. But he snapped plenty of photos and texted them to her. Still no reply. Maybe her phone was dead. His showed two bars.

How odd that his ex, in her important position, would let her lifeline stay dead for so long.

Rummaging through the kitchen cupboards, he found a box of dog bones and stuffed a handful in his pocket.

Jack, whipping his tail back and forth, whined as Nick approached. He flipped on the back porch light, but the bulb was burned out. Since he didn't have time to search for bulbs, the kitchen light shining through the window would have to suffice.

The Korg box, although not heavy, tilted at an awkward angle as he wrestled it through the door. As the box fell against the doorjamb, a corner of it jabbed Nick in the abdomen. Grunting, he doubled over, and the box slipped out of his hands. He dove to grab it before it hit the ground, but knocked his foot against the sill.

His injured ankle gave way, twisting beneath him, sending him crashing to the ground gasping in pain. Jack barked and came running, then stood, tail wagging expectantly.

Nothing but dark night surrounded him now.

He attempted to hoist himself up, but his left ankle couldn't bear his weight without intense pain. It better not be broken. He pulled the boxed piano toward him, worked his arms under it, and cradled it like a baby. The drop probably ruined it.

He sat, wishing he could cry. Wishing DeeDee was here. He wanted to nestle in her arms like a helpless invalid. Instead, he spit out every four-letter word he could think of. As more came to his mind, he sent them out his mouth like poison darts.

He'd crawl to the car if he had to. But right now, he needed to rest. Propping himself against the wall of the house, he leaned his head back and closed his eyes. If only blocking out the pain were so easy.

Chapter Ten

DeeDee, vaguely aware she'd crossed the line from tipsy to drunk sometime during her fourth beer, clutched Renee's arm and staggered to the parking lot. Her wails drew attention from other patrons, but she ignored them.

Once in the car, Renee forced DeeDee to look at her. "Don't call Nick."

She sobbed. "I have to." The warm river of beer inside her had turned into a flash flood.

"You're in no shape to. Let me call."

She sniffed and agreed to let Renee make the call. "It went straight to voicemail," Renee whispered after she dialed. "Hey, Nick. It's Renee, just making sure everything's okay." DeeDee reached over to snatch at the phone, but Renee held up a warning finger. "We're a tad concerned, so please call." She hung up.

The roaring in her head bellowing louder by the minute, DeeDee grabbed her own phone.

"Put that away." Renee's voice pulsated through her. "Think about how you'll feel in the morning if you send him a bunch of drunken messages."

"But…" DeeDee wailed again. "He went to his ex-wife's place."

"You don't know that. Just because a map was in his pocket doesn't mean it's where he was going."

"I overheard him setting up a rendezvous with her."

"He wouldn't. He has no reason to."

Her sobs crescendoed. "Then where is he? And who

was he talking to last night?"

Twisting in her seat, Renee clamped her hands on DeeDee's shoulders. "Calm down. He said he'd be home by ten, which is still hours away." Facing forward again, Renee put the key in the ignition. "Let's get you home and into bed. When you wake up tomorrow, Nick will be there."

"Promise?"

"No, I can't promise." Renee huffed, exerting near eye-rolling exasperation. "But he's always been a man of his word, hasn't he?"

❧ ❧ ❧

Nick jerked awake, glancing around at his pitch-dark surroundings. Either the frigid temperature or the excruciating pain in his ankle awakened him. To his left, a beam of light pierced through. To his right stretched unending black.

He was sprawled in the cargo van's front seat. But he couldn't recall why.

Awareness came slowly, bit by bit. After he fell on the back porch, he'd crawled through the yard to the van to retrieve some pain-numbing weed and whiskey. He'd left his prescription painkillers at Renee's, thinking he wouldn't need them. Then he must have fallen asleep. Or, judging by his dry mouth and nausea, he'd passed out.

He groped for the seat and pushed himself to a sitting position, his head throbbing in sync with his ankle. Through clenched teeth, he sucked in a breath. The light came from the cabin's kitchen window. A vague memory teased him, and he felt for the ignition. He heard the clang of metal and jangled a set of keys. The ignition was on.

A chill raced up his spine. Oh no! Surely, he hadn't.... His whole body sagged. Yes, he had. Stupefied with pain, he'd switched the ignition on in order to work the heater.

How long had it been on? His backpack, on the passenger seat, contained his phone. The weather app told him it was thirty degrees outside. The display showed 8:14 p.m. But no signal. And a low battery.

He jerked forward and turned the key. The telltale clicks of a dead battery rewarded him.

He cursed loud enough for the stars to hear. How could he have been such an idiot?

Reaching into his pack, he pulled out his tablet, still fully charged, and opened the browser to search for a Wi-Fi connection. He found one requiring a password, which he didn't have. Next, he checked for unsecured connections, knowing the odds were not good, with the nearest neighbor living a quarter mile away.

No Wi-Fi available. No Pam. The cold chill prickled to stabbing fear.

He had no way to notify Pam or DeeDee or call roadside assistance. He couldn't use the jumper cables or his phone's car charger. So much for emergency preparedness.

"God!" he yelled. But God didn't reply. The Almighty was finally giving the prodigal son what he deserved.

He'd have to stay here tonight, crawl to the road tomorrow morning, and pray he could find a ride back to town.

So be it. He hoisted his backpack and muddled out of the car, hopping on one foot toward the porch steps where Jack slept. Jack opened his eyes and scrambled to his feet, barking. And not in a friendly way. Nick reached in his pocket for a dog bone, but the pocket was empty. He fumbled in the other one, also empty. Jack growled and leaned back on his haunches.

"Easy, boy," Nick crooned. "It's your old buddy, old pal, Nick. Remember me?"

Jack growled louder. Nick took a longing look at the

porch, then remembered the trail mix in his backpack. He scooped a handful and threw it to the ground. Jack pounced on it.

Too late, he remembered chocolate was poisonous for dogs. But he had to get in the house, or he would freeze to death.

He hopped to the steps, throwing more handfuls as he went. With Jack sniffing around for morsels, he shuffled to the porch and fetched the gun, hobbling past the Korg box he'd left there, into the warm, lit kitchen, then to the front room.

He left the pack on the floor, the gun beside within easy reach, and collapsed on the sofa. He needed to keep his ankle elevated. A nearby guitar box made for a decent leg prop. Folding his arms across his chest, he sank deeper into the corduroy cushions and resisted the urge to give in to body-racking shivers. Then, peeping open one eye, he pulled the thick throw draped over the back of the sofa to himself, wrinkling his nose at the musty smell. Several shots of whiskey later, the pain subsided, and he let oblivion take him.

⤞⤞⤞

A slamming door awakened him. Nick opened his eyes to a surreal dream. Shadowy geometric shapes formed an eerie backdrop, as though he'd somehow landed inside a video game. Two dark forms approached the sofa where he lay—one animal, one human.

The person kicked him in the legs, and he cried out. The bone-crunching pain—this was no dream.

Leon, his hand around Jack's collar, snarled, "I knew I'd find you here, you backstabber."

Chapter Eleven

DeeDee awoke at two a.m., shivering and dry-mouthed. No doubt, her breath smelled like the inside of a keg. Out of habit, she reached for Nick. But grasped only empty air.

She bolted upright, memories flooding back, pain knifing through her head. Nick was supposed to be home by ten. Bounding from the bed, she ignored her headache, grabbed her robe and slippers, and shambled to the living room in case he'd crashed there.

But the sofa was empty.

A sob burst from her, and she hurried back to the room. Even before she picked up her phone, she knew he hadn't contacted her.

She started to throw the phone down, then stopped herself. A broken phone would do her no good. A vision of her twin invaded her mind, and a ray of hope brightened her spirits. She needed Livy and her calming presence.

She tapped her sister's contact.

"Deeds?" Livy's voice crackled with sleep.

"Livs, I need you!"

She heard Livy yawn. "Why for?"

"Nick is missing. He's been gone all day, won't answer his phone, didn't come back when he said he would." Another sob choked her words. "Please, Liv, you've got to come be with me."

"Why don't you just come home and wait for him here?"

"I can't leave while he's missing! What if he comes back

and finds me gone? Please, please. I'd do it for you."

Livy croaked out, "I can't leave the studio in Ella's care—"

"Yes, you can! She's very trustworthy."

It took some doing, but DeeDee finally persuaded her sister to come stay with her until Nick returned. A settled peace rested on her now, and the tight band around her head eased a few degrees.

"Sorry I woke you, Livs. I've been so upset. But now I feel better just knowing you'll be here for moral support. I didn't interrupt anything, did I?"

"Interrupt what?"

"You and Scott—"

"Deeds. I told you we're not—"

"You're engaged! Why don't you want to sleep with him?"

Livy huffed an exasperated noise. "It isn't that I don't *want* to. I wouldn't marry him if I didn't want to."

"I don't get why it matters to you what some fictitious God thinks."

"De–e–eds." An unmistakable warning rumbled through the phone, and DeeDee bit her lip. Ever since last year, when Livy decided she believed in God, she'd adopted all kinds of strange ideas. According to her, God wouldn't bless her and Scott's relationship unless they did things God's way, including waiting until their wedding night to have sex. Any God who'd deprive a couple of a pleasurable way to get to know each other didn't sound like a very nice God. She recalled Livy's exact words: "Scott says I'm worth waiting for, and I think he's worth waiting for, too."

Ha. With the chemistry between those two so thick you could fill ten beakers, she doubted they'd truly succeed in waiting even a month. DeeDee shook her head. She'd never understand religious folks and their quaint ideas. "Okay,

okay. We won't talk about that. How soon can you be here?"

❧❧❧

Nick winced at the sudden light from the lamp Leon switched on and resisted covering his eyes. He shivered hard, both from the bone-piercing cold and the way Jack the Rottweiler made it clear he was no longer Nick's friend. Growling low in his throat, the dog glared at him with eyes gleaming in the lamplight.

Where'd he put the gun? Yes! On the floor. Fortunately, the blanket hid it from Leon. Nick dropped his hand toward the floor, but Jack saw the movement, lunged, and barked. Nick pulled his hand back, then sniffed. Something smelled foul, like a dead animal. "What did you drag in?"

Leon abandoned the hostile act, reverting to his high-strung persona. A false persona. Releasing Jack's collar, Leon stared at Nick from slitted eyes. "Jack upchucked. What did you feed him, anyway?"

"Sausage."

"Don't you know dogs can't digest sausage?"

Nick shrugged, then winced when pain shot up his head. "How did you know I was here?"

"Apparently, your girlfriend was asking a lot of questions at Dad's pub. She found a map."

A surge of relief hit him. Would DeeDee show up here soon to rescue him? Then his spirits plunged. If Senior had helped her find him, she would've shown by now.

"You must think you're pretty smart to have caught me, eh?"

Nick groaned. "No, not that smart. You just didn't cover your tracks well." He tried to keep the contempt out of his voice. It would only make Leon angrier.

"Oh yeah? How so?" A hint of doubt tinged the bravado.

His teeth chattered so hard, Nick had to force the words out. "Y–you dropped a receipt on your living room floor. For a ferry trip from Wednesday matching a transaction on my credit card statement. A round trip for two from Victoria to Vancouver. Sound familiar?" He paused for a quick breath. "That huge p–purchase from Rockstar confirmed it."

Leon said nothing, but shifted into a Clint Eastwood stance—legs three feet apart, free hand on hip.

Nick, his teeth chattering with a mind of their own, gripped the edge of the cushion. "Remember when I stayed behind to use the bathroom? I ch–checked the receipt."

Leon merely sneered. "Next time I *will* cover my tracks." Hostility washed over his face in waves. "I brought a trailer, and I'mma haul this all away where you'll never find it." He gave a short chuckle. "Good luck getting out of here. You may have got by Jack the first time, but you won't be so lucky next time."

"Wait a minute." Nick tried to raise his head, but Jack's growl stopped him. "Wh–what makes you think you're entitled to all that stuff?"

"You broke your promise to help out. You owe me now."

"What universe are you living in? The music gods didn't endow you with talent. W–why won't you give up your futile dream of rock stardom?"

"Don't need talent. Just a little luck and the right connections."

"Your dad should be your go-to guy, not me."

"No, you promised to fund the band's start-up costs."

Nick shook his head, and pain knifed through his temple. "I'm not going to invest in a venture with no f–future." He kneaded the sore spot. "Especially after you stole all my money."

Leon spun on his heel.

"By the way, where's your mom?"

He half-turned to face Nick. "How should I know?"

"She said she'd meet me here. She wanted to see the evidence with her eyes."

Leon pressed his lips together. "I haven't seen her for days. I've been honeymooning, remember?"

"She hasn't answered any of my calls or texts, and I'm worried about her."

Leon shrugged. "She must not want to talk to you."

If Nick weren't lying here helpless, he'd wring Leon's pencil neck, take pleasure in yanking that thick skull back and forth. He started to lower his hand, then stopped. Digging around on the floor would be too obvious. A white-hot surge chased away the cold, but he clamped down on it. *Don't show emotion.* "Why don't you try calling her yourself? If you're right, she'll answer."

Leon rolled his shoulders, removed his cell phone.

"And while you're at it, call a tow truck for me."

He ignored Nick and punched in a contact. Seconds later, he disconnected. "It went straight to voicemail. I bet it's dead."

A niggle of worry only heightened Nick's discomfort. "Sure hope she's okay. Hey, try her husband, will you?"

Leon cast him a wary look. "He's already called me twice wondering where she is."

"Really? Even he hasn't been able to reach her? Why didn't you say something?"

"What's to say? She can take care of herself."

His stepson's indifference mystified him, and heat surged through his limbs. "What is wrong with you? People are worried about your mom and all you do is shrug it off?"

Leon spun to the door. "Okay, I'm outta here."

"Wait!" Jack and the pounding pain rendered him powerless to stop Leon. "You're just going to leave me here?"

Leon moved closer to the front door.

"DeeDee is obviously worried about me. She's a smart lady. She'll figure out where I am."

Ignoring him, Leon opened the door, accompanied by a current of cold air. Jack sat on his haunches and watched Nick with beady eyes as if waiting to see what Nick would do about it.

"You son of a..." Nick yelled at the closing door. But no, he couldn't call Pam the B-Word. His ex might have her shrewish moments, but right now, his apprehension supplanted all the unpleasant memories.

Chapter Twelve

"Dear God," Nick moaned and burrowed deeper under the blanket, but something dug into his side. "Please help me get out of here." Leon had left hours ago with a trailer full of band equipment. His ankle throbbed, swelling larger with each passing hour. Now he needed medical care. If he could just get to the road, someone would help him. But how to get by Jack? Distracting him with food wasn't an option. Leon had filled the dog's bowl, and Jack had gobbled half of it down.

His heart rate surged. If Pam had shown up, he wouldn't be in this predicament.

And Senior...Hard to believe the man couldn't see through his son's fun-loving façade. But then again, he'd always been an addlebrained, head-in-the-sand parent who believed his kid could do no wrong. Who believed his son could be the next Nick Rush, even encouraging his son's vain ambitions. Either his tone-deaf ear or too much weed had skewed Senior's thinking.

A glimmer of sunrise wiggled through the eastward-facing blinds. He'd better leave soon. He'd allowed himself a few hours of much-needed sleep, but now he had to get moving.

Another prayer sprang from his lips. He hoped God cared for him as his mother claimed. Faith in Christ came easy for people like his mother. She'd never wanted anything more than to be married and raise children. But he'd always gagged whenever he considered a traditional future for himself. His father had wanted him to attend university and major in Business. But music had sung in Nick's soul at an early age, and the powers in charge of meting out talent had granted him an abundant portion.

Mom said God had blessed Nick with talent and wanted Nick to use it for His glory. But Nick couldn't stand the idea of playing church music the rest of his life. After his band won a local talent contest, it was easy to walk away from the faith he'd been raised in.

He shifted around, trying to get comfortable, and something poked him again. Exploring with his fingertips, he tried to grasp the object. It protruded from the sofa's crease into his rib. He rolled to his side, which alerted Jack, but the dog merely watched him. His fingers found the object and pulled it out.

It emitted a squeak, and Jack barked.

A dog's chew toy.

Perfect.

Or Providential?

He squeezed it again, and Jack jumped up, his tail whipping back and forth at the speed of light. Nick threw it hard, and it bounced off the wall. Jack charged after it, and Nick wrested his backpack off the floor and set it on his chest, sucking in a breath from the pain.

Jack returned with the toy in his mouth and spit it to the floor with a whine. "Good boy!" Nick repeated the game, but this time he seized the rifle before Jack scrambled back.

Nick tucked it beside him, hoping he didn't have to use it.

He eased off the sofa by raising his head first, then rested his feet on the floor. Pushing his arms through the backpack straps, he dove to his knees and grasped the gun, tucking it under his left arm. Between groans of pain, he threw the toy as he crawled on his knees to the front door.

The dead-critter odor permeated the air around him, and his stomach heaved. He swallowed down the bile threatening to join the heap already on the floor.

He was almost to the door when Jack growled. Freezing, Nick tipped his head just enough to see the Rottweiler crouched behind him, ignoring the toy at his feet. Twisting, Nick grasped at it, and Jack lunged at his hand.

Nick yanked his hand back just in time. Apparently, Jack had lost interest in the toy, and now his true nature had emerged.

"Boy, don't make me shoot you." Nick put as much fierceness in his tone as he could, staring Jack down, refusing to show fear. It worked for Crocodile Dundee.

But Jack didn't flinch, and Nick inched closer to the door, keeping his eye trained on the dog, and his voice soft yet firm. "You think you're tough, dontcha?"

Drool dripped from the dog's jowls. Clearly, Nick had offended him. He needed out of here, quick, before Jack converted him into dog food.

Nick stayed perfectly still. The dog waited, crouching, his muscles rippling.

Nick eased the gun barrel toward the toy, slow and subtle. He let out a breath when the gun touched the toy. Still at a snail pace, he edged the blue plastic bone toward him.

Jack pounced at the gun, but Nick snagged the toy just in time, throwing it as hard as he could. It sailed into the kitchen. The dog bounded toward the echoing thud, and Nick sprang to his feet, ignoring the pain.

He lurched at the front door handle and had eased himself halfway out when Jack ran at him, toy in mouth. The dog stopped, growled, and the toy plummeted to the floor. The shift into attack mode was so subtle, Nick almost missed it.

Jack lunged at the closing door.

❧❧❧

DeeDee stood, staring out the rain-streaked window, her arms crossed. Her heart sat heavy in her chest. Twenty-four hours and still no Nick.

The angst intensified, tinged with an edge of worry. Suspicion needling her, she returned to the bedroom for her tablet and brought it back to the kitchen. Maybe he'd posted something on social media.

But Nick hadn't posted anything in a few days. She stared at his selfie of the two of them on the ferry, taken before he discovered the hacked account. He'd written, "Me and my sweetheart on our way to Victoria." Their happy smiles showed no hint trouble loomed ahead like a hidden cliff. A photo posted by "Neon Leon", a hashtagged video of a rock band, came next. She clicked on Leon's profile. He wore a multicolored Afro wig and a Jack Nicholson grin. She rolled her eyes, continuing to scroll through Nick's recent posts, but nothing hinted at who he'd gone to see yesterday.

She sighed. Nick hadn't posted updates for two days. At least Livy was on her way. She couldn't wait to unburden herself.

After hours of checking phone, e-mail, and social media, DeeDee climbed into Renee's car for the ride to the Sidney ferry dock to meet Livy. Rain slashed the windshield and thickened as they drove north. They talked very little, DeeDee lost in thoughts of Nick, Renee not pressuring her.

"See you at home." Renee waved as she dropped DeeDee off at the curb. The stately white vessel transporting her sister neared the dock, finally thudding to a halt.

DeeDee blasted Fall Out Boy on iTunes while border patrol released cars one by one. She peered at each one, watching for her sister's black Jaguar. Vehicles of all types marched past, but no Jag. DeeDee was ready to text her when she spied Livy's car. Waving her arms over her head, she broke into a run.

Livy parked at the side of the road and got out. DeeDee grabbed her in a tight hug, nearly knocking her over.

"Careful." Livy laughed. "I don't need another accident." Almost a year had passed since the car crushed Livy's leg, but Livy still harbored hope she would dance again someday.

DeeDee drank in the sight of her sister's face. A subtle glow had transformed it. What a difference a ring could make. "Let me see that sparkler."

Livy pulled off her striped glove. The stones glimmered even beneath the cloud-laden sky.

"Wow. That is breathtaking."

Livy's smile widened, and she sighed. "Words can't express how much I love it."

Something twisted inside DeeDee. How long before she had a sparkler of her own? She held out her palm for Livy's car key. "How about I drive since I know the way?"

Livy gave her the key, they piled into the car, and Livy tightened her coat around herself. "It feels colder here than in Seattle."

DeeDee merged into the traffic heading into town. "I wish we had our honeys with us to keep us warm."

"I miss mine already."

"Was he okay with you making this last-minute trip?"

"I think so. He seemed disappointed that he couldn't come, too."

"You could always come back on your honeymoon. Book a suite at the Empress."

The sparkles in Livy's eyes matched the ring's. "Oh là là."

The rain intensified, and DeeDee switched the wipers to high. "Have you set a date?"

"He says, the sooner the better."

She steered onto the main boulevard amid poor visibility. "Tell him to cool his jets. What's the rush?"

"I'm trying to keep my feet on the ground." But the dreamy smile on Livy's face said otherwise. "We're tentatively planning for a summer wedding." The smile vanished, and a cloud crossed her face, as though the storm outside had trespassed into her heart. "But, Deeds, I still can't dance. Not even the two-step! How am I going to dance at my wedding?"

"What's your physical therapist say?"

"She thinks by summer I might be able to do some moves without my leg collapsing."

"Keep thinking positive and keep it simple. Even if you can't dance by then, Scott will still love you."

"Easy for you to say. Try to imagine not being able to dance at your wedding."

DeeDee scrunched her face. Livy had a point. The vision in her mind wasn't pleasant. She pictured herself sitting on the sidelines, watching everyone else twirl and glide on the dance floor, envy eating away at her bones.

"I see what you mean."

To the left, the Quaking Aspen's neon sign flashed through the gloom. "Hey, are you hungry?"

"I am, as a matter of fact."

DeeDee swung the wheel into the parking lot. "So am I. You've got to try one of the burgers at this place." She parked. "Let's sit here and talk for a few until the rain lets up."

After a quick update on Nick, she said, "Maybe Grandma was right. This whole trip has been one strange event after another."

They unbuckled their seatbelts and leaned closer together. "His leaving you here alone for two days seems really out of character." A crease scrinched Livy's brows. "I hope nothing is wrong."

"Tell me about it."

"What else happened that was so strange?"

DeeDee told her everything, starting with the fraudulent transactions, Nick's injury, the clues in Nick's pocket.

The pounding deluge nearly drowned Livy's next words, but her eyes lit the way they did when she hit on an idea. "Maybe it was something to do with the fraud."

As DeeDee gawked, her sister grew more animated. "Maybe Nick found out his ex was responsible for the fraud and went to confront her. So, of course, he wouldn't want to involve you."

DeeDee grasped onto the logical explanation. "I hope you're right." She grabbed the door handle. "But I'm tired of sitting here. I want to go inside and pick Senior's brain."

They hurried through the torrent with Livy unable to run, arriving at the door as soaked as if they'd jumped in the ocean fully clothed. Inside, the place was mostly empty. DeeDee looked around for Senior. When she didn't see him, she asked a waiter if he was on duty.

"He is," replied the spike-haired young man. "Shall I get him for you?"

"Yes, please. And can you bring us two cheeseburgers with poutine?"

The waiter nodded and left. Moments later, Senior approached, but without the friendly manner from the previous evening.

He wiped his hands on a towel. "How can I help you today?"

Whoa. Maybe she shouldn't have stopped by. Maybe he was having a busy day.

"Is this a bad time?"

"We have a lot of phone-in orders we're working on. But I can spare you a minute."

"I want you to meet my twin, Livy. She just got in from the ferry. Livy, meet Nick's friend Senior."

He scrutinized Livy, then DeeDee. "Well!" He chuckled, his warm manner reappearing. "There's two of you! Except for the hair, I wouldn't know you apart."

"She came to keep me company until Nick returns."

"He's not back yet, eh?"

"No, and I'm worried about him. Are you sure you can't tell me how to find that place he went to?"

"It's pretty far from here. Look, don't worry. I'll send him a text, okay? Just to assure you he's all right."

"If he's not answering my texts, why would he answer yours?"

Senior smiled. "I'm not his girlfriend." He glanced toward the kitchen. "I need to get back to work. Would you like to chat with a couple of Nick's old bandmates? Clive and Erik, the dynamic duo. Erik is my new daughter-in-law's father."

"Jazzy's dad?"

"One and the same." Senior nodded and departed, and soon their food arrived.

Livy made appreciative noises as she chewed. "Scott asked me to Skype with him tonight. Let's tell him about Nick. Maybe his engineer brain will think of something we haven't thought of."

They were finishing their food when Senior brought Nick's friends over. He introduced them as Clive Kendrick and Erik Sterling. The beads in Clive's straw-colored dreadlocks clanged, brushing the shoulders of his Bob Marley shirt as he shook their hands. Erik, wearing a royal blue beanie with an insignia on the front, resembled an aging professor in square black glasses and goatee. A gold cross hung prominently around his neck.

Clive did a double take when he greeted them. "I'm

never going to get your names straight. I can't even tell you apart." He eyed her hair, studied Livy, and then slid his gaze back to DeeDee. "So is there a brown-haired girl hiding underneath all those red curls?"

DeeDee laughed as Erik took a seat beside her. "Yes, my natural hair looks like Livy's. Our mom used to call it 'sparkling brown sugar'."

She stole a glance at Erik's left hand. A shiny gold band flickered in the dim lighting.

Clive, also sporting a wedding ring, sat beside Livy. "Is this your first time to Victoria?"

Livy shook her head. "We've been here before and to Vancouver a few times, too."

"Vancouver's just a big, smelly metropolis. Victoria's a much nicer town."

"It's very quaint. And sweet."

Erik's stoic face relaxed a few degrees. "Sweet. First time I've heard it described that way."

Livy pointed at Erik. "I love the cross you're wearing. Are you a Christian?"

DeeDee stopped herself from rolling her eyes. Maybe she should go find the ladies' room while Livy talked religion.

But she stayed rooted when Erik nodded, his expression somber. "I am." He raised his palm to the ceiling. "Christ dragged me out of the mud and saved me, praise God."

Livy's smile widened. "How long ago was that?"

"Several years ago while I was in prison."

Livy's expression no doubt matched her own—eagerness to know what crime he'd committed, tamped down by caution against inappropriate questions.

"Yep." Clive's voice wrested DeeDee's attention to his animated face and wagging finger. "He's a preacher man now. He wants to get you saved, man."

Erik gave a good-natured chuckle. "What he means is, I

volunteer for a prison ministry, helping other ex-cons like myself get their lives back on track."

"Sounds like a worthy cause."

Her twin narrowed her eyes and cast her a suspicious glance. Livy always knew when DeeDee wasn't being sincere.

Not wanting to waste any more time on religious talk, DeeDee turned to Erik. "I understand you're Leon Jr.'s new father-in-law." At his inclined head, she went on. "Was the marriage as big a shock to you as it seems to be for everyone else?"

Erik rubbed his salt-and-pepper goatee. "Not really. The two of them were best friends since childhood. Always together. So yeah, my wife and I could see it coming."

"They've known each other since childhood?"

"Senior and I were best friends. So our kids saw a lot of each other. 'Course, we didn't call him Senior until after Leon Jr. was born."

"I see." She shoved away her empty plate. "Change of subject, but...can I pick your brain about Nick?"

Clive cut in, "If you can find any left to pick." He barked with a chortling laugh.

She offered an obligatory smile, but when Erik didn't reciprocate, she plunged in. "How long have you known Nick?"

Erik counted on his fingers, then held up his palms as though he'd given up. "A long time. We met through mutual friends. Clive, didn't Nick tour with us after we released our first album?"

Clive looked toward the ceiling, his fingers drumming out a percussion on the table. "The Bolts And Nuts tour? Yeah, he did. I remember because his wife kept calling him."

Pam again. Would she never be rid of that woman's shadow?

Clive went on, "So we decided to play a trick on her.

Next time she called, I answered and told her he'd been rushed to the hospital with acute Pamitis."

DeeDee and Livy shared an eye-rolling moment.

"She got mad," Erik took over the story, "and cussed us all out."

"Meanwhile, Nick was over there laughing his guts out…."

"But she got the message and quit calling."

"What instrument did you play?" DeeDee cut in before they could mention Pam's name again.

Erik indicated his friend across the table. "Clive was lead singer and keyboardist. Nick on guitar, obviously. We couldn't seem to acquire a decent drummer."

"What about you?"

"Me?" Erik pointed to himself and chuckled again. "I can't sing a note or play a lick. I'm a musical ignoramus. So they made me road manager."

"Did Senior tell you Nick took off and didn't tell anyone where he went?"

Erik shifted away from her. "He did. A bit of a surprise. The Nick I know wouldn't do something like that."

"In the nine months we've been dating, I've never known him to be flaky."

His expression softened. "He'll be back."

He was obviously trying to keep her spirits up, but she didn't want platitudes. She wanted Nick, in the flesh, at her side.

Chapter Thirteen

DeeDee set her laptop on the dresser and opened Skype. Since Scott didn't get home from work until six, she and Livy waited until five after to log on. A few minutes later, his handsome face appeared on the screen. He didn't look in DeeDee's direction at all. As usual, he only had eyes for Livy. Men had always been drawn more to Livy than to her, a baffling fact—until Nick came along. Thank goodness for Nick.

Livy's smile stretched wide when Scott's face appeared. "Hi, honey," she practically crooned. "How was your day?"

"I missed you." Mr. Serious brightened as though someone had flipped a switch inside him. He ran his hand along his five o'clock shadow.

"You're really rocking the scruffy look tonight, hon."

He chuckled and massaged his bristly jaw once more.

"You heard Nick is missing?" DeeDee cut in before they started getting mushy.

"Yeah." He nodded at her. "No word yet?"

"No. He's been gone for two days."

Scott frowned. "That doesn't sound good."

"But he left some clues, and we wanted to show them to you and get your take." She held up the map. "See this? Black Bear Lane? I Googled it and got a million possibilities."

Scott angled his head, then directed her to move it where he could make it out. "I can't read those numbers. Can you read them to me?"

DeeDee rattled off the digits. His face grew thoughtful. "Sounds like latitude coordinates to me. Forty-eight point nine-nine degrees north, most likely."

"Well, that narrows it down." DeeDee bit her lip. "Sorry, I wasn't trying to be sarcastic."

"It's somewhere north of here. Seattle's between the forty-seventh and forty-eighth parallels. You'll want to check online maps and see what falls on that latitude."

Livy nudged her and signaled with her eyes, a look DeeDee knew well. Livy wanted to talk to Scott in private. She thanked him for his input and left the two alone. Grabbing her tablet, she followed the scent of roasting beef to the kitchen, where Renee and Gavin prepared dinner. She told them what Scott had said and opened a map app.

Gavin offered a suggestion. "Try checking up near Nanaimo on Vancouver Island."

DeeDee did so. "Too far north." Further south, she located the latitude Nick had written on the map and groaned. "I don't see any roads. There's nothing but forest up there." She zoomed out to get a better look. A few towns dotted the island's east coast, smaller islands hugged the shoreline—some long and skinny, some shaped like fighter jets. Across the water, Vancouver.

"Do you think he could've gone to Vancouver? It's on the forty-ninth parallel."

Renee shrugged. "Not a clue. Sorry."

DeeDee threw up her hands. "This is like looking for a needle in a haystack. I'll have to check each of those Black Bear Lanes and see if any of them fall on that latitude. This could take a while."

Livy wandered in with a distracted smile, and DeeDee waved her over and showed her the map.

The landline phone blasted, a shrill noise that made them all jump.

Renee hurried to the counter to pick it up. "Hello?"

An expectant hush vibrated through the room.

"Hi, Mom." Renee listened for a few moments, then gasped and put a hand to her heart. "Where?"

DeeDee's heart jumped. She and Livy exchanged a look. News of Nick?

After Renee exclaimed, "Oh wow," and "Oh no!" DeeDee tried to meet her gaze, but Renee paced, the phone fastened to her ear.

DeeDee had to know more. She stepped in front of Renee and mouthed, "What?"

Renee stopped and cast her an anxious look, but clenched her grip on the receiver. "Nick's in the hospital," she whispered. Speaking into the phone, she added, "Mom, can you leave me the number, please?" She found a pencil and scribbled the digits. "We'll do our best to get over there soon."

By the time Renee hung up, DeeDee was a quivering mass of nerves. She grabbed Livy's hand and squeezed, as the two of them had done since childhood whenever one of them was upset. "Tell us what she said! Why is Nick in the hospital?"

A mask of worry tightened Renee's features. "He was found unconscious."

"Where?"

She went to sit beside her husband, who pulled her close. "On Mt. Sicker. The man who found him called emergency, and he was transported to the hospital in Chemainus."

"Where is Mt. Sicker?"

"About an hour north of here, exactly where you were looking."

DeeDee doubled over, fear washing over her in dizzying waves. She lay her head on her sister's shoulder, soaking in her soothing vibe. With her emotions shredded, she couldn't speak, so Livy, sensing it, spoke for her.

"Did they know why he was unconscious?"

"Hypothermia, the doctor said. It's thirty degrees on the mountain, with snow on the ground. The man who found him said he looked like he was sleeping, but couldn't rouse him."

"What's the prognosis?" DeeDee forced the words around the lump in her throat. Livy tightened her grip on DeeDee's shoulders.

"He's still unconscious. They're doing their best to raise his body temperature."

And she had doubted him. Remorse pierced her heart. Blinking back tears, she checked the clock. Endless hours of uncertainty separated her and her love. "I have to see him."

Chapter Fourteen

Nick reached out to the white-robed man with an outstretched hand floating toward him through the clouds. The man's smooth black hair fell below his shoulders, and he held a shepherd's staff.

"Jesus?" Nick rasped.

Instead of replying, the man gazed at Nick with eyes as soft as lambs' wool. Nick couldn't remember ever seeing such a heaping measure of love in anyone's eyes.

A burning peace invaded his heart, and he smiled. He wanted to utter "Lord" but couldn't get his mouth to work. But Jesus looked at him with such understanding, Nick knew he need not say a thing.

The storm in DeeDee's heart raged on, even while Renee urged Gavin to drive them up to Chemainus. For the first time, she considered the possibility of losing Nick. If he didn't make it, much more than a car ride would separate them.

"I don't want to wait till tomorrow," Renee insisted, echoing DeeDee's thoughts.

"By the time we get there, visiting hours will likely be over." An edge of exasperation lashed Gavin's words.

"Why don't I just call them, then? If it's not too late, will you take us?"

While Gavin and Renee argued, DeeDee rocked side to side, gripping Livy's hand as if holding a life preserver. She hardly noticed when Livy led her to the kitchen table and lowered her into a chair.

"I have to see him," DeeDee whimpered again, low enough for only Livy's ears. Livy, her eyes wide with concern, gathered her close.

"How about we pray?" Livy suggested, her voice quiet yet firm enough to carry over Gavin and Renee bickering in the background.

DeeDee grimaced, wishing she had the heart to glare at her sister.

"I've been praying since you called," Livy went on. "So has Scott. And see? God does answer prayer. Nick was found."

"Oh really?" DeeDee wrested herself out of Livy's grasp, holding her fingers a half-inch apart. "He's this far from death!"

When tears sprang to Livy's eyes, DeeDee regretted her harsh words. Softening her tone, she said, "But if Nick pulls through, I suppose I might believe someone out there can hear us."

⤜⤙⤜

After a rough night of frantic dreams, DeeDee awoke to a reality that made her wish she'd stayed in dreamland. Nick, flickering between life and death like a candle flame. Over coffee, Livy held out a ray of light when she offered to drive herself and DeeDee to the hospital. DeeDee could only clutch her in gratitude.

They followed the Maxwells up the island and through picturesque scenery DeeDee barely saw. Livy didn't try to get her to talk, just let her brood and sort through her yo-yoing emotions. As soon as she dared be optimistic that Nick would be okay, fear crowded in, drenching her spirit in a cloud cover as impenetrable as the one above. Twisting, whirling, like a strenuous typhoon inside her.

By the time they reached the hospital, her spirit was drained, numb. She gasped when she finally laid eyes on Nick's unconscious form. As she bent over him, Livy and the Maxwells hovered next to the nurse in charge. Nick lay so still, DeeDee froze for a second, thinking he was dead. Then his eyelids twitched, and his mouth moved.

"No," he whispered as creases furrowed his forehead.

DeeDee eyed the nurse, whose name badge said Carol. "Is he having a bad dream?"

Carol nodded. "Ever since he came in. He says the same thing over and over again."

"What's he say?"

"Leon, no. Over and over."

"Leon? Leon's his stepson. Why would he keep saying his name?"

"I don't know. Sometimes he talks to someone named Jack."

"Jack? I don't know him." DeeDee pursed her mouth and picked up Nick's hand, as cold as a mannequin's. At least he hadn't been with Pam.

Carol turned to Renee. "Are you next of kin?"

Renee spun to the nurse. "His sister. Our parents are on their way and should be here soon."

"I'm his girlfriend. Does he ever say my name? DeeDee?"

A soft smile curved the nurse's stiff lips. "He has mentioned you a few times."

A little of her sorrow eased, and Gavin asked Carol to fill them in on the details. "How long had he been lying in the snow?"

"There's no way to know. He was bundled up pretty good, so there's no reason his body temperature should have dropped. But the paramedics said his clothes were wet. Which would explain the hypothermia."

DeeDee searched Nick's ashen face. "Why was he wet?"

"We're not sure. His jacket was ripped, and there were traces of blood on it. The man who found him thought he may have been attacked by a wild animal and somehow got away."

A vision of Nick getting attacked by a black bear made DeeDee nearly collapse, but Livy caught her just in time.

Carol's next words drifted through a fog. "He may have tried to wash off the blood in the creek. He was lying near the edge of it."

"He has a sprained ankle. Did someone get X-rays?"

Carol studied Nick's drawn face. "We did. It was pretty severe, poor guy."

Renee cleared her throat. "Nick wouldn't have tried to wash himself off in a creek. Not in freezing weather. He's smarter than that."

"He might have fallen in," said Livy.

"Yes." Dee nodded. "He could hardly walk Saturday."

"We can speculate all day," Carol gestured to the charts, "but we won't know for sure what happened until he wakes up."

If he wakes up. DeeDee tried to shove the thought away. If she lost Nick, how would she ever feel joy again?

༺༼༻

DeeDee's appetite had fled somewhere back on the Trans-Canada Highway. Still, she allowed Livy to talk her into having lunch at a diner across the street, where she picked at her food. Gavin, who needed to report to work, took Gabe and headed home after Livy agreed to bring Renee back.

Across the table, Renee brooded while Livy stepped outside to call Scott with an update.

"What'll I do if he doesn't make it?" DeeDee croaked.

She picked up a fry, then set it back down. The last one she'd eaten felt like a potato ball in her stomach, growing larger each second until it threatened to bulge over the waistband of her Adriana jeans. The vision made her want to hurl, and she glanced around for a restroom, just in case she lost her lunch.

"Do you want to finish these?" She slid the platter across the table. "I'm not hungry."

Renee shook her head, still silent, her eyes shrouded.

Were Livy and Scott praying? DeeDee hoped they were. What if they were right and there was something to this prayer thing after all? Livy seemed so grounded and peaceful now that she believed in God. She called it a relationship, and God her Heavenly Father.

"Are you a Christian?" The question blurted out before she could stop it.

And seemed to shake Renee out of her stupor. She met DeeDee's eyes and nodded. "Growing up, we went to church, but Gavin and I don't attend very often."

"Why not?"

Renee lifted her cup and sipped her herb tea. "We'd rather sleep in on Sunday. Gavin works hard during the week, and Sunday is R and R day."

"Livy started going to church last year." DeeDee studied the plate of American-style fries in front of her. The thin strips were scattered across the china like straw on a barn floor and tasted the same. "Her fiancé, who was just a friend at the time, persuaded her to believe in God. She's been really different ever since."

"Different in what way?"

DeeDee glanced out the window. Livy still paced outside, her phone to her ear. "She doesn't party with me anymore."

"A lot of Christians won't touch alcohol."

"She'll still have a glass of wine with dinner or an occasional beer, but she won't hang out with the band we used to sing with. She's got all these churchy friends now."

"I know the type you mean."

"Whenever I use swear words, she gives me this *look*. And she got rid of all her spiritual books."

"What kind of spiritual books?"

"You know, channeling energy. Chakra. Practicing the divine feminine."

"That sounds a little too woo-woo for me. I'll take old-fashioned religion any day."

DeeDee bit back a defense. Renee didn't know she and Livy had been raised on New Age beliefs and DeeDee still tried to live by those ideals. But Livy had taken her spiritualism and narrowed it down to one person: Jesus Christ. "Things were kinda tense between us for a while. Livy told me she didn't need all those other spirits, because she has the Holy Spirit inside her. Doesn't that sound a little woo-woo to you?"

"Not really. I recognize the saying. Christianese was the language of my childhood."

"Are you saying you have the Holy Spirit inside you, too?"

Renee regarded her through narrowed eyes. "I doubt it. I'm pretty sure God gave up on me a long time ago."

"Nick says the same thing."

"Yes, Mom calls him our prodigal son."

"What does she mean?"

"The story Jesus told of the runaway son who blew his father's money on wild living, then came to his senses and went back home. When the dad saw him coming, he threw a big party."

DeeDee took a sip of water. It flowed in a cold river down her parched throat. "Why would he?"

"Because his son who was lost had come home. Mom's been praying for years Nick will do the same."

"You mean, get religion?"

Renee smiled for the first time all day. "Yes, get religion. She calls it getting saved."

DeeDee shuddered. "Please, no more religious nuts. It's bad enough my sister got bit by that bug."

As though Livy had heard DeeDee, she flounced back inside, the door chime tinkling behind her. Sliding into the booth, she exclaimed, "Scott found something."

Both heads turned toward her.

"After we Skyped last night, he did his own search for a Black Bear Lane at that latitude. And guess what?"

"Tell me."

"There's one on Mt. Sicker. Not too far from here."

From the gleam in her eye, DeeDee knew what was coming next.

"Do you want to drive over and see if we can find the place?"

Chapter Fifteen

Crystallized snowflakes crunched under DeeDee's feet when she and Livy exited the hospital. A light brushing of snow glittered on nearby windshields, but the road was clear. Renee had stayed with Nick to wait for her parents. "We'll be back in an hour," DeeDee assured her.

DeeDee rattled the key at Livy. "How about I drive, you navigate?" she suggested as they climbed into Livy's Jag. She handed Livy the printed map. "Okay, we're set. Let's do this."

A twenty-minute scenic drive brought them to the bottom of a seven-thousand-foot mountain. Livy's phone directed them north, past stately homes spaced far apart and surrounded by tall, thin evergreens. The supermodels of the tree world. When they had nearly arrived, the road narrowed and made a sharp right turn up an incline.

"Are we going the right way?"

Livy frowned at the phone. "The phone thinks so. Keep going. Black Bear Lane should be just around this corner to the left."

"I hope there are no bears around."

"Turn here."

DeeDee steered to the left onto a one-lane dirt road gutted with deep crevasses packed with snow. The wheels sank into the ruts, undulating the car up and down. DeeDee cursed. "This can't be good for the suspension." The speedometer dipped below five miles per hour, but the car still bounced them around like a trampoline.

"Ow!" Livy clutched the top of her head. "That hurt!"

"Oh, sorry." DeeDee slowed to a crawl. Within a hundred feet, the tree-lined road smoothed out into a flat dirt lane mixed with gravel then launched up another hill. Thin patches of day-old snow dotted the road.

"Where is this place, anyway?" DeeDee muttered.

"Almost there." Livy swiveled to face her. "How about we pray?" She cupped a hand on DeeDee's shoulder.

DeeDee felt a slight flinch where Livy's touch rested. How could she get out of this?

"What for?"

"I'd just feel better knowing we have prayer cover. Especially with wild animals around."

"You go ahead." This would be something to hear. Livy normally kept her prayers to herself.

Livy closed her eyes and lifted her face to the ceiling. "Father God," she began, "please watch over us and protect us. We didn't really think about the possible dangers, God, but we're here and we can't turn back now."

She prayed as though she were talking to a real live person. Squeezing DeeDee's shoulder, she said amen. The next moment a one-story log cabin came into view. With her foot on the brake, DeeDee sized it up, estimating it to be about a thousand square feet. Faded patches and chipped wood on the logs gave the exterior a ragged look. A chain-link fence wrapped around the property, forming a tight wall between the bare front yard and the woods, like a security guard holding back invading trees.

"This isn't at all what I expected, but it has to be the right place. What's our latitude?"

Livy peered at her phone. "Spot on."

"It looks deserted, doesn't it?" A gate with a padlock interrupted the stiff line of fence, but she couldn't tell if it was locked. "Let's go check out the inside."

"No."

"No? Why?"

Livy's eyes grew wide. "This is someone's home. We'd be breaking and entering."

"You're the one who suggested this."

"I didn't mean we should break the law. I just wanted to help you figure out where Nick disappeared to." She hung her head. "I admit, I was dying of curiosity myself."

DeeDee thrust a hand toward the house. "But I still know nothing. I don't know who lives here or why he was here." She clutched the door handle. "I'm going in."

"No, Deeds."

"Yes, Livs. You want to stay here, be my guest."

She slammed the door over Livy's protests and approached the gate, eyeing the rusty, unfastened padlock. Probably so corroded, it no longer shut. DeeDee removed the lock and stepped inside. Two large dog food bowls, one filled with food, sat next to the fence. A metal chute fed into them from the other side of the chain link. Clever. Obviously designed for someone to pour the dog's food and water without stepping inside. She glanced around. No dog. Only a faint, yet insistent, barking from inside the house. No other signs of life, no movement, except the sigh of the wind through the tree branches high above.

"It's so quiet here." Her whisper seemed to boom through the void, and she glanced again at the front door, half-expecting it to burst open and an angry resident to appear. But the door and the window blinds stayed as tightly closed as a fortress, strengthening her sense that nobody was home.

Unsure what to do next, she picked her way over a carpet of pine needles to the side yard. A line of trees formed a barrier between front yard and back. She continued around the corner, through the trees, until she reached a doghouse and a decrepit shed. Glancing to the right, she froze. A U-Haul van sat beyond the fence in front of a sagging carport. But no yellow Alfa Romeo.

She sniffed. An odor, reminiscent of a dead animal, filled her lungs. She wrinkled her nose, and an odd sight near the shed caught her eye.

Someone sprawled facedown on the other side of the fence, head resting on a tree root, matted black hair hiding the face. A jagged hole marred the back of the person's leather jacket like an angry scab. Below the jacket, long, black-denim-clad legs in a pair of knee-high Saint Laurent suede boots perched toe-first on the pine-needled dirt as casually as if they'd returned from a stroll at the mall.

Her heart accelerated, but she made herself kneel despite her trepidation. The head was lying with its face toward her, and chiseled features lurked under the wild, shadowing hair.

Pam!

Her wide, lifeless eyes stared back at DeeDee.

She gasped and jumped back. Then screamed loud enough to send pine needles hurtling to the ground.

She pivoted and ran back the way she came. Her heart pounded so hard, she was sure Livy could hear.

Doubling over, she fought to catch her breath, couldn't reply to Livy's frantic questions. She could only hand Livy the key and gasp out, "Get us out of here!"

Ignoring Livy's anxious glances, DeeDee hastened around the car as though ghosts chased her, landing in the passenger seat with her heart still in overdrive. Livy clambered over the center console and jammed the key into the ignition, fishtailing the car in her haste to turn it around.

"What? What's wrong?"

DeeDee tried to pull herself together as the car jostled down the rough lane. "Pam's back there!"

Livy gasped. "What?"

"Someone murdered Pam. I found her in the back yard—shot."

Braking to a stop, Livy reached for her as her screeches crescendoed, but her sister's embrace couldn't erase the vision—the staring eyes, the mouth open in mid-scream.

Nothing could.

Chapter Sixteen

"Aren't you going to call the cops?" Livy barreled over a rut, sending their heads on a collision course with the roof.

"No way. You know what'll happen once they find out Nick was in the area. Especially when they learn of his relationship to the victim. They'll never believe he didn't do it."

"But it's obstruction of justice."

"Then so be it. By the time someone finds her body, nobody will remember Nick was here."

The ride back to Chemainus passed in grim silence. At the hospital, Renee and her parents greeted them, their faces somber. Renee plied them with questions. Had they found the place they sought? It took all DeeDee's strength to pretend they'd found nothing, especially with Livy casting her perturbed looks. Did Livy really expect her to reveal what she'd seen? And risk incriminating the man she loved? Seriously?

Hard to believe Renee didn't see the truth on her face. But she seemed to believe them as she relayed Nick's unchanged condition, his uncertain prognosis. "He could stay this way for days. Weeks, even."

DeeDee's shoulders drooped with the effort of maintaining her charade. How could she keep this up for indefinite days or weeks? The truth would burst out of her and bring trouble on her head.

Finally, tears prickled her eyes, and her mouth trembled. "I just want to go home."

"Home as in Seattle?"

She nodded. "Sorry. I'm a basket case. You'll keep me updated, won't you?"

At Renee's wide-eyed nod, she explained, "A couple days ago, Nick told me it's been one bad thing after another ever since we stepped on the ferry. And he was right."

Renee came to her and hugged her, patting her back and murmuring, "I understand."

DeeDee pulled away and made a show of wiping her eyes, even though the tears had frozen inside her and wouldn't fall.

Forcing visions of Pam's staring eyes out of her mind, she went to Nick's side and massaged the top of his head, pressing her lips to his cheek. She and Livy drove back to Victoria, stopping at the Maxwells' for the rest of their things. She stared blankly out the Jag's windows on the drive to Sidney for the drawn-out ferry ride home, made even longer by her surreal state of mind.

Every jutting island, every wave of the sea reminded her of their happy journey last week. Oh, if only they'd never come to Victoria. Livy kept squeezing her hand and didn't expect her to talk, for which DeeDee was grateful.

The early dark of winter had fallen by the time the ferry docked at Anacortes, bringing with it a chilling rain. She climbed into the Jaguar's passenger side and leaned her head back while the car crept through the customs queue, then closed her eyes against the terrible visions. In another couple hours, she'd be home.

Home never sounded so sweet.

❧❧❧

DeeDee hadn't realized how much she'd missed the animals until they both came running the moment she and Livy walked through the door of their spacious red home on

Laurel Court. Murf, Livy's elegant Samoyed, always quivered as if he were about to burst with coiled energy. He yipped at them and shimmied his short, fluffy tail in greeting, his claws loud on the hardwood floor. Miss Piggy, the cat, round and orange like a furry basketball, dropped to her haunches and eyed DeeDee with an impassive gaze as if she regretted giving away her excitement. Lifting a paw, she ignored them and proceeded to bathe herself. But her telltale purr when DeeDee scratched her behind the ears betrayed her pleasure.

After depositing her bags on top of her yellow-striped comforter, DeeDee peeked out the matching curtains at the drenched backyard. The porch light illuminated the patio where Nick barbecued burgers for her last summer. Would they ever feel so carefree again? Steeling herself against the memories, DeeDee took her laptop to the kitchen and leaned against the island, an old dresser she and Livy refurbished, topped with faux-marble, and painted banana yellow. She scoured the news from Victoria, but saw nothing about a woman found shot on Mt. Sicker. She checked her map app again. Nanaimo was the nearest sizable town to the murder site, so she skimmed their news as well. Then Chemainus.

Nothing.

She might as well retrieve her stuff from his place. No telling how long before he returned home. After a dinner of rice and beans chimichangas, she drove to Nick's townhouse in the U District and let herself in with her key, breathing deep. The place smelled like a home that missed its owner. Gone was the welcoming warmth of a cared-for home that she'd always loved. In its place, a cold, sterile emptiness, like a showpiece house nobody wanted.

She shivered.

From habit, she dropped the key on the hallstand. It clinged against a hardback book. She picked it up. *The Invisible Man*, by H.G. Wells, that she'd bought for him after he jokingly claimed that lead vocalists and guitarists got so much attention, bass players might as well be invisible. She bit her lip, desperately missing his self-deprecating sense of humor. When he opened the gift, a priceless look scrunched his face before he burst into laughter. To his credit, he'd finished the book in two days.

She moved from room to room, like the invisible man himself, almost as if Nick might appear around the next corner and catch her in the act. She gathered all the things she'd left over the months—a toothbrush, lingerie, books, food, clothing—and stuffed it all in an oversize satchel. In the spare room, where they watched TV, the stuffed Yeti Nick bought her in LA sat on the couch, his huge grin irresistible. She found herself grinning back, but then, reality hit, and a tear-filled knot, hard as a tennis ball, lodged inside her chest. If she'd known how hard this would be, how gut wrenching, she would've brought Livy. Even if her constant sniffles irritated her sister, Livy's very presence would be better than doing this alone.

With Yeti tucked under her arm, she ducked into the bedroom. And froze in the doorway. Red and gold packages, the Christmassy bows bright and shining, perched haphazardly on his bed. She tugged on her heart necklace, twisting it around and around her finger until the gold links shattered in her hand. Stunned, she watched the tiny pieces bounce on the polished maple floor. Was this a sign of her future with Nick? As Yeti slipped to the floor, she knelt and groped around, but could only salvage the gold heart. She clutched it, head down, eyes shut tight against reality. Maybe she'd fall asleep right here on Nick's floor. And when she awoke, he'd be here.

But no. She'd likely be spending Christmas without him. And she needed to finish before she had a meltdown. As she dared lift her head, the colorful gifts drew her forward. She stood and picked up each package and examined the wrapping, picturing Nick taping and folding the perfectly creased corners. None of the five festive boxes had name labels yet. She set down a gold-wrapped one and touched one splashed with poinsettias. He knew she loved poinsettias. Was this one for her? And did one of them contain those mouthwatering Moonstones he'd ordered? Much as Nick knew she adored chocolate, she didn't think he'd really buy her a gift from his ex-wife's store. Maybe they were for his mom or sister.

Stiffening her sloped shoulders, she set the boxes back on the bed and resumed her task. With the bag full, she marched it out to her car and slammed it in the trunk. She hadn't known she'd accumulated so much stuff at Nick's. When he came home—*if* he came home—he'd surely notice their absence.

Back inside, she made one more walk-through in case she'd forgotten anything. In the kitchen, she opened the dishwasher and stared at the neatly-stacked dishes from their last dinner. Happy memories mocked her. She and Nick had laughed and fed each other savory scallops in brown butter, unaware of the ordeal ahead.

She might as well unload them. And empty the garbage. She gathered up the garbage under the sink, took it out to the dumpster, and then went to fetch the recycling, which he accumulated in a box under his desk. She pivoted toward the TV room and, bending at the waist, looked inside the box. It contained only a few sheets—it could wait. As she pushed the box away with her foot, a name on the top paper caught her eye: Pamela. She sucked in a breath and, nearly touching her toes, pulled out the sheet.

And her hand shook as she read the heading of an e-mail from Pam to Nick, dated the same day as the map.

Hello, Nick. You're probably wondering

why I'd contact you after all these years. Well, I found out something interesting, something you will want to know about. But I warn you it could shake things up a little. Can we get together while you're here? Please?

PS – In case you're wondering why I'd discuss this with you instead of my husband, let's just say it's not the sort of news he would want to know.

She gripped the desk chair, then sank into it, her emotions teetering on a precipice. She read it again, twice more. No mistake. Nick had lied to her. He *had* gone to meet his ex.

She recalled the conversation, verbatim:

Who were you talking to?

An old friend.

Not just any "old friend." His gorgeous ex-wife. Why had he hidden his true intent? Either he didn't trust her, or he was afraid of her reaction.

He had to have known how much it would hurt her.

Was his real reason far more ominous? The first frisson of doubt needled her. Could Nick be guilty of a horrendous crime?

She sprang to her feet. She had to get home and tell Livy.

�-�-�

"Livy!" DeeDee wailed, her pent-up grief sailing through the living room to Murf's empathetic ears. Miss Piggy gave an indifferent tail swish and blinked lazily.

But Livy's car was gone. As DeeDee leaned against the garage door, the knot in her heart diminished little by little, until it had finally shrunk to the size of a pebble. She tissued away the last vestige, sniffed hard, and set her laptop on the kitchen counter. Rushing through the Victoria news sites, she almost passed by a tiny article about a missing woman, then did a double take at the name Pamela.

> A Saanich woman has been reported missing. Pamela Campbell, founder and president of Moonstone Truffles, Ltd., was last seen by her husband, Bryan Campbell, on Monday morning about eight o'clock when she left home presumably to report to her office. "She seemed quieter than usual," said Campbell, 43, "like she had something on her mind." He attempted to reach her several times throughout the day, but she did not answer any of his calls. Her assistant at Moonstone informed Mr. Campbell that his wife was not expected in the office that day. She never returned home that evening.

> If anyone has any information about her possible whereabouts, please call this number.

DeeDee's heart knocked against her chest. Surely, someone would eventually find the body. Maybe by then, Nick would have recovered, and no one would ever know Pam had gone there to meet him.

She picked up her phone to text Renee. *How's Nick? Any change?*

He's getting restless. Dr. thinks he will regain consciousness soon. Planning to visit him soon?

DeeDee chewed her lip as she pondered several responses, then discarded them like old socks. She couldn't simply forget what Nick had done. But there was no avoiding the inevitable. *I'll come see him as soon as I can arrange it.*

But the thought of an hour-long drive to Anacortes, then a two-hour ferry ride and another long drive up the island...the very idea left her exhausted. If only she could fly to Nick's side.

Livy glided through the front door, her arms laden with Nordstrom bags. DeeDee ran to her, led her to the sunroom, and told her everything.

Livy swung the bags back and forth after DeeDee read the incriminating e-mail. "Hmm. She had news her husband wouldn't want to know. Sounds highly suspicious to me."

"He lied to me."

"True, but..."

"What?"

"That seems like the less serious issue."

"Huh?" DeeDee dropped to the tropical-print futon.

Livy plunked the shopping bags on the ground and joined her, pointing to the e-mail. "This sounds huge. Didn't you wonder what she had to tell him?"

"Sure I did."

"I can understand why he wasn't ready to tell you. He'd want to hear the news first so he'd know whether it was shareable."

"But he still should've been honest with me. It just ticks me off that he didn't trust me with the truth." DeeDee groaned and lowered her head to her hands. "I need to go see him. Maybe he'll be awake and explain everything. But I can't stand another ferry ride through the San Juans. Too many memories."

"Does Chemainus have an airport?"

"I don't know. What are you thinking?"

"Remember Maggie the pilot? The wife of Dad's old bandmate?"

"I do. I bet she'd be willing to fly me up there in her little Cherokee. If Chemainus doesn't have an airport, she could drop me in Nanaimo, and I'll rent a car." She leapt to her feet. "I'll call her today. Oh, before I forget..." She palmed her forehead and sat back down. "Look what I found." She angled her laptop toward Livy and showed her the news article. Livy, beside her, leaned toward the screen, her hair brushing DeeDee's shoulders. They breathed in sync as they absorbed the news.

"Wow." Livy straightened, her face taut. "I've been feeling so guilty, keeping this news to myself. I haven't even told Scott, and I feel like a little sneak."

"You can't tell him or anyone. We need to pretend this never happened and let things take their natural course."

"But it's obstruction of justice—"

"Which needs to stay between you and me."

Livy's face sagged. "But what would Scott think of me, knowing I'm suppressing evidence of a murder? Not to mention, what does God think of me?" Livy whirled and hurried from the room.

DeeDee dashed from the futon and scurried after her, grabbing her arm and swiveling her around.

"Don't you dare tell," she warned through clenched teeth. "I wish now I hadn't told you anything." She let go of Livy's arm when she saw her stricken look. "If you snitch and he gets arrested, I might never speak to you again."

DeeDee watched Livy's eyes closely to see if the words hit hard. Her twin's eyelids twitched as though something were trying to escape. Her gaze darted around the room, evading DeeDee's fierce stare. Finally, her shoulders loosened and her face relaxed, and DeeDee knew she'd won over Livy's tender conscience.

"Okay," she croaked, her focus steady on DeeDee. "I won't say anything."

DeeDee, nearly crying in relief, wrapped her sister's shoulders and squeezed.

Chapter Seventeen

Nick heard DeeDee's voice from behind a high black wall. He moved to the wall and tried to push it away, but it wouldn't budge. He pushed harder, longing to see her. He missed her adventurous spirit, her glimmering smile, her cayenne-pepper curls. He needed to tell her he wanted to spend the rest of his life with her.

"God, help," he murmured. "Please bring DeeDee to me so I can see her again."

A sliver of light shone around the wall, and the wall began to move. It rose, the light behind it glowing brighter. Now he could see the woman he loved, far away and indistinct. He reached for her, and at the same time, his eyes flew open. Golden light formed a halo around DeeDee's hair and filled his vision.

"DeeDee?" he tried to say, but it came out garbled.

She turned a startled face to him, then let out a cry. "He's awake!"

❧❧❧

On trembling legs, DeeDee rushed to Nick's side, and the room seemed to darken around her. With his gaunt complexion and cheeks sunken like craters, he resembled a famine survivor.

An unfamiliar nurse bustled through the door. "Did I hear right? Our patient woke up?"

Still staring at Nick, DeeDee nodded. The young nurse examined him and said a few words, and he mumbled something in response. "His vitals are looking good." She lifted his bed to elevate his head. "How's the handsomest patient in the hospital today?"

DeeDee rolled her eyes, then faced the nurse. "Do you mind giving me some time alone with him?"

Renee and Ms. Desperate White Female left, and Renee's voice floated back into the room. "You were flirting with a taken man. That's his girlfriend."

She leaned closer. "Hi, Nick," she ventured, keeping her voice even.

He gazed at her and smiled. "Dee—" he said, lifting his hand toward hers. Instead of clasping it, she crossed her arms. A flicker of surprise creased his face, morphing to a ripple of confusion. His next words came out clear but weak.

"I...miss you."

She said nothing, merely waited.

"Dreamed...about you. And Je–sus—"

"You dreamed about Jesus? Are you religious now?"

He shook his head, his eyes darkening like a storm over the San Juans. "God—Father."

"You dreamed about the Godfather?"

He shook his head harder, his shaky hand stretched toward her. She stayed motionless. "I love...you." He forced the words out with great effort. "Get...married?"

She wrapped her arms tighter around herself. He'd trysted with his ex, lied about it, and now expected her to marry him? The words she'd planned to say fled like a flock of startled birds. He continued to gaze at her, his eyes filled with yearning as innocent as a baby's.

She wiped her sweaty palms on her jeans and took a deep breath. "Nick, I–I..." She swallowed hard. "I don't know." She was gabbling with nerves, squeezing her chin, her tight throat constricting her words.

His eyes darkened again, and a strangled sound—like "why?"—came out of his mouth. Deep creases crisscrossed his brow.

Because you shattered my trust. She had to get out of there. Swiveling to the door, she peeked out and saw Renee and the nurse chatting halfway down the hall to her left. She sidled out of the door and headed right, hugging the wall to remain inconspicuous. Finally reaching the stairwell, she hurried down two flights of stairs to her rental car, where she broke down and let all the dammed up tears sweep her away.

✧✧✧

Back in Seattle, DeeDee hopped from the little Cherokee to SeaTac's pavement. "Bye, Maggie, and thanks."

Maggie's long gray hair lifted in the wind. "Not a problem. I love Vancouver Island."

"Dad said send the bill to him."

"I will." Maggie waved, then turned her attention to the shiny four-seater Piper PA-28, her pride and joy.

After clearing customs, DeeDee dug her phone from her purse and strode to her car. Sure enough, the expected text from Renee awaited her. She waited until she'd settled in her car to read it.

Where did you go??

She'd already planned what she would say. *Sorry I left in such a hurry. I was upset.*

Nick was upset, too, but he wasn't able to tell me why. When will you be back?

Will be busy finishing up prep for Christmas in the next few days. Don't know when I'll make it up there.

She could visualize Renee's puzzled expression. DeeDee clenched her lips. When a fresh batch of tears stung her eyes, she had to blink over and over before they receded and she could begin her journey home.

Livy met her at the door and searched her face. DeeDee fell into her sister's arms and clung there, her voice muffled against Livy's sweater as she narrated her day. When the words had all spilled out, Livy nudged her into the kitchen, parked her at the island, and thrust a cup of coffee into her hands. Grateful, unable to speak of it anymore, DeeDee sipped and stared out the window. The cherry tree in the side yard spread its leafless, twiggy branches to the sky, trying in vain to absorb nourishment from the nonexistent sun. Like DeeDee's barren soul.

For two days, no updates on Pam appeared on any news sites. DeeDee mostly kept to herself because Livy's guilt-ridden face got on her nerves. And shouted that she was keeping DeeDee's secret against her better judgment. Whenever Scott came over, DeeDee could see the effort it took for Livy to act naturally. Fortunately, he appeared clueless that anything was wrong.

"How's Nick?" he asked Thursday evening as he and Livy prepared to leave for a movie.

"He woke up yesterday morning, but he was still very weak and could barely talk."

"But he'll be okay?"

"They seem to think so." DeeDee meandered out of the room to keep Scott from asking any more questions, like why she wasn't keeping a vigil in Nick's hospital room. If he started quizzing Livy, she'd better not give anything away.

But judging by Livy's starry-eyed face after Scott kissed her goodnight, neither of them had been thinking about DeeDee or Nick. The ugly twinge squeezed DeeDee's heart once again.

◈◈◈

A dark figure came for DeeDee in the night and called her name. Fear paralyzed her.

"Diana McCreary?" A blurry canvas shimmered where the face should be. "You're under arrest." The black hood billowed off the figure's head. Pam's white-rimmed eyes glared at her. "You've committed obstruction of justice."

As Pam reached a translucent hand toward her, a scream ripped from DeeDee's throat. She flung herself to a sitting position, her breath coming hard and fast.

Heart racing, she snapped on the bedside lamp, and blessed light chased away the phantom. She bent over her outstretched legs, heaving in air until her pulse and breathing settled back to normal.

She glanced at the faint numbers on the clock—3:12 a.m. What if someone found out she'd been at the cabin? Would she become a murder suspect? She could see the headlines: SEATTLE WOMAN ARRESTED FOR SHOOTING BOYFRIEND'S EX-WIFE.

She wouldn't be going back to sleep tonight.

∝∝∝

On Saturday, despite the twinkling lights lining the Christmas tree, the damp, gray morning seeped into the house and into DeeDee's soul. How long would this darkness in her spirit linger? How long before she snapped back to her natural upbeat self?

Leaning against the kitchen counter, she sipped coffee in one hand and held her tablet in the other. A headline from the Victoria *Times Colonist* jolted her to attention.

WOMAN FOUND SHOT AT REMOTE CABIN

Her hands jittered, and she nearly dropped the coffee cup. Setting it on the Formica, she peered at the words, trembling in her hands like paper in the wind.

> On Friday afternoon, Leonard Wilson of Chemainus found the body of a woman at an unoccupied log home near the southern edge of Mt. Sicker. She was identified as Pamela Marie Campbell, 42,

of Saanich, British Columbia. Mrs. Campbell's husband, Bryan Campbell, reported her missing on Monday evening. Wilson found her body when he stopped by to feed the homeowner's dog. He told authorities that he usually goes to feed the dog every day, but on Monday, he found the tires on both his vehicles slashed.

"It took me two days to get them all replaced," he told our reporter. "It infuriates me, those punk kids these days. Anyway, when I finally got there, someone had locked the dog inside the house. Jack always barks whenever I drive up. But that day, the yard was empty. So I walked around the property and heard him inside barking. That's when I saw her. So I called emergency."

A U-Haul van was found at the site. The office manager at the U-Haul lot in Victoria released the name of the last person to rent the vehicle and said it had been due back Monday evening. This person remains a person of interest, but no arrests have been made. The victim's car, a late-model Lexus, was found at the bottom of an embankment about five hundred feet from the property boundary.

Mrs. Campbell, a former fashion model in Vancouver during the '90s, left behind a son, Leon Brown Jr, and a three-year-old daughter, Sofie Campbell. She was founder and president of the popular

Moonstone Truffles in Victoria.

DeeDee sprang to her feet and followed the aroma of English Garden tea to the sunroom. Livy perched in the Papasan chair, hugging her laptop.

"Look." DeeDee thrust the tablet at her.

Livy's head jerked up, and her eyes moved back and forth with the text. Her mouth froze in an *O* as DeeDee waited, hands on hips.

Livy gaped up at her. "A 'person of interest'. Could it be Nick?"

"I don't know. I can't imagine why he would rent a U-Haul."

"Then where is his car?"

"Good question. He drove it when he left Renee's Monday morning, but what he did with it after? I wish I knew."

Livy set the laptop on the round white table next to her. "W–what will you do if he gets arrested?"

DeeDee sat and closed her eyes. For the first time, she realized she might be facing an immediate future without her man, a future as bleak as the rain-sodden clouds outside. Despite Nick's attempt to deceive her, she loved him more than she'd loved any other man. That kind of love might not come around again for her.

She eyed her sister. "You have that look on your face again. What are you thinking?"

Livy curled her lip over the rim of the cup and didn't look at her. A wispy river of steam floated around her face, casting it in an ethereal look.

Finally, she met DeeDee's eyes. "Isn't it usually the husband? Maybe he followed her—"

Livy stopped and twirled her hair around her finger as though her brain waves were fueling the movement. "Maybe

Nick never got to the cabin. Maybe he was on his way when he passed out. And the husband found out and went there to put a stop to it."

"Yes." DeeDee crinkled her face, visions from the Scott Peterson trial filling her thoughts. "Maybe he concocted the story in the newspaper. Or he could've shot her that morning before work, and then reported her missing."

She visualized a heavy burlap sack filled with guilt hanging from her shoulders. "Wow. I feel both wonderful and terrible. Wonderful because deep down I know he's the noble, trustworthy man I knew him to be, but terrible because I could've thrown away the best relationship I've ever had."

Chapter Eighteen

To get her mind off Nick, DeeDee drove to the mall with Livy, where they loaded up on Christmas gifts and décor. Hoping for something to chase away the clouds in her soul, she opted for the brightest of reds and greens. Then she and Livy spent the rest of the day arranging it all around the house. While they worked, she inhaled the piney fragrance of Deep Woods, her holiday candles, which brought to mind visions of Robert Frost's poem "Stopping By Woods On A Snowy Evening".

And visions of the snowy woods on Vancouver Island.

She shivered. So much for getting her mind off Nick.

Later, she went clubbing with her friends from the band Free The Defendants, the band she and Livy sang and danced in until last year, shortly before its leader, Nils Nelsson, passed away from a heroin overdose. Nils, Dad's best friend, had died the same way her mother died over twenty years ago.

She couldn't forget her mother's struggle with "bad medicine" when they were children. As a result, DeeDee avoided hard drugs with the same fervor that she avoided GMO foods and artificial sweeteners. But her band friends were unapologetic substance experimenters.

She squeezed into a semicircular booth with five others. Beyoncé blared. Tiny lights lining the dance floor pulsated with the beat. Ryan, the pony-tailed drummer, kept eyeing DeeDee, a question in his brown eyes. She caught a wink from him and winked back.

"Where's your guy tonight?" he shouted across the table.

"In the hospital."

A flash of disappointment creased his chiseled face. No doubt, he hoped they'd broken up. Ever since she and Ryan parted ways after dating for a year, they'd stayed on friendly terms.

He got up and skirted the dance floor toward the soundman. Seconds later, an exasperating tune sung by a familiar growling baritone pounded in DeeDee's ear.

Oh no...

"What a shiny gown...beneath her plastic crown..."

Ryan, you didn't just ask the sound guy to play my dad's song.

Couples flailed their limbs on the parquet floor.

"She's gonna bring big trouble on me ...."

Ryan stood next to her and held out his hand, and she cast him a purposeful glare.

"She's gonna be trouble...Trouble...Yeah–eah, double trouble...."

Instead of taking Ryan's hand, she gave it a light slap. But his mischievous grin was hard to resist, so she clamped her lips and let her glaring eyes do the talking.

"C'mon, babe, lighten up."

"I'm not your babe."

His grin faltered a tad. "Consider it my song to you."

"You trying to tell me I'm trouble?"

"Are you?"

She crossed her arms, blocking off his charm, then sprang to her feet and threaded to the deejay. "Can you play 'Roar'?" she yelled over the din. "And dedicate it to Ryan?"

She stalked back to the booth, triumphant grin intact, and slid in next to Taylor, the band's Goth backup singer. "Hey." DeeDee tossed her head toward Ryan's bemused face as Katy Perry began her plaintive wail. "Someone's gonna hear me roar."

Taylor shouted into DeeDee's ear. "Where've you been hiding lately?"

"Nowhere. I've been around."

"Still seeing that gorgeous hunk?"

DeeDee swallowed a chug of beer, thankful Taylor couldn't see the pain twisting her gut. "Well, sort of." She bent her head close to her friend and updated her on Nick's ordeal, leaving out the murder.

"Hello? What was he doing out in the middle of nowhere?" Taylor's snapping brown eyes prodded her from a chalk-white face.

She cast about for a safe answer. "He didn't say." Bodies gyrated on the dance floor as Rihanna's voice soared into the stratosphere. "Drunk On Love". She hummed along with Rihanna, who must be seeing right into her heart. She'd let herself get drunk on Nick's love. And what did that leave her with?

A big, fat nada.

The already dim air around her thickened. She had to get out of here. She should've known being here wouldn't help her forget Nick.

Nothing would.

She and Taylor stood at the same time, catching the others' attention. "Going out for a joint?" yelled Ryan.

DeeDee shook her head. "No, just need some fresh air." She poked Taylor, who recoiled, then elbowed her out of the booth. "Excuse me."

From the corner of her eye, she saw the others gawking as she fled from the club and into the darkened parking lot. Grappling for her phone, she leaned against a streetlamp next to her parked car. She breathed deep, pulling crisp, cool night air into her lungs. There was always something about the air in December, a special nostalgic quality evoking memories of smiling snowmen and soft sweaters, happy songs and aching longing. Mile-high stacks of Christmas gifts that took her and Livy a good hour to work through.

Neon lights blinked along the boulevard and lit up the night. "The Boulevard Of Broken Dreams", as Green Day so eloquently put it.

All she had to do was call Renee to make that connection with the man she longed to spend the rest of her life with, if she were honest with herself.

She couldn't fathom life without Nick and shuddered at the memories assaulting her from her pre-Nick life—a life marked with fruitless quests for love in all the wrong ways.

Chapter Nineteen

Nick almost felt back to his old self by Saturday. He stood beside his hospital bed, nurses hovering and smiling as they helped him prepare to leave. Renee darted in and out, ready to get him out of there and back to her house to recuperate.

"Renee?" he croaked.

She poked her head through the door. "Did you say something?"

"Where's DeeDee?"

Renee's face closed in on itself, and she turned away, opening his black duffel bag and stuffing his clothing inside with jerky movements. "She went home. Couldn't handle seeing you like this, she claimed. She hasn't been here since, I don't know, Wednesday?"

"I need her." He remembered his awful dream. "Did—did she break up with me?"

She whirled to face him, her fist clutching neatly-rolled socks. "Why would she?"

"I—" He eyed the backpack, ran his finger along the zipper. "I had a dream she broke up with me."

"Very strange."

He spun his gaze to her. "Maybe it wasn't a dream. I was so doped up I couldn't tell dreams from reality."

He reached for his phone in the backpack's side pocket. No messages, no missed calls from his ladylove. He scrolled back several days, his movements frantic, jerky. Nothing from DeeDee. He blew out a disbelieving breath and glanced around. No trinkets, balloons, or flowers—the sort of gifts girlfriends brought to their men in the hospital.

She'd discovered his sordid secret and decided he wasn't the man she'd thought he was. That had to be it. But how could she possibly have found...? His thoughts raced. He sensed a presence enter the room. Something—someone—cut off the hall light in the space of an eyeblink.

He spun around. Two uniformed police officers blockaded his path to the door, badges flashing, faces stoic. Renee, gaping, dropped the duffel bag. Carol hesitated in the doorway, her eyes wide and worried.

"Mr. Nicholas Rush?"

"Uh..." Words lodged in his suddenly dry throat.

"What's going on?" Renee's voice cut through the roaring in his head.

"We're looking for Nicholas Rush."

"What for?"

The heavier cop scrutinized him. "Are you Mr. Rush?"

At Nick's slow nod, the skinnier cop said, "We need to see you at the station."

The ominous words hung and echoed in the air. Renee's gasp punched them away. "He can't go anywhere right now, except home to rest."

They ignored her. The larger man, his name badge identifying him as Holmes, took hold of Nick's arm and ushered him to the hard vinyl chair. His grip, although light, held authority, discouraging resistance.

Fear squeezed Nick's heart as he dropped into the chair. "Please tell me what this is about."

Holmes folded his arms, swaying with forced casualness on the balls of his feet. "This is about Mrs. Pamela Campbell."

"Pam? What about her?"

"You're her former husband?"

"Yes."

"She was found dead this week. Shot."

Nick lurched forward, shock morphing into comprehension. They couldn't possibly suspect... "Who shot her?"

"We don't know." Holmes's partner, Williams, gave Nick a hard look from steel-gray eyes. Stereotypical cop eyes telling him he was suspect number one.

Nick's gaze darted to the door, but no means of escape presented itself. "Are you saying she was murdered?"

"It sure looked intentional."

Nick slumped, his head in his hands.

"You need to come with us to answer a few questions."

"Why me? I haven't seen Pam in months. Did you try her current husband?"

Williams shifted closer, a threatening tower. "A U-Haul was found at the site." His mild voice betrayed no emotion. "Your name was on the rental documents."

The rental documents...The van! He'd left them at the cabin, intending to retrieve them when he could.

"Your phone number was on her call log. Dating from last Sunday evening through Monday afternoon."

The text messages...The photos. Sent from his phone to hers.

A tremble began in his legs, traveled up his spine. They thought he shot his ex-wife. They were going to arrest him, take him to jail.

He'd certainly done plenty to incriminate himself.

ৰ৾ ৰ৾ ৰ৾

When DeeDee arrived home, Livy was gone. She glanced at the time. Ten thirty. Renee might still be up at this hour.

Renee, can we talk? She paced the sunroom, waiting for Renee's reply. Renee might be upset she hadn't attempted to

123

contact Nick for days. But she had to find out how he was. Had to know if any hope remained for them.

It's about time!! came the reply. *Where have you been?*

DeeDee dialed the number. Renee picked up on the first ring.

"How's Nick doing?"

Renee made a noise—an attempt at a laugh, morphing into a cry. "Well, before I tell you, I want to ask you something."

DeeDee waited, holding her breath.

"Did you break up with Nick?"

Not the question she'd expected. "Um—why do you ask?"

"He seemed to think you did. But he wasn't sure...thought it could've been a dream."

She had to get Renee off this line of questioning. "Do you think I'd be calling to see how he is if I'd broken up with him?"

A long silence. Then, slowly, "He's not doing well. He was detained by a couple of police officers and taken in for questioning."

Her legs buckled. She sank to the futon, fear filling her chest, ripping the breath from her lungs.

Renee took advantage of her speechless state. Her voice dipped and soared as she told about Pam being shot, Nick's rented van at the scene, cops taking him in for questioning. "You should've been here, DeeDee. He didn't understand why you gave him the silent treatment all week."

DeeDee couldn't speak. So Nick *was* the person of interest. Chills shuddered through her.

"Nick is not a murderer," Renee was saying. "In fact, I can't think of a single reason he'd benefit from Pam's death."

Tears swelled behind DeeDee's eyes, but didn't fall, as frozen as the rest of her. Until a thought fingered and poked into her consciousness…

"Renee, what about the test results? The blood on his jacket? Did they…?"

"Oh right, I haven't heard anything yet. I need to ask."

"And what about the bullet? Whose gun was it?"

"I don't know." Renee gave a little cry. "Wait a minute. DeeDee, you were there. At the house. Didn't you see anything?"

She gripped the futon's wicker seat, thankful Renee couldn't hear her accelerated heart rate. "Huh?" she managed.

"You and your sister drove to the house where Pam was found."

"Yeah," she whispered.

"You must have seen *something*. They said Pam was probably shot sometime on Monday."

"No."

"No what?"

"I saw nothing."

"Odd. Did you just drive up without getting out?"

"Right. I heard a dog barking, so I stayed in the car."

"I can tell you're really upset." Renee's voice softened. "I'm so sorry to be the bearer of bad news. I'm upset, too."

Good thing Renee didn't know the real reason she was upset. The evidence *was* incriminating. Nick disappeared the same day as Pam. He must have been at the cabin when she arrived. But that was all she knew. They wouldn't have needed to meet at a deserted remote cabin if it was something simple. Maybe they'd argued.

Because if he'd shot her, it would've been in the heat of the moment. The Nick she knew wasn't capable of a cold-blooded shooting, even on his worst enemy.

She tightened her grip on the seat. She had to stop these seesawing thoughts before her head exploded.

Chapter Twenty

Nick sat in the Chemainus police station, swinging his foot like a pendulum, trying not to breathe too deep. Someone had gone overboard with the chemical cleansers. Probably an attempt to snuff out the odor of human depravity. But it didn't work. The spray stung his nostrils and worsened his nausea. After they'd brought him here, handcuffed in the back of the patrol car, he explained to Holmes and Williams—at least ten times—the details of his time at the cabin and his subsequent injury.

They had no reason to detain him. Flimsy proof at best. The only clues tying him to the murder? The U-Haul. All those text messages. And the twenty-minute phone call Sunday night.

Apparently, the bullet that killed Pam came from one of the guns in the carport. No prints.

The blood on his jacket was human. His own. Courtesy of Jack.

"Pam never showed," he said, over and over, to their skeptical faces. They remained unfazed by his testimony of the unlocked storage room and the unknown trigger exciting Jack. "I should've gone over to investigate," he told them. "It was probably her body he was barking at."

He'd requested his attorney, even though they hadn't said he was under arrest. "Why don't you go arrest my stepson? He's a thief and a liar. And he was there. Maybe he did it."

"We've already extensively questioned him and all the

family members. Unless we find an inconsistency in his testimony, we have no cause to detain him."

He huffed. Once he was out of here, he was calling his attorney, Adam Vernon. He needed to go home. Call DeeDee. Get back to a normal life. He'd do whatever he had to do to divert the cops' attention from himself. "I have proof he hacked my credit card."

Williams gave him another hard stare. "Again, we only have your word. You didn't file a police report, did you?"

Nick opened his mouth to reply, but Williams held up a restraining hand. "We're going to keep you in custody a little longer. We need to verify your story and do some further investigating."

Nick sat forward. "What? You're arresting me?"

Williams pulled him to his feet as Holmes said, "You have the right to remain silent. You have the right to an attorney...."

Nick tuned out the rights recitation as adrenaline spread throughout his body. His heart pounded out a frightening rhythm. The two officers led him to the booking area where they fingerprinted him and made him change into a jumpsuit. Then to the cellblock, where they deposited him in a metal cage with two other inmates. The gates closed and locked behind him, echoing with finality.

He sat on a metal ledge and dropped his head into his hands.

He was screwed.

⊰⊰⊰

The city, the homes, the very air, was filled with Christmas, just days away. DeeDee and Livy boarded a plane for Southern California to spend the holiday with their dad, brothers, and Dad's new girlfriend, Brittany, widow of his late friend and bandmate, Nils Nelsson.

DeeDee had laughed when Dad called and told them he and Brittany started dating. "Each new woman in your life gets younger, Dad. Will the next one be my age?"

He'd been a good sport and chuckled. "We're just two lonely people who have some things in common."

Fortunately, she and Livy had known Brittany for many years and liked her. True, she wasn't Joy, the woman who'd been with Dad for twenty years until last April, when he kicked her out. Thanks to Livy, he found out Joy withheld vital information about Mom's death all those years ago. But Dad seemed content with Brittany. "At my age," he told them, "love isn't fireworks all the time." His voice had softened, and she knew he was thinking about Mom, the love of his life, who'd died when DeeDee and Livy were six.

On the plane, DeeDee did everything she could to get her mind off Nick. According to Renee, he'd been charged with murder and was rotting away in the Chemainus jail. The words on the magazine she tried to read ran together, made no sense. Crazy. She couldn't picture Nick shooting a deer, much less a person. Yet the evidence was incriminating. Numerous text messages from his phone to hers. The U-Haul van he'd rented, left at the site.

"Do you know why he rented a van?" she'd asked Renee.

But Renee hadn't known, either.

DeeDee sniffed and swiped away tears as the plane began its descent to LAX.

"I miss my honey." Livy sighed.

DeeDee missed Nick, too…rather, the good memories of Nick. "I'm sure your honey is missing you, too." Livy and Scott planned to fly to Dallas later in the week to celebrate a late Christmas with his family, where she'd meet them for the first time.

After they disembarked, they grabbed lunch at one of

the airport's restaurants and hurried to where Dad's limo waited. The chauffeur ferried them up and around steep, curved streets lined with grand stucco homes to the community of Los Feliz. Tiny colored lights adorned the eaves and windows of Dad's forty-five-hundred-square-foot white house. They must look spectacular when lit.

Dad and their teenaged half-brothers, August and Dominic, greeted them with hugs. The last time they'd been here, in April, Livy had hit Dad with devastating news. But he appeared well recovered and smiled his old Dad smile at them. Both her brothers had grown out their red hair. Dominic's reached halfway down his back now, like a real rocker wannabe. The boys' mother, Joy, wouldn't be joining them. Dad had made it clear he wanted nothing more to do with her, so she and Livy planned to spend the day after Christmas with her, the brothers, and Joy's new man in her Hollywood home.

Dad's Christmas tree brushed the top of the twenty-foot-high ceiling, poking its way past the loft. Every year he hired a professional decorator who went all out making the tree sensational. Huge wrapped boxes covered every inch of the floor beneath the tree, including the ones DeeDee and Livy shipped down last week.

Livy settled on the green leather sofa. "Where's Brittany, Dad?"

"She'll be over in an hour or so. We'll have dinner, then head to the Lakers game. Sound good?"

DeeDee dropped next to Livy. "Sounds like awesomeness."

"Why didn't you bring Nick?" He flashed a proud grin, having introduced her and Nick last year at Nils's memorial service.

DeeDee's festive mood fled. "Um…it's a long story. We're sort of on hiatus right now."

Dad's eyes widened. "Seriously? He's perfect for you, kiddo."

Her shoulders sagged. "I know. Like I said, it's a long story."

"We have all day. Tell me your long story."

She started with the Victoria trip, shared the highlights up to and including her last phone call with Renee.

"What do you think, Dad? Do you think he's guilty?"

He gazed at the ceiling, his eyes glazed over as if he hadn't heard her. "The justice system is corrupt. Innocent men getting locked up. Guilty men set free." He rubbed his hand down his face, leaving behind a frown that sank to his jowls. "I hate to see Nick get sucked into that black hole. They're going to eat him alive, then spit him out for breakfast."

⚘⚘⚘

Christmas morning, while DeeDee and the family opened gifts, carols piped into the room, so she almost didn't hear her phone chiming out "Jingle Bells". Brittany leaned on Dad's arm, her long dark hair draped over the back of the sofa. When DeeDee first saw Dad and Brittany holding hands the previous evening, she did a double take. Last time she'd seen Brittany with a man, she'd been holding her late husband Nils's arm. This was going to take some getting used to. But Dad beamed—a positive sign Brittany was good for him.

Ripping sounds from Gus and Dom's spot on the floor ended with grins and whoops as they held up a Kenwood satellite car stereo and a Sony PlayStation 4 respectively.

"Jingle Bells" chimed again. "Your phone, Deeds." Livy pointed to the table. DeeDee had received several Merry Christmas texts from friends, but most of them also went to Livy's phone. All morning, their phones had chimed and pulsated in unity at each incoming text.

But this time, only DeeDee's phone chimed—an urgent undercurrent to it. The call she'd been subconsciously waiting for. Like the ringing of the phone at midnight—it sounded exactly like any other ring, but somehow, a tone in it made her snatch it off the table.

Had Nick been released? Her heart raced.

Merry Christmas from the Maxwells, said Renee's text. *I saw Nick last night. He has a message for you, wants you to know he didn't do it. And I believe him.*

Her grip tightened and her breath accelerated. Livy watched her, eyes wide and knowing, while the rest of the family went about their business, oblivious. Livy moved next to her, and DeeDee tipped the text her way, finger tapping the side of the phone while Livy read.

"Are you going to reply?"

DeeDee shrugged. "Should I?"

"I would."

She punched in a reply. *Merry Christmas to you, too.* She bit her lip, mulling over, then rejecting, possible responses. *How is Nick? Bummer of a way to spend Christmas.*

The phone chimed in her hand before she'd even hit send. *He wants to see you.*

Livy's mouth dropped when DeeDee showed her the text. "Yes." She nodded. "Tell her yes."

DeeDee toyed with her hair, wrapped a curl around her finger. Could she handle seeing the man she loved behind bars?

Finally, her fingers tapped out a message. *OK. I'll go see him as soon as I get home.*

Great! He's been moved to Victoria. Let me know what day. I'll pick you up & we'll go together. But you can't wear jeans or jewelry. Here's the jail's website…they have a ton of rules for visitors and restricted visiting hours.

If my friend Maggie is available to fly me there, I can be there in an hour.

She and the family spent the rest of the morning tending to the roasting turkey, baking pies, mashing potatoes. Dad called them all to the table. To her shock, he requested a moment of silence to thank the Lord for the food, then smiled at Livy as though they shared an inside joke. What? Dad was going religious, too? She cast a glance at Livy, noting the smug smile curving her lips. But she couldn't say a word.... Silence descended as eyes closed. Even her brothers'. She glanced around as awkward as she'd been at the Maxwells'.

Dad said amen, opened his eyes, and motioned them to sit. Roast turkey and mashed potato aromas mingled with savory stuffing scents and tickled her nose. Dad cracked jokes, Brittany responded with bubbly laughs. Gus and Dom shoveled food in their mouths as though they hadn't eaten in a month. Bottomless pits, Joy called them when they were little.

During dessert of apple, peach, and rhubarb pies topped with vanilla bean ice cream, Dad caught DeeDee's eye. "You're quiet today. Thinkin' about that con man of yours?"

"Dad! How can you call him that? Even you don't believe he's guilty."

"Yeah, but even if he's acquitted, once word gets out that he was a suspect, the label's gonna follow him the rest of his life."

She hunched over her apple pie. "Wow, you're such an encouragement."

His eyes hardened, belying his mild reply. "It's not gonna be easy. But you'll be okay. You'll find someone else."

"You want me to give up on him?"

"Well, if he's found guilty, won't you want to move on?"

She couldn't reply. There would never be another Nick

Rush.

❧❧❧

Livy reached for DeeDee's hand and squeezed. Poor Deeds. Her Bright Peony mouth drooped like a tired flower, and her shoulders bowed. Surely, Livy would feel the same if Scott were imprisoned for a crime he didn't commit.

Dad's voice broke through her ponderings. "Livy. Have you and Scott set a date?"

"Only a vague promise that it'll be sometime next summer."

"You're looking happy these days."

"I'm ecstatic. Scott is a kind, loving, wonderful guy."

"I hope he's as good for you as your mother was for me. The connection your mother and I had…well, it's a rare treasure. Do whatever you have to do to hang on to it."

His words brought to mind one of Jesus' parables. The pearl of great price. But Jesus referred to the kingdom of heaven. Dad, who held to a secular mindset, likely had no clue he was borrowing an example from Jesus to make an earthly point.

"Have you talked about a honeymoon yet?"

"He did mention Hawaii…."

"How about a two-week European tour? My wedding gift to you. You two could hit all the romantic spots…Paris, Venice…"

Oh, to see Europe again! Ancient yet modern. Enlightened yet traditional. Not to mention exotic. The perfect honeymoon destination. Scott would love Italy, home of his ancestors.

"Oh, Dad! Would you really?"

She met DeeDee's envious gaze, whose eyes snapped green sparks. *He'd do the same for you*, she wanted to say, but instead let her embrace do the talking.

She could hardly wait to tell Scott. In fact, she'd Skype him today, just to see his face when she told him.

❧ ❧ ❧

Livy tilted her laptop when Scott appeared on her screen, relishing the love radiating from his eyes. "Merry Christmas, honey." Would his face still light up at the sight of her twenty years from now? Would her heart still pitter-patter? "I've got some really cool news."

His smile widened. "I can see it all over your face."

"Wait'll you hear what Dad's going to do for our wedding." Deep breath. "He's offered to pay for a European honeymoon for us. We'll get to see Paris and Rome and..."

The smile left his eyes, then froze on his lips. "That's really generous of him."

Why the flat tone? Where was the pleased grin she'd expected? He should be relieved they had one less thing to plan and pay for. "And Italy! The land of your heritage. Aren't you excited to visit Italy?"

He nodded, but not in his usual decisive, confident way. "Sure. I'd love to see Italy someday."

"Someday? Like in six months? I can't wait."

Finally, a glimmer of his usual easygoing grin poked through. "I'm glad you're happy. But I'll be happy just being with you, whether in Italy or Hawaii. Having a fancy, expensive honeymoon isn't going to change that."

Oh, so it was about money, was it? She needed to reassure him her feelings for him transcended finances. "Honey, you know I feel the same way. It truly won't matter where we start our married life as long as we're together." If only she could reach through the screen and clasp his hand or give him a hug or sit on his lap inside his tender embrace...

"Right." He gave a jerky nod, then went on to tell her

about his Christmas with his girls. His forced cheer masked the earlier tension, but the memory of his less-than-enthusiastic reaction teased her, like the aroma of a nearby fireplace snaking through the cracked-open window.

Chapter Twenty-One

DeeDee's stomach wound tighter with each passing mile to Victoria. She glanced at Maggie, calmly in control of the flying tin can, then below at the Salish Sea, its dull gray mass broken up by odd-shaped humps as though someone had tossed ill-fitting puzzle pieces into the sea. The San Juan Islands. Less than an hour had passed since Maggie took off from SeaTac. With the piper's engine whirring in her already scrambled brain, it felt twice as long. Even blasting Fall Out Boy on her iTunes app hadn't calmed her nerves.

Per the jail's rules, she wore a simple white pullover sweater paired with linen slacks she rarely wore. Saving them for jailhouse visits, apparently. Out of nervous habit, she reached for the gold heart around her neck, but groped only bare skin. A sour taste built in her mouth when she remembered she'd broken it.

When Maggie descended into Victoria International Airport, the sign for Quaking Aspen appeared to wave them down—closer, closer—and with it, the emotions DeeDee'd been squelching rose to the surface. Fingers knotting, she nearly choked on the sudden bile. Everything about the place evoked memories of Nick. Nick as a fifteen-year-old musical rookie, playing his heart out. Nick as a twenty-something rocker, a young Sting entertaining the crowd on his Fender bass. In her mind's eye, she and the present-day Nick sat at a heavy wood table, holding hands and sharing poutine and ale. But now…she didn't know if this imaginary scene would ever blossom into reality.

An ache threatened to overtake her heart. She turned to Maggie. "I should be back in about two hours."

Maggie nodded. "Got your customs paperwork and passport ready?"

"Yep." DeeDee clutched them to her chest.

"Great. Follow me, and I'll take you to customs. When you're ready to go back, I'll be in the pilot's lounge."

જ⚬જ⚬જ

Once she'd been cleared for entry into Canada, DeeDee found Renee, a frown twisting her coral-glossed mouth, waiting for her at the prearranged meeting place. They embraced. Then Renee drew back, tucking a wayward blown curl behind DeeDee's ear. "I'm so glad you could make it. Nick will be so glad to see you."

A tense twenty-minute drive brought them to Vancouver Island Correctional Centre, an imposing brick place bearing no resemblance to DeeDee's mental image of a jail. More like a haunted old schoolhouse, where ghosts of long-dead students, or in this case prisoners, still roamed the halls. The place where Nick lived 24/7 now.

She stifled a shudder. "What a ghastly place."

"I know, right?" A sheen glazed Renee's eyes as she opened the car door.

DeeDee's footsteps dragged while she followed her friend to a somber off-white lobby. Impenetrable glass and steel covered one wall. A guard with equally somber expression directed them to the security queue to get their bags and persons photographed and scrutinized.

"Who are you here to see?"

"Nick Rush."

"This way." They followed the guard's direction to the visitor's room. Two more grim-faced uniformed guards stood near the exit and blocked access to a thick steel door, presumably the one opening into the heart of the prison.

When Nick appeared behind the glass, DeeDee stifled a gasp. His coverall, an unhealthy shade of burnt orange, reflected on his face, inducing a jaundiced appearance. He rubbed his eyes, deepening the bluish-gray blotches underneath. But his expression relaxed in a half-smile when he saw her.

She picked up the receiver. And gulped, tongue cleaving to the roof of her mouth.

"DeeDee." He drew in a harsh breath. "Your face...it's like a light in the middle of a nightmare."

"Nick," she managed.

"I didn't kill Pam." A keen light burned in his eyes; his face stiffened. "You've got to believe me."

She searched his eyes through the glass, trying not to flinch. Such desperation muddied their clear blue.

"This place is the worst." His hard breathing echoed in her ear. "Like a bad dream I can't wake up from."

She shuddered. "What's being done to get you out of here?"

His mouth twisted. "Unless someone finds the real killer, I'm stuck here until my trial. No bail for first-degree murder."

"Nick, why did you plan to meet her?" Her voice wobbled, and she swallowed the lump in her throat.

He drooped lower. "She begged me to. But she never showed." His gaze shifted to somewhere behind her. "If I ever get out of here, I'll tell you all about it."

"Why didn't you just tell me?"

His shoulders sagged. "I wish I had now."

"Why would someone kill her?"

"That's what my attorney is trying to find out."

"Was it her husband?"

Nick gave a quick shake of his head and lowered his

voice. "I don't know. He and everybody were already questioned. They all have alibis."

DeeDee strained to hear his softened words. "Who's everybody?"

"The husband. He claimed he was at work all day. Her son, Leon. He and Jazzy hadn't seen Pam since their wedding, they said." He clamped his mouth shut. "Anyway, my attorney advised me not to talk about this, my love."

Speaking of love... "Nick, what about us?"

Those beaten eyes caressed her face, the edge of sorrow deepening in the crinkles around them. The familiar tingle jittered up her spine.

"Is there still an us? In the hospital, I dreamed you broke up with me."

She sucked in a breath. What could she say? Particularly with his questioning gaze pinned on her. "You did?"

"Please tell me it was just a bad dream." The questioning gaze turned pleading. "On top of everything else I've lost, I can't lose you, too."

She gave a feeble shake of her head, not flinching under his steady gaze. "Just get out of here as quick as you can."

"Absolutely, sweetheart. As soon as they nail the real killer."

Wasn't that O.J. Simpson's line?

"We'll get our life back. We can get married."

A gasp burst from her mouth, and her heart thumped. "You truly want to get married?"

"Of course. If you'll have me."

Two weeks ago, she'd have been overjoyed to hear those words. But two weeks of upheaval had turned her life into a wasteland, as though a volcano had spewed destructive lava all over her and Nick. Smashing all her hopes in its wake.

Waiting expectation shone in his eyes as her father's words rang in her head: *Even if he's acquitted, the label's gonna follow him the rest of his life.*

"I—I'll give it some thought, Nick."

When the hopeful gleam in his eyes dimmed, she hastened to whisper, "Everything's different now. What if..." But she couldn't finish the thought. She couldn't put words to her worst fear.

"... I never get out?" he finished for her. "Believe me, not a moment goes by when I don't fear that very thing. I don't belong here. These guys"—he waved a vague hand behind him—"they're all hardened crooks."

Her whole body convulsed. How did he endure it?

"Will you wait for me, sweetheart?"

His question hovered between them. She stood at a fork, her gaze swinging between two equally murky options. Wait for Nick? Or move on?

Their time nearly at an end, she told him goodbye and moved aside for Renee. The desolation in his eyes told her he feared her answer would be no.

ॐॐॐ

Pam, clad in black leather, stood next to DeeDee's bed. "Help me," she mouthed as her frightened eyes pleaded.

"Help you, how?" DeeDee tried to utter the words, but her mouth refused to move. She tried to wrest her eyes open, but they stayed fastened shut. Yet here Pam floated, as tangible as real life.

"Save me!" Pam cried as if she'd heard DeeDee's unspoken reply.

"You're already dead!"

DeeDee jolted upright. *Already dead. Already dead.*

Heart in her throat, she threw off the comforter and padded across the hall to Livy's room, thankful for the first time Livy didn't share her bed with her fiancé. Last year, when Livy was having bad dreams about their late mother, she'd slip into DeeDee's bed in the middle of the night, clasping her hand like they used to do as children. This time, it was DeeDee's turn to seek midnight reassurance from her twin.

Murf, curled up in the corner, raised his head and thumped his tail once on the hardwood floor. But Livy didn't stir when DeeDee slipped in next to her. Soaking in her twin's warmth like a hot-water bottle, she soon fell asleep.

⋘⋘⋘

"You need to figure out what's bugging you." Livy, propped on her elbow, bunched her floral comforter around her hands after DeeDee had shared her dreams. "Just like I had to do last year."

DeeDee shifted to her side, Livy's purple satin pillowcase cooling her warm cheeks. "I agree. But how?"

Livy, her blue eyes shadowed in the dim morning light, tugged on the hair spilling over her shoulder. "Let's talk it through."

"Okay. You go first."

"The first dream had to stem from your guilt over having found the body and saying nothing—"

"But it's a moot point now."

"True. Then last night, Pam comes to you and begs you for help."

"I know. Freaky, isn't it?"

Livy's voice dropped to a whisper. "When I was dreaming about Mom, I realized later it was my subconscious screaming at me to find answers."

"But it makes no sense in this case. Why would my subconscious be screaming at me? I only caught a glimpse of Pam's body before I turned and ran."

"Want to know what I think?"

"Of course."

"I think your gut's telling you Nick is innocent."

DeeDee sat up with a jerk. "Of course, he is!"

"What I mean is, I think something you saw or heard at the cabin proves Nick's innocence, and your subconscious has filed it away. I've come to realize, often what we think is our gut is really God talking to us."

For once, DeeDee didn't have the energy to protest the God reference. "I heard absolutely nothing except distant barking. It was so quiet, I heard the ringing in my ears." She lay back and closed her eyes, visualizing the nightmare tableau. The cabin, the yard. The body sprawled on the bed of pine needles as though it had tripped and fallen.

"Her eyes were open." Something caught in her throat.

Livy grimaced. "That would haunt me, too."

"And the smell. I remember now. I smelled something heinous...."

"You smelled death."

DeeDee nodded, gripping her twin's hand. "Yeah. Death. It smelled like...like..." She clutched the comforter with her other hand. "If Hell were real, I imagine that's what it'd smell like."

Chapter Twenty-Two

Fired up by Livy's insights, DeeDee settled at her computer desk to learn more about Pam's history. To unearth any secrets that could give someone a motive for murder. Or learn who most benefitted from her death.

Morning sunlight streamed into her bedroom, lightening the ebony desk to a burnished gray. Pamela Campbell, she keyed into the search box. Tucking her feet to the side, she anchored one behind the other as she scrolled through several names, before landing on the right one: Pam M. Campbell, Saanich, BC. Pam and her husband smiled behind sunglasses, their heads micro-inches apart, the jagged peaks of the Canadian Rockies rising behind them into flawless indigo sky. Windswept black hair sailed around her face.

The top post brought a whimper to DeeDee's throat.

"My beloved wife, Pam, lost her life last Monday, December 15, at the hands of a brutal murderer, who is right now rotting in jail where he belongs." The comments string extended beyond the bottom of the screen.

Unable to finish, DeeDee dropped her face into her hands. Lifting her head, she called out, "Livy!" before remembering Livy and Scott were en route to SeaTac and their flight to Dallas, due to return in two days. She'd have to endure this slander against Nick on her own.

More diatribes and outraged comments from friends filled Bryan Campbell's page.

"So sorry, buddy. Thankful her killer has been locked

away."

"Can't believe Nick Rush is a murderer!! Hope he's put away for life!!"

"He's evil to the core...."

And so on and so forth. She blinked away the stinging in her eyes, her heart twisting. All the commenters assumed Nick had committed murder. Nobody even suggested any doubt, any other scenario.

Nothing on Bryan's page conveyed the tone of a man who'd killed his wife. But Scott Petersen had fooled everyone at first.

She jabbed open a new tab, away from the offensive reminders, then returned to Pam's page and opened her friends list. Leon, Jazzy, Senior—all present and accounted for. Clive and Erik numbered among her friends. But not Nick...Apparently, someone had unfriended him. Pam's photos—all recent. DeeDee scrolled back looking for hints to her past, anything to give a clue to her life before Nick.

Ah...finally. Here was a younger Pam standing amidst a tapestry of flowers, her arm around an older woman. *Mom and I at Butchart Gardens – with Amelia Quigley.* Immediately DeeDee pulled up a search engine and typed Pamela Marie Quigley, crossing her fingers that she'd stumbled upon Pam's maiden name.

"Pamela Marie Quigley weds Leon Arthur Brown in afternoon ceremony," read the twenty-year-old article from Victoria *Times Colonist.* "Miss Quigley, 21, married Mr. Brown, 25, at two o'clock in the afternoon on June 24, 1995, in St. Augustine's Chapel. Miss Quigley is the daughter of Adrik and Amelia Quigley of Langford. Mr. Brown is the son of Mr. Arthur Henry Brown of Victoria and Mrs. Susan Whitaker of Surrey." DeeDee scanned the unfamiliar list of bridesmaids and groomsmen, none of whom she recognized except Erik Sterling, the best man. "The couple's two-year-old son, Leon Jr., served as ring bearer. The best man's daughter, Jasmine, also two, was their flower girl." She smiled at the mental image of Leon and Jazzy as dressed-up tiny tots.

She studied the black-and-white photo of the beaming couple. Pam in a simple bridal gown—a younger, no less beautiful version of herself. The groom—Senior—virtually unrecognizable. His long, kinky Sammy Hagar hair frizzed as though he'd run through an electrical storm, and his smirking wink only emphasized his '80s rock-god look.

Amazing how some people changed so little, and others so much.

Changing her search, she typed in Moonstone Truffles. With Pam dead, would the business remain open?

The website appeared to be current. "Come Nibble On Heaven," the motto beckoned. Pam stood next to the banner, smiling her isn't-life-grand smile, her eyes partially hidden under cropped bangs. A pang seized DeeDee. Pam would never broadcast that glad smile again. DeeDee read through the company's history. Pam had launched it ten years ago in her kitchen. Instant popularity caused avid expansion, and today, twenty employees operated the two-thousand square foot factory. Visitors could even drop in for tours. "Come see how your favorite truffle is made...from cacao seed to decadent treat."

Pretty impressive. Clearly, Pam and chocolate got along beautifully.

DeeDee hunted around for a news or updates option, scrolling past mouthwatering photos of truffles in varying shades of white, milk, and dark chocolate. Petit fours adorned with ribbons of icing, pastel butterflies, and dainty flowers made her stop and gaze in awe, tongue tingling in anticipation.

Little wonder the place was well known as far away as

Seattle. On impulse, she placed an order for a variety box, threw in a quartet of White Russian truffles, and received an immediate e-mailed reply. Her order would be delivered in three days.

Three days to wait for her first nibble of heaven.

Chagrined over allowing her sweet tooth to distract her, she perused the site, but still found nothing about Pam's death. Most likely, the assistant Nick mentioned still did all the work. Pam's absence might not have made a ripple in the operations.

So who'd inherited Pam's share of the business? Her husband, probably. Or maybe Leon.

She filed it away in her mind as a puzzle to resolve later, then clicked open Jasmine's profile photo. Jazzy, in heavy makeup, leaned in toward the camera. The thin lips she'd inherited from her father pressed into a sultry pout. Curly strands escaped the pile of hair atop her head and glistened against her cheek. DeeDee clicked the friend request waiting for her, which Jazzy sent before Nick's arrest.

You are now friends with Jasmine Sterling Brown.

DeeDee took a few minutes to peruse the photos of the happy newlyweds. The two must have been inseparable for years. How odd, then, that it was such a surprise to the family when they decided to wed. Perhaps the relationship had been merely platonic until recently. She knew of other couples who started out as platonic friends, then realized one day that love had bloomed between them.

An aged photo caught her attention—a little boy and girl on a porch swing, holding hands. The boy bared his teeth, a say-cheese smile spanning his entire face. The girl's mouth hung open as though in mid-speech. *Me and Leon as kids*, read the caption.

She couldn't help a goofy grin at their tiny carefree faces. Still, nothing here shed any light on Pam's life. She returned to Bryan Campbell's profile, avoiding the comments section. Maybe he'd found out Pam was on her way to meet Nick and flew into a jealous rage.

Or had he been having an affair, and, like Scott Petersen, chose to off his rich wife instead of divorce her? DeeDee scrolled through all 417 of his friends in search of *the* female face. Unsure what a home-wrecker would look like, she still felt certain she'd recognize one if she saw her.

Even better, which attractive females had liked and commented on his vicious post against Nick?

She sighed. This would take a while. Clicking on the uppermost female name, she settled back in her chair, prepared to stick it out for the long haul.

⛧⛧⛧

Unfortunately, Bryan had many attractive female friends on social media, rendering DeeDee's task virtually impossible. If he were having an affair with any of them, nothing jumped out.

Next, she searched through his posts to see if any one female seemed to comment more frequently than others. She finally threw up her hands. Shelley Campbell Duncan, his sister, commented most often.

Perhaps one of his photos contained something significant. But no. Pictures of him and Pam in various activities with their cute little girl dominated his photo albums.

If Pam's husband had another woman in his life, the two of them covered their tracks well.

Livy offered sympathy when DeeDee called and shared her findings. "If you really want to know who Pam was, you need to go talk to the people who knew her best," she declared over the background noise of children shouting and squealing. Scott's daughters, Kinzie and Lacie, no doubt.

Maybe even some nieces and nephews.

"Where are you?"

Livy raised her voice. "In the back yard, watching Scott push the kids on the swing set." Her tone dipped, and DeeDee strained to hear. "He's so good with kids." Her voice oozed affection.

DeeDee didn't want to talk about kids. Her mission rang urgently in her head. "You think I ought to go back to Victoria?"

"I do," said Livy.

☙☙☙

Livy hung up and took a swig from her water bottle, basking in the mild Dallas afternoon. This day felt nothing like a Seattle winter. Sixty-three-degree temperatures in December were almost unheard of in the Northwest. And these squat little Texas trees! Most of them would no doubt suffer a self-esteem crisis if they were to stand next to a soaring Northwest evergreen.

She removed her navy fleece vest and leaned back in the porch swing, then crossed her legs underneath her, letting the swing carry her gently back and forth, a boat drifting beneath partly-cloudy skies. Sweet pea vines curled around the trellis beside her, enveloping her in their warm, sweet scent like a fragrant sauna.

Kinzie and Lacie's delighted squeals from the swing set belied the girls' earlier crankiness on the plane. Livy, not yet entirely comfortable disciplining Scott's kids, had let him deal with it. She had to admire the firm way he took charge, promising both girls pecan pralines if they'd be good until the plane landed. He'd kept his promise, steering them to the first gift shop he found, and bought two packages of the wrapped goodies. The crunchy treat was hard to find in Seattle, but plentiful here in Texas and well worth waiting

148

for.

"Livy?"

She turned at the sound of Scott's mother's voice. She'd warmed to Jeannie immediately, at last understanding what the term "Southern hospitality" really meant. Both parents had greeted her at the airport with enthusiastic kisses on the cheek, a gesture she wasn't accustomed to in the reserved, polite Northwest.

"Hi, Jeannie." She got up and met her future mother-in-law at the back door.

Jeannie's dimple flashed as her kind eyes surveyed Livy. "Jerry just unloaded the rest of y'all's luggage and put it in Scott's old room for y'all," she said in a drawl far more pronounced than her son's. Fifteen years of immersion in the flat West Coast speech had worn down Scott's southern accent to a faint trace. "There's a nice new bed in there. You'll like it, I'm sure." Jeannie turned to go inside, then swiveled back to Livy. "Oh, and he's fixin' to put the girls' stuff in the smaller room next to it. Hope that's all right."

"Sure. But, um, but where will Scott sleep?"

Jeannie's smile froze on her face. "Why, in his old room. Don't worry, the bed is big enough for the both of you."

Ah. Scott's parents had assumed they would share a bed. Apparently, he had neglected to mention that one detail. Now what would they do?

Livy's face burned under Jeannie's puzzled gaze. "I see. I'm sure it will be fine."

Jeannie patted Livy before returning to the house, and Livy made tracks to the swing set. "Scott?"

He looked up, his lips shifting into a smile. "Having fun yet?"

"I love it here. It's so warm! Anyway, we need to talk."

His expression stiffened. "What's the matter?"

She gestured him to the porch swing. He held up an

index finger, then scooped Kinzie off the swing, setting her on the ground, and repeated the same for Lacie. "Girls, go inside and ask Grandma if she needs help with dinner."

Without a protest, Kinzie ran to the back door, disappearing inside, Lacie on her heels. "Grandma!"

Scott joined Livy on the swing and drew her close. "What's goin' on?"

Just an hour in his parents' presence had deepened his drawl.

"Your parents think we're sleeping together. Your mom put all our luggage in your old room."

His eyes narrowed as he tilted his head. "Huh. I told my mom I'd be sleeping on the couch. She must've thought I was just being gallant."

"You haven't told her we're …uh…"

"Abstaining? Not in so many words. They know I'm a Christian, but I guess they're still fuzzy on what exactly that means."

"Can you talk to her?"

"I can." He took her hand and went inside. "Right now."

⚜⚜⚜

While Scott set his parents straight, Livy opened her purple Samsonite carry-on and started unpacking. She held up a pair of jeans identical to the ones she had on and wondered what Scott was saying. The jeans passed inspection, so she rerolled them and stored them in a plain white dresser, half-wishing she could hear the conversation, half-relieved she couldn't. Next, she grabbed her velvet lilac robe and hung it in the closet. How awkward to be put in this position, but she had to laugh at the irony. She and Scott were committed to purity, yet his parents encouraged them to share a bed. Polar opposite to Nick's parents, who wouldn't let him share a bed with his lover under their roof.

A wall hanging wrested her attention away from her task, and she moved closer to study it. She smiled as a glow lit her heart. A large brass carving of Jesus on the Cross hung there. Christ's head lolled to the side, and His tiny eyes were closed as if He were sleeping. Scott's parents must be Christian.

A light tap sounded from the door, and she opened it to Scott's smiling face.

"Okay, it's all good. I think they were a little embarrassed, but they understood."

She pulled him inside, and his brawny arms surrounded her waist. His hands caressed her back.

"Thank you, hon. What did you tell them?"

"Just explained that you and I had decided to wait till our wedding night to sleep together. Then my dad asked if it had something to do with the church I go to now. I said no, we just wanted to be obedient to the Lord."

"Aren't they Christians, too?" She pushed away from his embrace and pointed to the Cross. "See that?"

Scott glanced over. "Oh, that's a crucifix. Very common among Catholic families."

"They believe in Jesus' crucifixion."

"Yes, they do. But sometimes I fear many churchgoers rely too much on the symbols of Christ, and not on Christ himself."

"Oh." She wasn't quite clear on what he meant. "Do your parents go to church?"

"On and off. Only one of my two sisters is a faithful church attender. All of my other siblings have forsaken the faith."

The distress on his face was so palpable, she had to lower his head and give him a kiss. What a caring man.

From the look on Scott's face, he wasn't thinking about

crucifixes anymore. His eyes moved over her face, and she could feel the mingled love and yearning coming off him in waves.

He rubbed his hands on his jeans. "It's going to be hard," his deepened voice grew husky, "being here tonight with you under the same roof."

"I know." Her arms itched to pull him close, longed to let him tug her down onto the bed, just inches away. Oh, why did he have to be so ridiculously good looking?

Not for the first time, she wondered why God would be displeased if she and Scott fully expressed their love before their wedding. She tried to remember what the pastor had said in their Christian Dating seminar last month. Piece by reluctant piece, it came to her. Rejecting God's moral standard equaled rejection of God. First Thessalonians Four.

She sighed. What a difficult road. Yet there wasn't anything better than knowing the living God. How could she ruin that?

She recalled the pastor saying that husband and wife became one in the marriage bed.

I am my Beloved's and he is mine....

She liked the sound of that.

As thoughts skidded through her mind, Scott ran his fingers through her hair, the green of his eyes intensifying.

"Daddy?" said a little voice at the doorway.

She and Scott whirled to see Kinzie watching them, a question mark in those solemn blue eyes.

"Grandma says dinner's ready."

Livy's relief at the interruption echoed in Scott's eyes. *Close one.* Chuckling, they went hand-in-hand to the dining room. He leaned his mouth close to her ear. "When we're married, remind me to lock our bedroom door at night."

Chapter Twenty-Three

The familiar scent of grilled burgers hit DeeDee when she walked through Quaking Aspen's front door the next day. Renee's presence beside her grounded her and kept her from feeling exposed and vulnerable. On the flight north, she'd kept her mind and heart carefully blank, shoving away visions of Bryan Campbell shooting his wife. But once she stepped foot into the nightclub and sensed every eye turn her way, she had to fight the urge to flee back home.

What must they think of her, the murderer's girlfriend, waltzing in here as brazen as a half-drunk babe looking for action?

They were partly right. But the action she was after wasn't what they thought.

Renee had seemed a little surprised when DeeDee called and informed her she was returning for a couple days. "I've booked a hotel, but I hope we can get together."

"Oh, don't do that. Come stay with us again."

DeeDee had agreed, then the story of her visit to the cabin poured from her. Once she'd spilled her guts, she held her breath, torn between regret and relief.

Silence on the other end convinced her Renee highly disapproved of her behavior. "Please don't judge me for keeping it a secret."

"I'm not judging you. Just a little shocked is all."

"Not as shocked as I was. I've been holding this in for too long. I've even had a couple dreams about Pam calling for help. Livy thinks I saw or heard something to prove Nick didn't do it, and now I'm dying to know what it was. I want to learn more about Pam's life to see who could have a reason to murder her."

Renee replied in the clipped tone she used whenever she stuffed her emotions. "I've been wondering if her husband is the culprit. Not that I've ever met him, so I have no reason to think so, except I'm convinced Nick didn't do it."

"So am I." DeeDee paced her kitchen floor, the phone fastened to her ear. "And if you could come with me and lend me moral support, I'd be ever so grateful."

It was still a little early for the evening rush at four thirty. She didn't see a single familiar face. Elation fought with disappointment as they found a booth and ordered burgers from the spiky-haired waiter.

After what seemed like hours of small talk, interspersed with door watching, a familiar figure strode inside. Senior gaped when he saw her. Then his face darkened.

"Sure wasn't expecting to see *you* here ever again." His head shook back and forth, sending thick chestnut curls bouncing as if he were shaking away a hallucination. He backed away, still staring.

DeeDee shrunk a little inside—she'd known her presence would get attention, but she hadn't foreseen this level of hostility. Senior behaved as though she'd pointed the gun at Pam and pulled the trigger herself.

If this continued, she wouldn't be getting any answers.

"Wait a minute." Renee's uncharacteristically sharp tone halted his flight. "Don't run away."

He halted, and his face smoothed over like the work of an invisible hand.

Renee shot a quick glance at DeeDee before offering Senior a forced smile. "We're just here to offer our condolences."

His normally merry eyes hardened. "Condolences, eh?

Did you spend your Christmas helping to plan a funeral?" He returned his attention to DeeDee just as the front door opened, letting in a blast of frigid air. Clive sauntered in, followed by Erik, and started toward the back of the restaurant before spotting Senior.

"Hey, hey, the gang's all here," Senior chanted, waving at his friends. His sudden mood swing reminded DeeDee of a giddy child. The three men congregated near the kitchen door.

Snatches of conversation from the surrounding booths, all normal and ordinary, mocked her. "He hates me," she stage-whispered across the table at Renee, then dropped her chin onto her clenched fists.

Livy. Her twin's face floated onto her mind's canvas. She needed her sister. "Excuse me a minute. Be right back."

Renee's mouth elongated in surprise when DeeDee leaped to her feet, but she nodded. DeeDee grabbed her red Anne Klein peacoat and rushed out the door, punching Livy's number before she'd even stepped outside.

"Deeds? Did you find anything out?"

"No!" DeeDee cringed from the wail in her voice, then hurried toward the dark parking lot when a nearby couple eyed her on their way in. "They hate me and won't talk to me."

"Why would they hate you?"

She pulled on her gloves as she relayed the events. "I feel like a fool, showing my face in there where Nick has so much history. It's obvious they believe he's guilty. Senior treated me like I was a pile of vomit on the ground."

Silence.

"What? What are you thinking?"

"I'm thinking a change of approach is in order."

"A change of approach, huh? I'm listening."

❧❧❧

DeeDee strode back inside, her spine straight, her head high, ready to channel Jennifer Lawrence. As Livy promised, she wouldn't even have to lie.

When she slid onto the seat across from Renee, her friend sat deep in conversation with Senior, who cast her another what-are-you-doing-here look. She ignored the look and motioned a waiter over. After she'd ordered a beer refill, she listened to the chatter across from her.

Renee was updating Senior on Nick's case, what little she knew of it.

"And I'm here to get closure," DeeDee cut in. Both heads swung toward her. She ran her thumb along the bench's vinyl piping.

"Closure?" Senior's abrupt echo poked a hole in her high hopes, but she plowed on.

"Yes. Closure. How would you feel if the love of your life killed their ex? Wouldn't you want to understand why?" Her voice surged in a movie star-like climax, edged with gasping angst.

Renee wrinkled her brow, clearly confused.

DeeDee sat forward, rolled her shoulders in an exaggerated slump. "I just want to know why he would do it."

From her peripheral vision, she saw Renee's mouth drop open, felt her probing gaze.

A laser-beam glare shot from Senior's eyes. "Well, why don't you ask him? It's what we all want to know."

"You're joking, right? He says he didn't do it."

Senior pushed a contemptuous snort from his compressed lips.

"But I thought you said..." Renee paused mid-word, but DeeDee hushed her with a tiny headshake.

"Nick never really talked about Pam," she cut in, addressing Senior. "I'm guessing it was a bitter divorce...?"

Senior had stopped glaring at DeeDee. The old jolly warmth, this time tinged with sorrow, softened his eyes. "Funny thing about Pam," he began, his finger tapping the roughened wood surface. "None of her breakups were nasty or bitter. She and I parted the best of friends. As did she and Nick. You couldn't really stop loving Pam."

Not the sentiment she expected. "You honestly believe Nick still loved her?" Now the angst was real and curled around her heart, contorting her emotions.

"I wouldn't doubt it." Senior's hard visage had morphed into compassion as he gazed at her. "Nothing against you. Pam just had that effect on men."

Like she needed to hear that. "How strange, then, to think he shot her." Not exactly a lie.

Senior nodded. "Strange indeed. Even stranger that it appeared premeditated."

Premeditated. What a sinister word. But Senior's voice rang with conviction.

Before she had a chance to ask about Pam and Bryan's marriage, a swift breeze from the front door wrestled her attention toward two figures hurrying in from the cold. Leon clasped Jazzy's mittened hand and pulled her in their direction. At Leon's entrance, the very air became charged, as though the oxygen molecules danced and celebrated his arrival.

He stopped and tilted his head when he saw her, his eyes loaded with disbelief, while Jazzy flung off her parka's fleece-lined hood and stared. DeeDee tried to read her expression, but her stage-worthy makeup job obscured it.

Leon looked at his dad, thrusting a thumb in DeeDee's direction. "Never thought I'd see her again."

"She's here for closure," Senior explained as DeeDee clenched her teeth to dam a flood of annoyance. They acted as though she couldn't hear them. She studied Leon's face.

If he was grieving his mother's death, she couldn't tell.

"I'll give her closure." Leon's sudden venom startled her. He turned on her. "May your boyfriend rot in prison, and may Bubba choose him to be his girlfriend."

Jazzy snickered, but DeeDee's stomach churned. While she wavered between the urge to slap him or crawl under the table, Senior came to her rescue.

"Son. It's not her fault."

Leon ignored his father. He yanked off his Blue Jays baseball cap in one quick movement and scratched his head. Thinning hair on top of his scalp contrasted with the black strands hanging over his ears and added ten years to his face.

The couple settled in the booth behind DeeDee. Leon's spastic chortles carried across the seat and scraped DeeDee's already-raw nerves. He must have been raised on Beavis and Butthead.

Jazzy's rebuke carried straight to DeeDee's ears. "I can't believe you said that."

DeeDee leaned toward Senior, trying to block out the couple's murmurs. "When is the funeral?"

"Done and past. Yesterday. Quite a somber affair."

She strained to concentrate on Senior's words, distracted by the hushed conversation from the newlyweds about someone's paternity test. Jazzy's intense whisper transmitted clearly. "I think you ought to just ask him."

DeeDee scooted further along the bench. "It must have hit her husband hard."

Senior again. "Under the circumstances, he held up well."

Had Bryan Campbell "held up well" due to Oscar-worthy acting ability? Or from genuine grief? If he wasn't the murderer, few other candidates presented themselves.

Odds were slim Pam had encountered a random bad guy in the deep woods. If she had, it could take weeks, months, perhaps never, to nail the perp.

Nick's stricken face floated in her consciousness. She *had* to do whatever she needed to get him back to a normal life. If she had to stay here indefinitely to get at the truth, then so be it.

Chapter Twenty-Four

Bryan Campbell, DeeDee discovered when she searched the Internet, lived in Saanich with his preschool daughter. As the CEO for Cottingham Property Management in Victoria, he looked the part, with his clean-cut, businesslike attire and not a strand of black hair out of place.

Pam's male counterpart.

Over morning coffee, DeeDee merely told Renee she planned to take a drive. No need for Renee to know her true intention. She'd arrive at Cottingham Property Management by eight a.m., so she could find out what kind of car Campbell drove and follow him after work. Maybe she could catch him in an incriminating situation.

She parked her rental car at the curb opposite a six-story brick building as nondescript as the structures around it. Whenever a car drove into the lot, DeeDee scrutinized the driver as they got out. Finally, a silver Mercedes pulled in, driven by a man resembling Bryan Campbell's Internet photo. He strode the paved walk to the double-door main entry. By now, rain was misting down, and she needed to get a better look. Keeping the man in sight, she heaved her hood up and entered the same glass doors.

She caught up with the Campbell look-alike at the elevator, but kept her hood covering her head. He didn't glance her way as he stepped into the open elevator and held the door for her. She glanced at his left hand to see if he still wore his ring, but the gloves he clutched blocked her view.

He punched the fifth-floor button. "What floor?" His

head finally tipped toward her.

She scrutinized him from the corner of her eye, but kept her face angled away. "Same."

He was unmistakably her quarry.

"Do you work for the attorneys?"

She shook her head. "Job interview." Her voice came out terse, and he got the message. He asked her no more questions. On the fifth floor, he veered right, so she went left, found a ladies' room, and then returned to her car.

"See you at five, Bryan Campbell," she muttered.

⊰⊱⊰⊱

Nick lay back on the reeking mattress, his hands beneath his head. He blocked out the incessant noise, a task made easier over time. DeeDee's beloved face hovered in his mind's eye as he reminisced on her recent visit. The naked compassion in her eyes had startled him. His sweet, hardheaded ladylove, whose mouth could hurl a mean left hook, who never said no to an adventure, felt sorry for him. Shame crawled up his torso, sending a shudder out his shoulders.

He tried not to be annoyed at Adam Vernon for taking so long on his case. Nick had stressed the urgency of getting out of here. He had gigs to play, a life to live. But Vernon insisted the best way to get the case dropped was to find Pam's murderer.

"Well, how many people have you interviewed?" Nick had demanded.

"All the family members. None of them were anywhere near the site that morning."

"Well, one of them's lying. What about the husband?"

"He was at work all day, he says."

"He says."

Vernon had shrugged. "Naturally, we verified it with the

office staff."

Thoughts churned—the same thoughts that kept him awake for nights on end. Who would have reason to kill Pam, except a greedy husband? Bryan benefitted financially from her death.

"He could've hired someone. He could've killed her at home that morning. And transported her body later."

The same could be true of Leon. Could his stepson have had a more sinister purpose when he came to the cabin? Nick visualized the scene—the forested yard, Jack barking at something beyond the fence. Felled trees on the ground...No, not trees. He was almost certain Pam's already-dead body had excited the dog.

If Leon had shot his mother, he wouldn't have hesitated to shoot Nick, too. Yet he hadn't.

"What about Leon's alibi?" he'd asked.

"He says he had the day off, so he stayed home and worked on his car while his wife got some Christmas shopping done," Vernon had said. "He was nowhere near the cabin."

"He's lying."

He'd recapped his conversation with Leon that fateful night, and Adam had promised further questioning of Leon. "You realize, don't you, if you press charges against Leon, the defense could claim you were hallucinating. Whiskey and marijuana were found in the U-Haul."

Nick balled his fist. So much for his brief reconnection with God. Apparently, God was severely punishing the prodigal for an indiscretion from four years ago. The little face he couldn't get out of his mind floated like a phantom into his brain. Pam's little girl, Sofie, with the face so like his own.

"Okay, God, I get it now." It made a certain twisted sort of sense, punishing him for someone else's crime against his ex-wife. Until the day he died, he'd regret trysting with Pam while both of them were in committed relationships. And now, his sins had found him out. "But it was just one time. Wasn't losing Gracie punishment enough?"

Apparently not. He shifted, clenched and unclenched his hands, and fought a persistent thought—by the time he got out of here, would he have any sanity left?

⌘⌘⌘

It took all DeeDee's persuasive powers to convince Renee to accompany her in pursuit of Bryan. "If I catch him in something incriminating, I could be in danger. I'll need you there to call for help, or in case I need to make a swift getaway."

"Gavin will kill me if he finds out."

"Then don't tell him."

They set out in Renee's car through the driving rain, arriving at Bryan's office building by four thirty. As they waited across the lot from Bryan's Mercedes, pop tunes from the stereo broke up the nail-biting silence. Every forty-something male who emerged from the glass doors underwent DeeDee's scrutiny.

"He could be working late tonight, you know," Renee reminded her. "How long are you going to wait?"

DeeDee, shrugging, chewed her lower lip. "I don't…Oh look. Here he comes."

Campbell, brooding over the phone in his hand, and two other businessmen, strode briskly along the drenched walk.

"The one in the middle."

Renee started the engine, and DeeDee shifted upright, her shoulders loosening once the awaited moment arrived. A surge of excitement jolted her heart, and she grinned. "Watch out, Mr. Campbell, you've got a couple of Charlie's

Angels on your rear."

DeeDee squinted at the distinctive wing-shaped taillights, never once letting her eyes wander. Dusk neared and, coupled with the dense rain, compromised her visibility. They trailed him north toward Saanich—was he heading straight home?

After about five kilometers, he exited the highway and turned left, away from Saanich.

Renee switched the wipers to high. "Where could he be going?"

"To visit his paramour?"

Their quarry swerved into a strip mall parking lot. Renee followed him to a spot near a Fitness World and found a space directly across. He made a brief call on his cell, then got out and retrieved a duffel bag from the back seat.

DeeDee brought her hands down hard on her thighs. "Great. He's living a double life as a gym rat."

Renee chuckled. "Or he could be meeting his paramour inside."

DeeDee grabbed the door handle. "I'm going in."

"Wait. What am I supposed to do?"

DeeDee pointed across the lot to a Wal-Mart. "Go shopping. Then you have a legitimate excuse for being gone so long."

"You're just going to spy on him?"

"You bet I am." She hurried to the entrance, where a red-haired young man held the door for her. She thanked him, then blinked, her eyes stinging against the brightly-lit interior. She glanced around, finally spotting Campbell heading to the men's locker room. So she'd do the same.

After purchasing a guest pass and new fitness gear from the attached shop—nondescript black tights and leotard, metallic running shoes, red headband—she quickly changed, then scoped the place. Campbell was puffing along on a treadmill, next to a young ponytailed blonde woman.

DeeDee claimed the empty treadmill on his other side, thankful he hadn't seen her face that morning. She sensed him checking her out as she studied the display. The settings were in kilometers, giving her a perfect opportunity to strike up a conversation.

"Excuse me." She turned to Campbell, whose face betrayed his interest. So, the blonde wasn't his paramour. Up close, she could see a slight redness around his eyes, leathery skin stretched over protruding cheekbones. "Can you help me? I don't know the metric system." At his raised-brow stare, she hastened to explain, "I'm from the States. I usually start it on four miles per hour."

"Ah." He nodded. "I think that's equivalent to about six kilometers." His voice reminded her of Nick's. "Try it and see if it feels right."

She fiddled with the selections. "Feels a little slow." She moved it up to seven, and it sputtered to life beneath her accelerating stride.

"Just visiting, then?" The words broke into her thoughts.

"Yes."

"Whereabouts in the States?"

"Seattle." She immediately regretted the admission. Bryan must know Nick lived there, too. Then she relaxed, knowing that, out of a metro area of three million, he wouldn't necessarily connect the two of them.

"What brings you to visit us this time of year?"

This wet, dreary time of year. "I have family here." That is, family-to-be, if she could nail this guy for murder, spring Nick out of jail, and marry him.

"I'm Bryan, by the way."

She hesitated, unwilling to reveal her name. "Diana. Di for short." He wouldn't recognize her childhood nickname.

"Glad to meet you. Welcome to BC." He refocused on the row of TVs mounted from the ceiling. She followed suit, staring at a sitcom she didn't recognize.

He punched the treadmill settings, and his belt began to slow.

"Cooling down already?"

He glanced over. "Yeah. Need to hit the weights next."

Wrong order, she wanted to say. *Weights before cardio.* Yet his sinewy physique and well-shaped legs suggested frequent workouts, so maybe he knew something she didn't.

She increased her speed two notches. So far, she'd seen nothing that screamed "wife-murderer." She'd just have to keep pounding away on this treadmill until he was done, then tail him home.

His cell phone rang.

She held her breath, suddenly irritated at the overarching roar, the high ceiling creating poor acoustics. Attempting nonchalance, she slowed her speed to warm-up level so her pounding feet wouldn't drown out his voice.

"Hey." His tone came out clipped, impatient.

Her steps decelerated in sync with his.

"No, I stopped at the gym."

A distinctly female voice came through his phone, but she couldn't discern the words.

"Did you remind them I've already talked to them three times?"

DeeDee's ears perked up. Apparently, the cops still had questions.

"Anyway," his voice lowered to an undertone, "I can't talk about it now. I'm leaving in about twenty minutes." He clicked off and pocketed the phone.

DeeDee couldn't resist. "Your wife checking up on you, I take it?"

He didn't take the bait. "No, my mom. She babysits my

daughter."

She watched his eyes for any hint he could be lying. But he averted his gaze, betraying nothing.

She stopped the treadmill and texted Renee. She needed to get showered and changed and be ready to leave in twenty minutes. With any luck, she'd see cops lying in wait for him when he arrived home.

Chapter Twenty-Five

"This is getting boring." Renee, smothering a yawn, checked her phone while DeeDee kept watch. Renee was right—nothing was happening at the four-thousand-square-foot Campbell mansion. No cops awaited. Bryan had gone inside where he presumably planned to spend an uneventful evening with his little girl. Gavin had sent Renee a couple of worried texts, but she merely told him she and DeeDee were out shopping.

"I need to get home now."

DeeDee reluctantly agreed. "Per Murphy's Law, something exciting will happen as soon as we leave. And we'll miss it."

"The way Gavin's talking, there's going to be plenty of drama if I don't get home," Renee drolled in a dry voice. "You'll get more excitement than you bargained for."

"Oh wait." DeeDee grabbed Renee's arm. "Wait. He's coming out the front door."

"Really?" Renee craned her neck to see.

Bryan strode with purpose toward his Mercedes, cradling a bundle. "He's holding his little girl." When Bryan kissed the small cheek and settled his daughter in the back seat, DeeDee braced herself against the tender emotions the gesture wrought. She didn't want to go feeling warm fuzzies toward a possible murderer.

Campbell climbed into the driver seat and started the engine. DeeDee opened the GPS on her phone. "Look out, Mr. Wife-killer, we're right behind you."

Renee groaned. "I need to get home, I told you."

"Let's just see where he's going, then go home."

Renee sighed and took off after Bryan. "This better be short." He wound through the neighborhood, onto a boulevard for a short distance, and into another, shabbier neighborhood.

DeeDee peered at the street sign, but couldn't make it out in the dark. "Do you know where we are?"

"Vaguely." Renee followed Campbell as he made a left at the next street. "I wonder if he knows he's being followed."

Around the corner, Campbell was pulling to the curb in front of a box-shaped fourplex with two units upstairs and two below. "Here we are. This must be the other woman's place."

Campbell retrieved his daughter, then approached the lower right unit and stood for a minute before someone let him in. Each unit's front door was on the side of the building. No matter which way DeeDee craned to see, she couldn't see the person's face, couldn't even tell if it was male or female.

Renee plopped back against the seat. "Well, that told us one big, fat nothing."

"Oh, I don't know." DeeDee held up her phone. "The route's on my GPS, so all I have to do is come back tomorrow during daylight and get the address. Then I'll Google it and find out who lives there."

Renee shot her a smile. "Good thinking, my friend. Isn't technology wonderful?" She pulled into the street and headed home.

"How pathetic he'd take his daughter with him to his girlfriend's house."

"Then again, she's only three and likely to sleep through everything."

"Now that Pam's not around, he must be loving his freedom."

ᰔᰔᰔ

DeeDee's stomach growled as she stood at the door of Unit 1, shivering against the morning chill. She regretted leaving Renee's with an empty stomach. After following Bryan to work, she'd mustered her courage and vowed to knock at the apartment he'd visited last night.

She gave a couple of hesitant raps, almost expecting Bryan's silver mobile to come humming to the curb. She flinched. She'd sure have some explaining to do.

A black pickup rumbled by, but no silver Mercedes.

Two more knocks, harder this time, her planned speech running through her mind.

The door opened, and she looked into a lined, thin face and half-worried gaze. Frizzy gray hair, cloudy hazel eyes. A woman, as DeeDee expected. An elderly woman leaning on a cane, not expected.

"Can I help you?"

Yes, why did Bryan Campbell visit you last night? There was something familiar about the woman. DeeDee forced an all-business tone. "I understand there's a unit for rent. Are you the manager?"

The woman frowned and cocked her left ear closer. "A unit for rent?" Her voice croaked like an ancient door hinge. "I don't believe so. We're full here. Where did you hear that?"

"An ad in the paper."

"You must have the wrong address. Our property managers don't advertise the addresses of their rentals. Only their office phone number."

A wisp of a hunch floated into her mind. "Who is your property manager?"

"Let me see if I can find a card for you." She shuffled into the dim interior. Laughter and voices came from the TV.

She returned with a folded-up business card and handed it to DeeDee.

Cottingham Property Management.

Now we're getting somewhere.

"Thank you." DeeDee stopped, held out her hand. "By the way, I'm Olivia. And you are…?"

"Amelia." The woman's feeble grip barely lifted DeeDee's hand. "Good luck with your search."

Amelia. She'd heard or seen the name recently.

She studied the woman, noted her tall, thin frame, classical bone structure, and a memory intruded. *Mom and I at Butchart Gardens – with Amelia Quigley.*

Pam's mom.

This woman was Pam's mom. Bryan had brought his daughter to visit Grandma last night.

Probably not something a wife-killer would do.

Suddenly, DeeDee felt two inches high. She turned and slunk to her car, then drove back to Renee's slower than usual. If she could kick herself with the heel of her mid-calf Mizrahi boots, she most decidedly would.

She needed to call off this whole wild-goose chase. After all, if the experts hadn't found the real killer, why did she think she could?

⊰⊰⊰

"Liv, answer your phone!" DeeDee muttered after the fourth ring. From her vantage point, face-up on Renee's guest room bed, she watched the sunbeams disappear from the ceiling as a cloud floated over the sun. Livy had flown home yesterday. No reason for her not to answer her phone.

"Deeds?" Livy's breathless voice burrowed like a warm puppy into her spirit.

"Liv! You won't believe what I just did." It felt so good to unburden herself. Livy merely listened, occasionally injecting an appropriate "wow!" or a "hmm". "I feel like I've wasted my time."

"Why?"

"The cops would've already searched Bryan's e-mail and online activities, I'm sure."

"That's one of the first things they do."

"So I'm guessing they didn't find anything incriminating, or he would've been arrested by now."

"Yeah, good point." Livy sighed. "Sorry I didn't answer my phone right away. Scott and I were in the bedroom and…"

"No wonder you were out of breath." DeeDee snickered. "Finally decided the nun act wasn't for you?"

Livy tsked. "Stop it. No, we're watching a movie with his daughters."

"I'll let you get back to your movie. Miss you."

"Double ditto."

"Triple ditto."

"Oh, hey." Livy uttered a squeak. "I almost forgot."

"What?"

Livy paused. Background voices carried over the line, then faded. DeeDee could picture her twin throwing Scott a reassuring kiss before she left the room. "I had a little brainstorm the other day and meant to call you."

"Tell me about your mini-brainstorm."

"Okay. You know we've had this murder on our minds so much, we haven't even thought about the hacked credit card."

"Right…"

"You said Nick ordered something from Moonstone using his credit card, which was later hacked."

DeeDee scrunched her face and saw a pattern clearly

unfolding in her mind.

And suddenly, she knew what Livy was about to say.

"Haven't you wondered how the thief got hold of Nick's credit card data?"

"Oh, Livs. Of course. Why didn't we think of it sooner? Someone who works at Moonstone."

"And who do we know that works at Moonstone?"

"Leon Jr." Another memory intruded. "Rockstar Guitar was one of the merchants. According to his wife, he wants to be a rock star in the worst way."

Livy chuckled. "I think we found our credit thief."

Chapter Twenty-Six

DeeDee, determination firming her jaw, gripped the vinyl steering wheel and pointed the car toward the highway leading to Quaking Aspen. If she timed it right, she'd arrive before the lunch rush. Leon had some explaining to do, and she was going to see that he did.

If Leon wasn't there, she'd corner Senior and demand some answers. She visualized his gentle face, his soft hands seemingly incapable of shooting an animal, much less a person. Now Junior, on the other hand...

"Oh snap." She'd driven right past the highway and into an unfamiliar neighborhood. Brick buildings, their once-stately storefronts faded like aging divas, lined the street. A few cars, as old as the buildings, hunkered about potholed parking lots.

A rather sketchy street to get lost on. And the barricade dividing the lanes prevented her from turning around. She had no choice but to keep driving until the barricade ended and hope she could find her way back.

A seaplane, purring low for a landing in Victoria Harbour, anchored her with a vague sense as to her whereabouts. The buildings grew shabbier as the street veered right, then left, until she was no longer sure in which direction the highway lay. She bit her lip and eased in a deep breath. *Do not panic. Not all who wander are lost.* She'd have to pull over to the side of this questionable street to check her GPS and hope the slump-shouldered, shuffling residents left her alone.

A chill sent a shiver through her, and she turned up the heat, longing for her forgotten gloves. She stopped at the curb in front of a nondescript building, all opaque windows and striped awnings, and felt for her phone.

A familiar figure appeared on the sidewalk. Although his face pointed to the ground, she recognized him straightaway. Erik Sterling in a polo shirt, tailored denim jacket, and newish jeans, his head covered in a red beanie. He looked the way she imagined she must look: as though he'd been transported from Renee's neighborhood and somehow ended up on the wrong street.

But what was he doing around here? Relieved to see a familiar face, she rolled down the passenger window and hollered.

His surprise morphed to a friendly smile. He poked his head in the window. "Hey, you. What's a nice girl like you doing in a place like this?"

The tautness in her face relaxed a small degree. "I might ask you the same thing."

He waved behind him, his gaze following. "These are my stomping grounds. That's the place I volunteer at. Across the street." She turned to the spot his finger indicated—a mirror image of the building next to her. Victoria Mission read the letters on the awning. "The place I was telling you and your sister about the other day."

"Then you can probably tell me how to get back to the highway."

"Sure. Where are you headed?"

"To Quaking Aspen." She immediately regretted her words, his expression startled. She hurried on. "But I'm lost."

"Yes, I'd say you are." His intense tone somehow managed to infuse the simple words with a deeper meaning. She narrowed her eyes at him, unsure if he was insulting her.

"You're as lost as I used to be," he went on, further baffling her.

"I'm not following."

He glanced at her white-knuckled hands, still clasped like a vice on the steering wheel. "You look upset. Would you like a cup of coffee?"

Boy, would she.

"There's a nice café in the next block. You look like you could use a listening ear."

The kindness in his tone reeled her in, and free coffee sounded irresistible after a stressful morning. She checked his hand for a wedding ring, saw the brassy flash, and then at his eyes radiating puzzled concern. No interested gleam shone from them; no sly grin hovered on his lips.

"Won't your wife mind?"

A slight lift of his lips. "She works there." At her raised brows, he explained, "We're pretty secure in our relationship. She knows this is what I do."

"Well, okay."

Once on the street, she strolled beside him to a shabby, faded door set in a decrepit structure, its glory days long over. When he opened the door and gestured her inside, she stepped into another world. A fifties-style diner spread before her, complete with black-tiled floor, shiny chrome stools, and red vinyl booths. A jukebox proudly dominated the side in all its gleaming retro glory. She almost expected to see teenagers in poodle skirts and ankle socks perched on the stools sipping root beer floats.

"Ooh, nice."

"Yes, Stella's Diner is popular with the folks around here." About ten guests, as opposite of innocent youth as you could get, occupied the stools and booths, lending credence to Erik's words. Most of them appeared rumpled and unbathed. A couple of them waved when they saw him, and he returned the wave. She sidestepped a woman dressed like an aging Janis Joplin, big round glasses and all, heading for the jukebox.

DeeDee hung back, reluctant to sit on the possibly dirty or greasy bench. She didn't know what kind of critters the street people might have left behind. But Erik didn't seem bothered. He ushered her to a booth. "Let me go tell my wife I'm here, and you can meet her."

The happy strains of "My Boyfriend's Back" launched from the jukebox. The colorful hippie woman couldn't have picked a more ironic song. DeeDee grabbed a wad of napkins and spread them on the bench, then sat gingerly, afraid to touch the table's Formica surface. No telling who'd sat here before her.

She looked up to see Erik watching her from behind the counter, his bemused expression mixed with something else…pity? She flinched against the unfamiliar surge of shame squeezing her heart.

A thin, longhaired woman appeared at his side, who kept eyeing DeeDee and nodding. Next thing she knew, the couple strode toward her, their broad smiles lacking even a hint of disapproval, which she appreciated. The woman placed two cups of steaming coffee on the table. Erik dropped to the bench opposite DeeDee. "This is my wife, Lisa. Lisa, DeeDee. Nick's girlfriend."

DeeDee exchanged greetings with Lisa, noting her youthful, makeup-free complexion contrasting her graying brown hair, her wide mouth forming a slant on her pretty face.

Lisa handed her a menu. "We're serving lunch right now. Tuesday's special is beef stew for five ninety-nine. Care for anything to eat?"

DeeDee shook her head. "Not right now, thanks." She planned to eat lunch at Quaking Aspen while she quizzed

Junior and/or Senior.

Lisa turned to go, and Erik rested his elbows on the table. "So tell me why you were heading to Quaking Aspen. Something tells me it's not just the food."

How much should she tell him? Her gut sensed his sincerity, but could he be trusted?

Instead of answering, she hedged. "Why do you think that?"

"Your boyfriend's in jail for murder, yet you're frequenting his old hangouts. Most people in your shoes would head home and move on with their lives."

She rested her elbows on the Formica, mirroring him, considering, and then discarding, several possible responses.

"Is there something going on you need to share? I'm willing to listen and help in any way I can."

"My Boyfriend's Back" segued into "Satisfaction". Like the Rolling Stones, she couldn't get any, either. She squeezed her fingers until they ached. "I think Leon shot Pam, not Nick."

From the way his head jerked back, it was clearly the last thing he expected to hear.

"They have the wrong guy locked up." *I just want my boyfriend back.*

Once the astonishment cleared from his face, he asked the inevitable question. "Why," his voice softened, "do you believe Leon shot his mom?"

"Because I'm ninety-nine-percent sure he hacked Nick's credit card."

The astonishment returned, mixed with a wary compassion. He thought she was nuts.

She plowed on. "Someone cleaned out Nick's bank account and racked up thousands of dollars on his credit cards. One of the merchants was Rockstar Guitar."

Judging from Erik's expression, this wasn't the first time

he'd heard this. But how could he possibly know?

She gripped the table edge, heedless of the germs. "The day Nick disappeared, he was heading to a place called Black Bear Lane…."

"Pam's father's home up the island, where her body was found."

"Right." She went on to share the conversation she'd overheard the last night she saw Nick. "I think it was Pam on the other end. He was talking about evidence and meeting someone—"

"Whoa. Slow down. That doesn't make Leon a murderer."

"Do *you* honestly believe Nick shot her?"

Before Erik could reply, an unkempt man, his frizzy beard matted with what looked like old food particles, shambled toward them and stopped at the table.

Erik offered an open-mouthed, gray-toothed smile. "Frank. Long time no see."

The man uttered a half-laugh, half-grunt and held up a shaking hand. Erik high-fived it. DeeDee shuddered, tempted to rummage in her bag for hand sanitizer and offer it to Erik. But she had a feeling he wouldn't appreciate the gesture. He'd probably give her that pitying look again.

Weird how he treated these people as though they were just normal folks, as though he didn't care what germs they spread. Or about the odors emanating from them like a foul-smelling bug spray they carried with them everywhere, coating them in a second skin.

Frank lingered, attempting to converse with Erik in a strange non-speak. She'd heard it before from the bums on Seattle's waterfront, but she always hurried by without looking at them. Men, and occasionally women, broken beyond repair.

How did they get that way?

"Frank, take care of yourself, okay?" The man turned away at Erik's words, and DeeDee allowed herself a deep breath. She hadn't realized she'd been holding it.

Erik returned his attention to her. "I would advise you not to go asking questions at Senior's restaurant."

"Why?"

"He was already questioned about the credit card transactions, and I don't think he would appreciate more interrogations."

"You don't believe me."

A flicker of doubt in his eyes confirmed her words. He rubbed his jaw as though he could scrape off the faint whiskers there. "Senior is my best friend, and Junior has always been like a son to me. I admit he has some growing up to do, but I never had a son of my own, you see. I'm having a hard time wrapping my brain around this."

"How do you know all this?"

"Senior told me. Nick named Leon as the suspect when he filed the fraud claim."

Another important piece of information Nick had kept from her. But why wouldn't he feel free to tell her who he suspected?

"Then why isn't Leon in jail?"

"Junior denied he had anything to do with it. They found no evidence linking him with those transactions."

"Seriously? He could easily get Nick's credit card data off his Moonstone order."

"Maybe so, but there's no proof he did. They never found any of those goods in his possession."

Her stomach dropped as hopelessness took root. "What about the wire transfer?"

"What wire transfer?"

DeeDee rubbed her thumb as she explained, watching his eyes for any hint of prior knowledge. But they remained alert and listening.

"Nick assumed the same person who hacked his credit card also made the transfer. Doesn't it make sense?"

He gave a partial shrug, obviously not fully convinced. "I'm not aware if the police questioned Junior about a wire transfer. But I doubt it was him. How would he have obtained Nick's banking data?"

"The same way he would've obtained Nick's credit card info. Through Moonstone's order history."

Erik lifted a shoulder, the compassion in his eyes back in full measure. "I know things look bleak for you right now, but I believe God is working on Nick."

She felt her face twist. "I want nothing to do with a God like that."

"What kind of a God *do* you want?"

Her kneading fingers stilled as her mind froze. Nobody had ever asked her such a question. She'd never even asked herself.

She squared her shoulders and mustered a fierce expression. "Life's been just fine with no God at all."

"Has it really?"

She glared at him, just about ready to jump up and head back to her car.

"You've lost your boyfriend as well as hope. You've lost your way."

"No, I haven't."

"You told me a few minutes ago you were lost."

"I meant I didn't know how to get back to the highway."

He merely nodded, his gaze still holding hers. "A great analogy for mankind's condition."

"Huh?"

Instead of clarifying, he launched a pointed question. "Last year your twin became a Christian. Do you mind if I ask why you didn't?"

Yes, she minded. This guy was starting to get on her nerves. But if she stalked out, she doubted he'd accompany her to her car, and she'd still be lost—No, make that temporarily disoriented.

Maybe if she answered his question, he'd be happy and stop asking them.

"She let a sweet-talking charmer indoctrinate her, and now they're engaged."

Erik slid his hand under his cap and massaged his head, the movement somehow familiar. Someone else she knew had the same habit, but she couldn't think who.

He opened his mouth to reply, but Lisa swooped over and refilled their coffee. DeeDee wrapped her fingers around the cup, enjoying the warmth seeping into her bones and chasing away the chill.

She'd rather stay in the warm, festive diner, fielding tough questions, than in the wintry outdoors where the biting wind tried to chew through her quilted black parka.

Lisa gave her a kind smile from her diagonal mouth. "Has Hubby helped you figure out the reason God sent you here?"

Now there was an unanswerable question. Lisa's penetrating gaze kept casting the question at her, so DeeDee forced out an answer. "Um, no, he hasn't." Despite Lisa's pleasant manner, something about this woman's no-nonsense body language discouraged DeeDee's usual flippancy toward religious subjects. Deep down, she suspected Lisa would only pity her if she derided the couple's faith.

"There's a reason you got lost." Lisa held the coffee pot suspended in air, as though she'd forgotten she was holding it. "Erik attracts lost souls like nectar attracts bees."

DeeDee could only offer a feeble smile. These people considered her as much a lost soul as the scruffy folks at the counter. Protesting would do no good, and, judging by their compassionate expressions, they clearly didn't mean it as an insult.

She was twenty-eight years old with a great career, looks, and a sparkling future. She ought to feel insulted. But something resonated inside her. She wanted to know more.

"Why do you keep saying I'm lost?" Her toes scrunched inside her boots while she clamped them firmly on the floor, as if they might rise of their own accord and launch her out the door.

Lisa smiled at her husband. "I'll let you take this one, honey." Pushing off the table, she turned and made her rounds to the tables, refilling coffee cups and offering friendly smiles to broken souls.

DeeDee steeled herself against Erik's searching look. Suddenly, like a yo-yo, she didn't want to hear his answer. So she blurted the first thing that came to mind. "Is Lisa Jazzy's mom?"

Erik's eyes grew soft. "No, Lisa is my second wife. Jasmine's mom left me after I got arrested in 2008. I married Lisa about..." He stopped, his eyes moving upward. "Two years ago. We started corresponding while I was in prison. She was a fine Christian lady, and after Christ saved me, she saw the changes He made in me and agreed to marry me when I was released." He clasped his hands and bounced them lightly on the tabletop. "She's the best thing ever happened to me. Never been happier in my life. Except for when I got saved."

The guy talked like Livy and Scott, with all his religious mumbo-jumbo. Plus, she desperately wanted to know what he'd been sent to jail for.

"I was in prison five years for robbing banks," he said, as though he'd read her mind. "Just like my old man. Like father, like son, as they say. I see that a lot at the mission…ex-cons who are sons of cons. One side of me is thankful I never had a son, for that reason. God's burdened my heart for these men. If I do what I can to help stop the cycle of crime, then maybe we can also save the sons."

"How? How do you stop the cycle of crime?"

Erik pointed at the ceiling. "Only through the grace of God."

DeeDee stifled a sigh. Everything came down to religion for this man.

A song melody nearby clashed with the jukebox tune. Erik reached for his phone. After a brief conversation, he ended the call. "Sorry, I have to get across the street. One of my guys is having a meltdown. Time for some crisis intervention." He stood and wrestled his arms into his jacket. "You're welcome to stay here. My wife will take good care of you."

The idea was tempting, but she needed to get going. "I can't stay." She thrust her arms into her parka. "May I get directions back to the highway?"

"Only if you promise not to go to Quaking Aspen."

Of course, she couldn't make such a promise, but she nodded anyway. He waved to his wife and a few other customers, explaining the route as they went, then saw her safely to her car.

"Thanks for the coffee."

"Come back anytime and talk some more," he called over his shoulder as he hurried across the street.

Studying her phone's GPS, she could see the way back clearly now. *See, I'm not lost at all.*

Chapter Twenty-Seven

The neighborhood grew gradually more attractive as DeeDee drove further from the mission. The surroundings, while unfamiliar, didn't fill her with churning dread or make her eyes dart this way and that to search for oncoming threats.

Almost there. At the stoplight, she checked her phone's map again, satisfied she was on the correct route, following the correct landmarks. Laughing Dragon Restaurant on the left. Wells Medical Clinic and CIBC on the right.

And around the corner—Moonstone Truffles, Ltd.

The light switched green, and on impulse, she took a right turn she hadn't intended to make. What a perfect opportunity.

Two short blocks brought her to Moonstone headquarters' ultra-cute storefront. Painted robin's-egg blue with gleaming white shutters festooned in stencil art, it could have passed for an artsy little home in Seattle's Capitol Hill. Blooms spilled from planters hanging from the eaves. Just like the website photos. What the photos didn't show was the monstrous boxlike warehouse abutting the office, its giant whale mouth in the act of swallowing the little building whole.

She wasn't sure what she expected, but she parked anyway and went inside the glass-paned door, accompanied by a cheery chime. A handful of customers formed a line in front of shiny glass counters displaying the prettiest assortment of treats she'd ever seen. Chocolate apparently came in all the colors of the rainbow. Pam's unique method of dyeing chocolate set her business apart from all the other chocolatiers and gained her a reputation for artistry that had made her rich.

DeeDee inhaled the chocolate ambiance, the air thick with it, giving her a distinct sensation of swimming in a pool of cocoa. Whitewashed walls offset hand-painted murals of oversized truffles and nuggets, each one labeled and described in a flowing teal script. A virtual sales catalog, blown up to a hundred times its size.

While she waited at the end of the line, she scrutinized the two employees behind the counter. A blonde forty-something woman—maybe Pam's assistant—kept glancing at the pony-tailed brunette on the other end who was swapping out an empty tray for one filled with blue-and-white-striped rectangles. Neither woman looked familiar, so she switched her attention to the tray of White Russian truffles looking delectable on the bottom shelf.

Made with real Kahlua and cream, said the tiny sign. Her favorite liqueur.

She'd placed her Moonstone order three days ago. It was probably waiting for her at home. She sent Livy a text, then grabbed a brochure from a nearby stack. The same smiling photo of Pam from the website dominated the cover, and DeeDee flipped idly through the leaflet while she waited for Livy's reply.

The couple at the head of the line retrieved their bag of treats and stepped aside. As the line crept forward, an inexplicable chill swept over DeeDee. She checked the front door, still tightly closed—so why the sudden prickles raising goose bumps on her arms?

Seeing no vents or any other draft source, she shivered and wrapped her arms around herself. "It's cold in here."

The woman ahead of her turned. "I hadn't noticed.

Maybe they need to keep the chocolates cool."

"Maybe." Or maybe it was just her. She kept talking, hoping the spooked feeling would leave. "What are you ordering?"

The other woman pointed. "Those delicious-looking Santas over there."

DeeDee glanced at the wall display of clearance items the woman indicated. And looked directly into a security camera. Aimed right at her.

Its red eye blinked like an alien UFO.

She stared at the camera, unable to look away from the pulsating red eye. Internal alarms were screaming at high decibels.

Behind that wall, someone was watching her.

A million thoughts arrowed through her mind. Obviously, her presence had alerted someone's suspicions.

She vaguely heard a customer behind her clear his throat.

A female voice penetrated the fog in her brain. "Miss?"

She looked up at the blonde clerk staring at her expectantly.

"What would you like?"

From her tone, it wasn't the first time she'd asked. How long had she been tuned out, focusing on the camera? "Oh, sorry. I'd like a White Russian truffle, please."

The woman bagged it and rang her up. DeeDee threw some cash on the counter and nearly snatched the bag from the clerk's hand, taking deep breaths to slow her jagged heartbeat. She forced herself to stride with nonchalance out the door, when all she wanted to do was flee.

෧෧෧

Once she settled in her car, her breathing slowed, and the shaking gradually subsided. She clutched her phone to read Livy's text. *Your chocolates are here waiting for you! I hope you don't mind sharing!*

She wasted no time calling Livy to tell her everything. "Erik said the cops found no evidence that Leon purchased anything with Nick's card. But Pam's murderer is somewhere in that building. I could feel an evil presence. I really believe Pam's spirit has been guiding me to find out the truth."

"No, she hasn't. God has."

"If God's so great, why doesn't He just tell me who it is?"

"If Pam's spirit were really guiding you, why wouldn't she just tell you?"

DeeDee grabbed the steering wheel and tried to wrest it back and forth as if trying to shake sense into it. "Look, I don't want to argue. Forget I said that."

"Where are you now?" Livy went on as though she hadn't heard.

DeeDee eyed the storefront's welcoming façade, the serene face hiding a sinister secret. "Still in the parking lot. Trying to calm down."

A gasp resounded from the other end. "You need to leave right now."

Her heart reacted to Livy's urgent tone, and trembles racked her limbs.

"You could be in danger. Especially now that whoever it is knows you're sniffing around."

She fumbled with the ignition for a few seconds before the engine roared to life. Livy, uncharacteristically firm, wasn't finished. "I'm going to stay on the line until you're out of that place and heading back to Renee's."

"I was planning to go to Quaking Aspen."

She knew what Livy would say before she said it. "No, you're not. I want you to get back on that road and head the opposite direction."

DeeDee barreled out of the lot a mere foot from a passing car, whose driver warned her away with a polite horn toot. She slammed the brakes. "Look, I need to hang up now. I just about hit a guy."

"You be careful, Sis. Call me when you're safely back."

Driving east, she debated complying with Livy's request or fulfilling her original intent. The highway loomed ahead, and she braked at the red light. If Leon had been watching her, he wouldn't be at Quaking Aspen anyway. But it had to be him. After all, who else at Moonstone could know who she was? She might as well head back to Renee's and find out for sure.

The creeped-out feeling had started to fade when prickles rose on her arms again. Glancing around to determine the cause, she caught a movement in the rearview mirror. The driver behind her was leaning to the side, arms in motion as though digging through something. A dark-colored scarf concealed the person's lower face, and large shades blocked the eyes. DeeDee thought of Dad and his disguises when they were children. Was this driver, like Dad, someone who didn't want to be recognized? Or simply bundled up against the cold?

The driver sat up and stared straight ahead. DeeDee couldn't tell if the person was male or female. But she felt their eyes boring into her.

The prickles intensified. Could it be Leon, bent on stopping her from finding out the truth? If a stranger followed her, why bother hiding the face?

Her clammy hands gripped the wheel tighter as she pondered what to do. She couldn't expose Renee by returning to her house.

The light turned green. She sped past the highway turnoff and drove mindlessly forward, unsure of her options. Livy was right. The real murderer was after her now, too.

❧❧❧

"Renee, can you come pick me up?" Panic tightened DeeDee's throat as she glanced across the convenience store lot. The burgundy Honda sat at the curb, the driver undoubtedly waiting for her to run in, make her purchase, and resume her trip. She wasn't going to give the guy the satisfaction.

At Renee's why, she went on, "I think someone is following me. I'm parked at a Mini-Mart about a mile from your house. Obviously, I don't want the guy to see where I'm headed."

She thought she heard a gasp. "I'll leave right now. Oprah can wait. Oh, and do not get out of that car."

"I won't. But he might follow you home."

"I'll drive around behind the store. When you see my car, go inside and see if there's a back exit. I'll wait for you."

Trembling, DeeDee sat tight. She rubbed her hands together against the chill in vain, then turned on the radio to get her mind off her ordeal. A jarring pop tune did nothing to ease her anxiety.

The burgundy car waited. DeeDee thrummed her fingers against the console and tried to focus on her Kindle app. But the words blurred, and she couldn't make sense of them.

Five minutes later, Renee's dark green car pulled in. Fresh trembles racked DeeDee's body, whether from relief or fear, she wasn't sure. Mustering up her courage, she got out and hurried inside to a small hallway marked Restrooms. Men's room to the right. Women's on the left. And straight ahead, a sign warned, "Emergency exit – alarm will sound."

This is an emergency. She pushed it open, ignoring the loud chime clanging near the front, and beelined to Renee's car crammed into a narrow strip of pavement.

"I could kiss you," she gasped out as she plopped into

the front seat. "But I set off the alarm. They're going to think I stole something."

Two large garbage receptacles blocked them in. Renee backed up and sped around the corner while DeeDee craned to see the door. So far, no one came after them. "Turn left," DeeDee urged. "If the driver tries to follow us, he'll have to turn around. We can lose him."

Two cars passed before Renee could turn. DeeDee kept her head down.

Renee cranked the wheel to the left. "Did you get the license plate?"

"Too far away." DeeDee sat up and watched the mirror, keeping her eye on the burgundy car. "He's not turning around. He didn't catch on to us. Awesomeness."

"What have you been up to, girl?"

DeeDee blew out a breath, then filled her friend in on the morning's events. Distress came off her friend in waves.

At the next red light, Renee faced her. "Have you thought maybe it's time to go home?"

"Oh no. I'm so close to resolving this—I can't stop now."

"I think you need to get yourself to safety."

"If I leave now, I won't have closure. I'll always wonder if there was more I could've done for Nick. Especially if he gets convicted." She sniffed against the tingling in her nose. "Time to do some more digging into Moonstone."

Chapter Twenty-Eight

The pesky burgundy car was nowhere to be seen as Renee drove home. "Whew!" DeeDee collapsed against the seat when Renee pulled into the driveway, then hoofed it into the house and to her computer. There, she again studied the Moonstone website, paying careful attention to the Board of Directors' names.

Not recognizing any names or faces, she moved on and clicked Our Staff which took her to a page filled with smiling, friendly faces. "We'll go the extra kilometer for you," their expressions declared, affirming the motto plastered across the top. She scoured each face, each name, from the Warehouse Supervisor to the Accounting Manager. No Leon. No other familiar name.

She dropped her hands into her lap, dismayed by the sheer number of possible suspects. In Pam's climb to the top, had she antagonized someone, turned a colleague into an enemy? It could certainly happen in the ruthless corporate world.

Unless Pam's killer was a family member. Which brought her back to where she started. If only she knew who inherited Pam's millions. Her husband or her son seemed the most likely prospects.

Beneath her hand, her phone chimed. A text from Livy flashed, wanting to know if she'd made it back safely. DeeDee rang her sister's number.

"I'm fine," she said before Livy even said hello. DeeDee recapped her harrowing drive home. "But now I'm stuck. I checked out Moonstone's Board of Directors and their staff."

"Are any of them the person who followed you?"

"I didn't get a good enough look at my follower. It didn't really look like Leon. And the staff all look as innocent as babes. Then I got to wondering who Pam left her money to. Her husband or her son?"

"Maybe Nick knows."

DeeDee went still, chewing on this. A twenty-minute drive to jail would answer that question.

"It's worth a try. Nick, my love, here I come."

৵৵৵

Nick's eyes held a terrible bleakness when he peered at her through the jailhouse glass. DeeDee stifled a gasp. What were they doing to him? After seeing his expression, she couldn't bring herself to pose the question she came to ask. A conversation about Pam's money seemed shamefully trivial at a time like this.

So she let him talk about whatever was on his mind while she listened with a sinking heart. The hearty, vibrant Nick who charged through life was gone, replaced by this furtive, jumpy stranger whose light had been snuffed out. She couldn't hold back a horrified shudder.

Nick's gaze slid upward, to something beyond her. His face changed as though a sculptor's hand had passed across it and lifted everything. Relief shone from his eyes. "Adam."

She turned. A man with salt-and-pepper hair stood behind her clutching a messenger bag, its gleaming Italian leather out of place in this concrete-and-steel wasteland.

The man's gray eyes stared down at her from above an aquiline nose. "Hi. I'm Adam Vernon." He thrust out a hand. "Nick's attorney."

She shook the offered hand. "I'm DeeDee."

His perfect teeth flashed, and then disappeared. "The girlfriend."

Pleased Nick had told him about her, she nodded, and then glanced back at Nick. His observant eyes finally showed signs of life.

She faced Adam. "How is Nick's case coming along?"

The man's face closed up. "I'm not at liberty to discuss it," he told her in an almost verbatim repeat of Nick's words.

"Well, I believe in his innocence." Certainty rang in her tone. She needed to get him to take her seriously. "I think someone at Moonstone is the guilty party. And—and I have proof."

Surprise rippled across Adam's otherwise stoic face. "Why do you—?" He stopped himself, then scanned the handful of other visitors chatting with prisoners. "Look, we can't talk about this here." He pulled a card from his breast pocket and handed it to her. "But call me tomorrow. I'm willing to listen to what you have to say." He crossed to a steel door guarded by a man as thick and unmoving as the door. Until he turned and hit a buzzer set into the wall. The heavy portal slid open, the guard stepped aside, and Adam Vernon disappeared inside.

"Babe."

She whirled to face Nick.

"I need to go back for my consultation now." The orange jumpsuit still cast a pall on his ashen skin, but couldn't erase the sweet hope in his eyes. "Thanks for coming. Love you."

"Love you, too." Slowly, she put the phone down and received his air kiss, then waved and blew one back.

She couldn't wait to tell Adam what happened today.

❧❧❧

With her phone to her ear, DeeDee gazed out the

Maxwells' guest room window at the taupe-colored clouds blanketing the new day.

And tomorrow, the new year.

Good riddance, 2014.

"So what's your proof?" Adam Vernon said after DeeDee told him everything. She paced the room as several possible replies flittered through her mind. All of which, she realized too late, sounded terribly lame.

"The disguise." She firmed her tone. "Why would the person wear sunglasses on a cloudy day?"

"So you believe this person, who presumably followed you, presumably in disguise, worked at Moonstone and killed Pam. Where's your proof?"

Stated that way, she sounded like an imbecile. Her legs stiffened as shame washed over her.

"He *was* following me. He even waited for me at the convenience store. Just moments after I saw that camera at Moonstone."

"You're aware, aren't you, that most businesses use security cameras?"

"But it was aimed right at me—"

"Prickles up your arm aren't evidence. You'd be laughed out of the courtroom if you were to testify to that."

She'd love to reach through cyberspace and smack some prickles into Adam Vernon's smug face for making an idiot out of her. Instead, she lifted her chin and mustered what was left of her shredded dignity. "Okay, then. Sorry to bother you."

She clicked off before he did, a defiant little gesture meant to tell him she was still in control. But now… another dead end. Plopping on the bed, she curled up in a ball until the shame shrank. Only to be replaced by anger. Mr. Smug might dismiss her suspicions, but she'd learned to trust her gut instincts. Too bad instincts weren't admissible in courts of law.

She hugged her knees to her chest, forming a shield to protect her from Adam's ugly insinuations. She had to do something. Talk to someone familiar with Moonstone Truffles.

Erik. The name came to her on silent feet, like a cat wanting a rub. She jumped off the bed, then stopped. She didn't know how to contact him. And, with a killer on the loose, she wasn't about to drive all over town looking for him.

She'd search online, starting with Victoria Mission. It took only seconds to find the phone number. But a wheezy male voice informed her Mr. Sterling wasn't currently on the premises. And no, he couldn't pass along Mr. Sterling's cell number.

She ended the call, racking her brain to remember the name of the diner. Something old-fashioned. Started with an *S*. Sheila's Diner? To stimulate her brain cells, she dug her fingertips into her scalp as though kneading away a headache, then crossed to her laptop on the dresser.

She found the answer on Google Maps—Stella's Diner—and rang the number. Lisa's low, untroubled hello settled her anxiety in an instant.

"This is DeeDee. I was in yesterday?"

"Oh, DeeDee. So glad you called. Do you need to talk?"

The woman must be psychic. "Um, yes, I do. Is Erik there today?"

"Not right now, but if you need to talk to him, I'll have him call you."

"Great." She left her number and hung up, already feeling better.

Chapter Twenty-Nine

In the booth across from DeeDee, a scraggy Jimi Hendrix lookalike sipped coffee, and, remembering yesterday's Janis Joplin, DeeDee wondered for a surreal moment if Jim Morrison and Alan Wilson might suddenly appear and join him—a beyond-the-grave reunion of the Forever 27 Club. She shook away the weird daydream. Yet something about Stella's Diner seemed to attract dead classic rockers.

She sat facing Erik, oddly reluctant to share yesterday's events. Maybe because it was, as Adam implied, all in her head. After all, security cameras were everywhere. People often wrapped themselves in scarves this time of year. She'd probably imagined the whole thing.

"What's on your mind?" Erik prompted, adjusting his fork to line up perfectly with the edge of the napkin.

She stared at the tiny black hairs on his fingers, floundering for a starting place that wouldn't make her sound paranoid.

"I think I need prayer," she blurted, surprising herself even more than him. "Something kind of unnerving happened yesterday."

He said nothing, merely intensified his gaze on her.

"Someone was following me." This time she'd omit the Moonstone connection. "I know because I drove into a convenience store lot, and the car pulled to the curb and sat there."

"Did you get the license plate?"

"No, unfortunately. I just know it was a burgundy

Honda. Not sure of the model, but it was a midsize."

His face was transforming before her eyes. Eyes dark with…concern? Lips clenched with…skepticism? "Burgundy Hondas are quite common around here. Even my daughter drives one."

Not the answer she'd expected.

But Leon could have borrowed his wife's car for the day.

"Does she work at Moonstone?" She shifted under his probing gaze.

"No." The drawn-out word told her he wasn't expecting the question. "What does Moonstone have to do with this?"

After picking through her mind for a plausible answer, she shrugged. "I passed the building on my way to the highway. And since Leon works there…" She lifted her hands in an oh-well manner to hide her agitation, "I wondered if she did, too."

"No, Jasmine is unemployed at the moment."

With a whoosh of damp air, the door flew open. The Janis Joplin wannabe stood there, scoping out the place with her magnified eyes, then sauntered to the jukebox and pushed a few buttons. Soon "Under the Boardwalk" announced itself from the lit-up contraption. The woman swayed, or rather, jerked to and fro, croaking out lyrics into an imaginary mike. Her private karaoke world.

Erik's wife immediately left her post behind the counter and got to the woman's side in seconds, where she embraced her, then escorted her to a corner booth.

DeeDee had to admire Lisa, who saw past the woman's ragged exterior to the hurting soul beneath. What a shallow, self-centered life she herself had lived by comparison. Something about this couple made her feel so inadequate for the first time she could remember.

Erik's next question gave her pause. "If you believe you're in danger, why aren't you on the next ferry home?"

She searched for a way to make this man understand her urgency. And then the answer came to her, as clear as the Drifters' honeyed vocals extolling the boardwalk.

She braced her arms on the table edge. "Yesterday, I asked you a question. But you didn't get a chance to answer because that man came to our table to visit with you."

He nodded. "Frank."

"Yes. I asked you, do you honestly believe Nick shot his ex-wife?"

He stared at her and tapped his fingers on the table, keeping time with the Drifters. Finally, he spoke. "I admit it's hard to believe. But sometimes people snap...."

"But he had nothing to gain from her death."

"The only person who gained from her death was nowhere near the house that morning."

"Bryan?"

He gave her a strange look. She'd slipped and used his first name, as though she and Pam's husband were old friends.

"Yes."

"Did he inherit her estate?"

"The little daughter was the main beneficiary, but as her legal guardian, he stands to benefit until she comes of age."

"But...what about Leon? Didn't he get anything?"

"Leon will get something, but Pam didn't trust him with her estate."

Interesting. Which ruled out a motive for Leon. "Why not?"

"His history of irresponsibility."

"Oh." Good on Pam for her shrewd assessment of her no-good son. "But in her position, she had to have had enemies. Wouldn't she?"

He shrugged. "She probably did. But the police interviewed several of her employees. If she had any enemies, I think the police would have found evidence by now."

She kept running into that same brick wall—evidence. Damning evidence that would earn her boyfriend life in prison. Unless someone could uncover the truth.

She shook her head at Erik. "If you believe he shot her…"

"I didn't say I believe it. I just can't see any other scenario. Everyone's alibis checked out." He rolled the saltshaker between his fingers. "As much as I care about Nick, I know he's not perfect."

"Are you saying he's capable of shooting someone?"

He leaned forward. She couldn't look away from the intensity in his eyes. "I'm saying I don't know. Our sinful human hearts are capable of great treachery. That's why we need God's mercy so desperately."

Before she could protest, a car squealed to the curb. She'd seen the '90s-vintage black Nissan somewhere. Then she remembered—in Leon's driveway.

But it wasn't Leon who emerged from the driver's seat. Jazzy lurched out of the car, wild-eyed, then reemerged at the diner door.

The door gasped open, bell clanging, and Jazzy, clad in a J Crew bomber jacket the color of rare steak, charged inside. Then jerked to a stop. Her eyes, dark with unmistakable resentment, stared at DeeDee as though she wished to shove her out of the booth.

Tears streaked the young woman's foundation as she hurried to her father's side. And understanding flooded DeeDee. Jazzy needed her dad, and DeeDee was intruding.

But curiosity kept her rooted to the sticky booth.

Erik scooted over and let his daughter plop next to him, then enfolded her in his arms. "What's the matter, baby?"

"Leon," she choked out against his shoulder. She lifted

her head and snuck another loaded glance at DeeDee, then returned to her damp resting place. No doubt, Jazzy would say no more as long as she remained.

Had Leon hit her or gotten hurt? Were they splitting up after only a few weeks of marriage? Clearly, Jazzy didn't plan to enlighten her.

"Can we talk in the kitchen?" Jazzy's lips moved against the shirt fabric. The two rose as one and passed the jumbo-sized Frank Sinatra poster to the back, then disappeared behind the counter.

They'd expect her to get up and leave, but she couldn't yet. Something told her this was significant. As she pondered whether to stay or go, Lisa came out from behind the counter, her kind gaze steady on DeeDee. Soon Erik's wife settled at her side.

"Erik told me to tell you he might be a while, but you're welcome to come back anytime and talk."

"What's going on?"

"Oh, I don't know all the details. Something with Leon has Jasmine upset. Erik doesn't know how long he'll be, so he suggested you come back later today if you still need to talk."

She knew a dismissal when she heard it. DeeDee gathered her purse and jacket, reluctance dragging her movements until Lisa spoke.

"Are you heading back to Seattle soon?"

"I might stay a couple more days."

"In case I don't see you before you leave, have a safe trip home. Let's stay in touch."

"I'd like that."

"Send me a friend request. Lisa Powell Sterling."

"Will do. You seem like a nice person. You and Erik both. I really admire what you're doing here." Her hand stretched in a sweeping gesture.

Lisa's slanted mouth widened. "It's the least we can do for our Lord."

Right. DeeDee glanced behind the counter. Through the kitchen entry, Erik crossed her line of vision, then disappeared as he paced, his face scrunched. "Is Jazzy religious, too?"

"Not in the least." Lisa's denial was emphatic. "She has a rebellious streak. Erik and I have been praying and witnessing to her and Leon for a long time."

"Okay. Well, I'll get going then."

As DeeDee stood, Lisa pulled her into an unexpected hug that sent warmth through her. "I pray God's blessings over you."

DeeDee turned and strode to her car, Lisa's parting words ringing in her ears and snaking into her heart. The feel of her hug lingered with a baffling persistence. Granted, hugs were supposed to feel good. But most people's hugs felt meaningless. Lisa's exerted authenticity.

She started her engine, and the radio, tuned to a news station, blasted to life. At the announcer's somber tone, underscored with urgency, she froze.

"Acting on an anonymous tip, police arrested him this morning after authorities arrived at the headquarters of Moonstone Truffles, founded by his mother..."

What?

"...who was shot, presumably by an ex-husband, on December fifteenth. After finding evidence of numerous fraudulent bank wires transferred to an offshore account, authorities are reopening Mrs. Campbell's murder case to determine whether Mr. Brown was involved."

Sweet hope rocketed skyward, and she whooped, entertaining visions of Nick back in her arms. Her love would soon be free. And Leon—liar, thief, murderer— would be behind bars.

Chapter Thirty

A fresh batch of questions and doubts chased each other, round and round in her brain, all the way back to Renee's. If Leon shot his mother, what was his motive? He didn't stand to inherit much, thus didn't gain much financially. Had Pam been referring to her son in her e-mail to Nick? Maybe she found out about the theft and went to confront him. Perhaps she'd threatened to turn him in, and Leon, in a panic, stopped her.

And Jazzy, in her pricey, elegant leather, had to have known what her husband was up to. DeeDee'd seen that same red jacket at Nordstrom. Five hundred bucks. Speaking of which…an elusive memory whispered to her, something important, just out of reach.

She shrugged. It would come to her.

When DeeDee reached Renee's and told her the news, Renee launched her fists in the air. "I don't want to get too excited. It may come to nothing. But now there's a little more hope he'll be released."

"Let me know if you find out anything more," DeeDee called over her shoulder as she hurried to the room for her laptop. The news about Leon dominated every local news site. As she scoured each one, she learned someone had phoned the Victoria police and named Leon as the culprit. Sure enough, when they seized his computer, they were able to trace the illicit wires. Not only had Leon wired money out of Nick's account, but also the accounts of several other Canadians, seemingly at random.

The cops had followed up on Nick's accusation of Leon and found no evidence of stolen goods. But when an anonymous tipster fingers him, they find what they should have found the first time? Talk about incompetence.

"Thank you, nameless tipster." She grinned at her reflection in the dark screen. "Leon, may you rot in jail, and may *you* get to be Bubba's girlfriend."

Still rejoicing, she opened social media and found Lisa's profile, then sent a friend request. Many of Lisa's photos showed her and Erik together, arms around each other, smiles glowing. Erik must own at least twenty caps. Apparently, he kept his head covered at all times.

Further down, she realized why. Lisa had caught him in a rare pose with his head uncovered. His completely bald head. Not a stitch of hair. Why he would try to hide his baldness she couldn't fathom since many men shaved their heads by choice. It couldn't be vanity. Erik didn't seem the type to care about something as trivial as baldness. Perhaps he only kept it covered in the cold winter temps.

In the midst of Lisa's friends, DeeDee couldn't resist opening Pam's still-active profile. The murdered woman's wall was filled with posthumous messages—outraged, grieved, wistful—bracketing family photos. DeeDee stopped at a photo taken in May. Pam's little yellow-haired girl grinned with open-mouthed glee at a pile of gifts in front of her. *Sofie's third birthday*, read the caption.

DeeDee's eyes widened, her hand frozen over the mouse. Baby Sofie was born the same year as Nick and Pam's divorce. Could it be…?

DeeDee stared at the little towhead girl sandwiched between her dark-headed mom and dad. From what she knew of genetics, the odds of two dark-haired parents producing a fair-haired offspring were one in four. But the odds that brunette Pam and blond Nick would? One in two.

Her heart seemed to stand still. If only she knew which month the divorce occurred.

Scrambling to her browser, she opened up a public records website and searched for Nick's name.

Ah ha. The divorce happened in January, four months before Sofie was born. She lurched under the blow of an invisible fist, then reminded herself that the marriage had ended months before, and both of them had moved on by then.

But maybe not.

Next, she searched Bryan Campbell's records. He and Pam were married that summer when Sofie was just a few months old.

She could no longer ignore the glaring question: was Sofie Nick's child? Could that have been Pam's earth-shattering news?

Maybe she'd had a DNA test and—

Wait a minute. This sounded familiar.

Fragments from a recent conversation floated into her mind. Leon and Jazzy, conducting a hushed, intense discussion in Quaking Aspen about a paternity test. She'd been trying to converse with Senior, but their words kept cutting in. "I think you ought to just ask him," Jazzy had whispered.

Surely, Jazzy didn't mean to ask Bryan if his daughter was not really his. After Pam's e-mail to Nick…

Certainty crashed over her. Pam had found out Sofie wasn't Bryan's and intended to tell Nick the child was his.

Which would have rocked Nick's world.

No wonder Pam hadn't wanted to tell her husband.

Still, she couldn't visualize a scenario in which Sofie's paternity gave Leon a motive for murder. It wouldn't have made a difference in the distribution of his mother's estate.

She carried her laptop into the living room where Renee

watched a documentary and plopped beside her, then showed her the photo. "Have you ever seen Pam's little girl?"

After frowning at the screen, Renee nodded. "A few times."

"Don't you think she looks a lot like Nick?"

The frown deepened, eyes narrowed as DeeDee held her breath. Renee studied the photo, tilting her head this way and that, for what seemed like a full minute. The seconds ticked by. Then Renee pushed reluctant words from her mouth. "Actually... she looks a lot like... like my baby photos."

A bolt seared through DeeDee. Then her entire body went numb. "When...exactly... did... Nick and Pam split?"

Renee's forehead scrunched. "Early in 2010. By the time the divorce was final, they'd been split for almost a year. Not to say they couldn't have gotten back together for a fling during that year. I suppose it's possible the baby was his."

Long pause. When DeeDee spoke, her voice teetered on the edge of a cliff. "The baby was conceived in August of 2010. Pam was already with Bryan by then. And...and Nick...he was already dating Gracie...."

"Wow. Just...wow." Renee enfolded DeeDee's sagging shoulders. "What will you do now?"

Sweat broke out on DeeDee's forehead. "I...don't know. I can't bring myself to ask him such a thing. Pam took the truth to her grave."

✧✧✧

DeeDee pulled to the curb outside Amelia Quigley's fourplex, cut the engine, and checked her reflection. Hair fully hidden under a cap: check. Drugstore reading glasses perched on nose: check. She'd switched her usual Bright Peony lip color for Dark Side, a deep burgundy shade that aged her face. With any luck, Pam's mother wouldn't recognize her as the apartment-seeker from last week.

She'd timed her visit to fall during Bryan's work hours. Couldn't have him dropping by and, God forbid, recognizing her.

Swinging her arms, she strode with forced confidence to the front door. The door opened seconds after she rang the bell. The same elderly Pam lookalike stood there, staring blankly at DeeDee from red-rimmed eyes.

DeeDee thrust the bouquet forward. "Mrs. Quigley?"

The woman's grip on the doorknob loosened. "Yes?"

"My name's Diane. I'm an old friend of Pam's."

Mrs. Quigley grasped the flowers and brought them slowly to her face. Her dark eyes swept once more over DeeDee's face, with no glimmer of recognition.

"I came to pay my condolences. I would have come sooner, but I've been out of town. As soon as I heard, I came over."

The other woman opened the door wider. "Thank you, my dear. Do you want to come in and visit for a while? I enjoy visiting with my daughter's old friends." The voice quavered, died away.

"Sure."

Mrs. Quigley gestured her to a faded old curvaceous floral sofa, then excused herself to the kitchen. DeeDee settled into the room cluttered with fragile-looking knickknacks, bags of yarn spilling over with partially-completed projects, and fabric scraps heaped on tables and chairs. It must be a challenge to host company with nearly every available surface holding crafts in progress.

A photo album lay open on the coffee table. DeeDee, moving closer, peered at the photos of a teenaged Pam, and a throb of sympathy went through her. These photos must be small comfort to Amelia after her daughter's murder.

Her hostess returned holding a steaming Butchart

Gardens coffee mug, handed it to DeeDee, then settled in a matching armchair. DeeDee took a sip and bit back a grimace at the weak brew. "This is a really cute apartment. Didn't Pam own this building?"

"No, her husband does. He's generous enough to let me live here rent-free, seeing as I'm family."

"How long have you lived here?"

"Since my divorce from Pam's father last year. They were building a house for me not far from here. But now…" She sniffed and held a tissue to her nose.

"I'm sorry."

She waited while Amelia composed herself. Pam's mother drew in a breath, squaring her shoulders. "How did you know Pam?"

"Well." From Pam's social media profiles, she'd gleaned plausible answers to possible questions. "She and I were in the same yoga class about four years ago. She was pregnant at the time, as I recall." She tilted her head. "I feel for that poor little girl, losing her mother. And the husband. Nick, right?"

Amelia shook her head. "No, she and Nick divorced. Pam is…" She jerked to a stop, then continued in a strangled tone, "…was married to a man named Bryan when she died."

"Oh, I see." DeeDee set the photo album on her lap and traced the outline of a uniformed Pam surrounded by identically-uniformed cheerleaders. "Will the little girl live with Nick, then? Since he's her biological father?"

"What? No, you must be confused. Bryan is Sofie's father. Haven't you heard the news? Nick is the one who murdered Pam. He's in jail."

DeeDee's heart twisted in her chest, but she arranged her features in a surprised expression. "I've heard bits and pieces of the news, but didn't realize…" She shook her head. "Wow. Poor Pam." Deep breath. "And then to hear about her son today…"

She eyed Amelia as her voice faded away. Awareness sharpened Amelia's eyes; a quick sharp breath betrayed her.

"I was shocked to hear about his arrest," DeeDee went on. "Pam had such hopes for him."

Fresh tears sprouted in Amelia's eyes. "In one sense, it's better that Pam didn't live to see this."

Idly, DeeDee flipped to the album's next page. "Mind if I look at this?"

"Of course not."

With each page flip, Pam grew older until DeeDee reached her high school graduation. After that, photos crowded each page: Pam with Clive and Erik surrounded by band equipment. Pam with the two of them, plus Senior, all of them dancing in someone's living room. Erik and her with beer bottles in hand. And below it, the two of them kissing.

Wow. Had party-girl Pam dated or married all of Nick's bandmates, then? Somehow, they'd all remained friends even though she apparently hooked up with one as quickly as she discarded the last. Like a game of musical chairs. Rather, musical band members.

She skipped over photos of Pam with Leon as a growing boy until she found what she sought—Nick and Pam's wedding day. Nick beamed, unaware of the turmoil he was in for. Pam's sweet smile never betrayed her adulterous nature.

Amelia cleared her throat. DeeDee glanced up. Had Pam's mother ever had an inkling of her daughter's true colors?

A small cry echoed from a dark doorway. There stood little Sofie, her thumb in her mouth. A feminine miniature of Nick gazed at Amelia with sad blue eyes.

The couch shifted beneath DeeDee, and she lurched forward. She grabbed at a cushion before she realized, the earthquake that nearly knocked her over came from inside herself.

Amelia's voice came to her as though through fog. "Oh look, my granddaughter is up from her nap."

The little girl ran to Amelia, staring at DeeDee as she climbed on her grandmother's lap. DeeDee couldn't pull her gaze away. If she and Nick ever had kids, they'd probably look just like this one.

Sofie's scrutiny gave way to a bashful smile. She didn't wait for DeeDee to return the smile, but ducked her head and buried it in Grandma's neck.

"This is Pam's little girl." Amelia shifted the girl to a more comfortable position on her knees. "Isn't she cute?"

DeeDee's heart constricted, and a delighted smile snuck out and planted itself on her lips. "She's adorable." She longed to point out the obvious, but refrained. If Amelia wanted to stay stuck in denial, it was no concern of hers.

"Mommy," declared the little girl, her muffled voice still hiding on Amelia's shoulder.

"Ssshh, Mommy's gone, honey."

"Went bye-bye?"

"Yes." Amelia caught DeeDee's gaze, and her breath hitched at the sorrow in the other woman's eyes.

Sofie let out a sob. "How come?"

Something unfamiliar had snuck into DeeDee's chest, something she couldn't identify. All she knew was, a craving to comfort the little girl had seized her.

She moved closer to Amelia. "May I hold her?"

"Sure, if she'll let you."

Amelia wrested the girl's clinging arms from around her neck, and DeeDee leaned over and scooped her onto her lap. She wrapped her arms gingerly around Sofie's tiny torso and inhaled the baby-shampoo-and-animal-cracker scent of her, overlaid with a faint hint of wet diaper. The vibrating ache in her heart expanded by the second.

Was this what baby hunger felt like?

Sofie gazed at her with quivering lower lip, a question in her sky-blue eyes. "I want Mommy." And just as quickly, she squirmed off DeeDee's lap and scurried back to Grandma.

This poor little thing was too young to understand her mommy had gone bye-bye forever.

Pressure built behind her eyes, but no tears came. She'd lost her mother when she was six and remembered the bewilderment, the constant hope that she'd wake up and Mommy would be there.

DeeDee stood, a little too abruptly, unsure how to process these unfamiliar emotions. Plus, Nick had some explaining to do. "I'd better get going. I'm sure it's been a rough time for you, and I'm very sorry about your daughter. She was good people."

Amelia walked her to the door, patted her back. "Drop by anytime, dear. I love company, especially if they knew Pam."

DeeDee fled, then texted Livy the moment she got in her car. *You'll never believe what just happened! See you in a few hours.*

Chapter Thirty-One

By the time Nick's eyes lit up at her from behind the glass barrier, pent-up words almost poured from her mouth. She'd decided not to drop a bombshell on him first, but to start on an optimistic note. She forced her tense shoulders to relax as shock, then hope, played across his face when she shared the news of Leon's arrest. "Remember when you said there's no need anymore to walk into a bank to rob it?"

He nodded. "I knew he'd done that wire transfer, and it frustrated me having no way to prove it."

When she told him the authorities planned to reopen the murder case, his mouth stretched into his first genuine smile in weeks. "It wouldn't surprise me if Leon turns out to be guilty of murder," he said. "He's a bad egg."

"But you know what else, Nick?"

"There's more?"

"Yes. I think I know why Pam wanted to meet with you."

He lifted his brows.

"I stumbled upon Pam's Facebook profile"—he didn't need to know she'd gone looking for it—"and I noticed something interesting. Her little girl. She looks more like you than like Pam's husband." She paused, dug her fingers into the phone receiver. "Nick." Calming breath. "You may not want to talk about this, but I have to know. Are...are you her baby's father?"

Her gaze could've bored holes through his head. If only she could peer inside his brain and watch the memories unfold. Was that twitch of his eyelid, the shifty gaze, a sign of guilt?

"Um…" he managed at last. "I…I don't know. Pam never said anything."

"Nick." DeeDee braced herself for his response to her next question. "Did you and Pam ever…um…"

A shuttered look settled over his face as if someone had reached in and closed the floor-length drapes. She had to tough it out.

"Did you two have a post-split fling?"

He hung his head. "I should've been honest with you, my love. I've regretted it ever since."

"But she was with Bryan by then." She hoped he didn't notice the tremor in her voice. "You were with Gracie."

"Yes, and it was just one time. It was wrong."

"But…but how…"

"Neither of us meant for it to happen. She asked me to meet her at Moonstone to discuss the divorce. She had a little sitting room behind her office, with a couch, and, you know, one thing led to another…" Remorse radiated from his hunched shoulders.

"Did it occur to you the baby might be yours?"

"Of course. But Bryan is her legal father. And there's no way to prove paternity unless Pam decided to get a test done."

"Well, um…" She swallowed hard and pushed out the words. "Maybe she did. I overheard Junior and Jazzy having a heated discussion about a paternity test."

"You did?" He shook his head a little too hard, as though shaking away the anxiety. "Why would Junior care about Sofie's paternity?"

"I wondered that myself. It was probably Jazzy enjoying the drama." She held his gaze for a long moment. "Nick, if it were true…would you do anything about it?"

"You mean, take her away from the only father she knows?" An agitated jerk of his head. "I couldn't."

She squared her shoulders. "But…would you want to be involved in her life?"

His blue eyes gleamed. "I doubt Campbell would be okay with that."

He had a point. Chewing her lip, she scrunched her face. "If that's what Pam meant to tell you, don't you think it's weird that someone killed her before she could?"

"But Leon wouldn't have reason to…"

"I know. Only one person would have a motive to shut her up."

Awareness widened his eyes.

"Her husband. Bryan Campbell."

⋖⋗⋖⋗⋖⋗

Nick plopped to his cot, arranged his limbs in the all-too-common stance lately: drooping head in hands, gaze on the floor. Ignoring the shouts and constant noises of daily jail life. He should have known DeeDee would be smart enough to guess his sordid secret. If only he'd been honest with her. She'd probably want nothing more to do with him now.

He breathed out a desperate prayer. "God," he whispered so his cellmates wouldn't mock him for praying. "Please don't let me lose DeeDee. I don't want to live without her. God, if she left me…" he pushed his fingers through his hair, "I wouldn't want to go on."

Chapter Thirty-Two

At the Stanwood exit pit stop, DeeDee checked her phone and found a text from Dad. *Happy New Year's Eve. Any plans for tonight?*

Don't know yet. Need to discuss with Livy.

What's new with you and Nick, kiddo?

I'll call you when I get home.

Her heart had finally recovered from its roller-coaster ride at the jail. Her breathing had calmed to its normal rhythm. She gripped the wheel hard as if it might leap from her hands and take control of the car. Did Nick truly regret his indiscretion, or did he say it just to appease her?

At least I was always faithful to her.

Granted, he hadn't lied. But he'd left out the most important detail: he'd been unfaithful to Gracie.

Had she guessed the truth, too?

DeeDee pulled back onto Interstate 5 behind a blue Audi with a British Columbia license plate. She'd bet it was the same Audi she'd followed off the ferry onto US soil. The clouds, heavy and deep, pressed down on her. A white flake splatted on the windshield, then a handful, turning to steady snowfall. The Audi's taillights taunted her, angry cat eyes glaring at her through the snow-studded dark.

Oh, if only Livy were here. DeeDee again tightened her grip on the wheel and squinted at the temp gauge. Thirty-one degrees. Snow flurries rapidly transformed to a blizzard before her eyes. And she was still an hour from home.

Her mind went numb as she concentrated on the

highway. The snow better not stick. She hadn't gotten her snow tires yet, and her little Miata didn't like the hill just before Laurel Court.

God, help me.

She jerked herself upright. Say what? *You don't believe in God.* Livy must be rubbing off on her.

Yet the anxiety had morphed to an uncertain peace. Strange. Livy would say the presence of God was with her. But Grandma Gaia would claim DeeDee's own internal strength had chased away the angst.

So who was right?

She fought with herself the entire hour, through the whirling, driving snow. God or self? Self or God?

No white stuff stuck to the pavement. No cars spun out. She tried to squelch the realization that life and death were beyond her control. But someone had to be in control of such things.

Score one for Livy's God.

By the time she walked through her front door, a half-inch of snow blanketed the lawn and the rhododendron bushes. She hugged an indignant Miss Piggy and a quivering Murf, before checking the garage. No Jaguar. She called Dad right away.

Dad just listened as DeeDee told him everything, finally commenting, "You really want to know about that paternity test, don't you?"

"Well, yes. Of course, I'm curious. If I'm right, it could shed light on her husband's motive."

"Just asking because I know a guy who could find out if she had the test done and tell you the results."

"Seriously?" Her mouth fell open. She sprang from her perch by the stainless steel refrigerator and paced the black-checkered linoleum. Her curiosity *was* multiplying like fleas on an alley cat. But what could she do with the information once she got it? She couldn't tell Nick she'd gone behind his back and...

"He's the best hacker on the West Coast. Even served prison time for cybercrime."

"I can't believe anyone could hack into a biolab database. Those places probably use firewalls and several layers of security—"

"He uses a worm to get past the firewall. A simple e-mail will do it. Usually to a lower-level employee who probably won't think twice about clicking it open."

"Sounds illegal."

"Well, it is. But he's good. Only problem is, he's on probation. So he'd be taking a huge risk and will expect payment accordingly."

"Is that an offer to pay, Dad?"

"It is. Unless you happen to have fifty grand laying around."

Propping against a metal barstool, she swiveled it back and forth and gave a small whistle. Fifty grand to hack into a database. But that was pocket change to Dad. And even though it hurt to know the man she loved had briefly reconnected with his ex, finding the real murderer was far more important than a few hurt feelings.

"I...I'd better write to Nick first and ask him. If he objects, we won't do it."

Chapter Thirty-Three

Remembering jail protocol for letters, all she could do was ask Nick to call her collect. With any luck, he'd get the letter by Saturday, three days away.

"Fifty grand?" Livy said when DeeDee told her. Livy and Scott sat hand-in-hand on the sunroom futon, skin-tight against each other, while DeeDee faced them from the ottoman. A pang twisted her gut. Nick should be here. They should be celebrating the new year together. And she wouldn't feel like a third wheel.

Livy shot a Scott quick glance before meeting DeeDee's gaze. "Is it worth that much to you?"

She shrugged. How do you quantify something like that? "It's not my moolah. If Dad wants to spend his money that way, I'm not going to object."

"True. He'll earn it back in one concert." Livy darted another glance Scott's way, longer this time. He gazed back at her, brows raised, his hand tightening on hers. Some sort of silent communication was going on between those two.

"And really, it's Nick's decision." DeeDee inhaled the steadying scent of her lavender candle. "Not mine, not Dad's."

Scott shifted to her. "His attorney can subpoena those records."

Adam Vernon's long-nosed face floated in her mind's eye. His haughty words echoed in her memory. He'd destroyed any credibility she may have had with him. "I think we'll get quicker results doing it Dad's way. Anyway, if Nick agrees to this, I'm sure he'd be willing to pay Dad back. *If* we can prove his innocence."

Livy's eyes now flashed yellow warning lights at Scott while her hand gave his thigh a nervous squeeze. Meanwhile, his chiseled jaw clenched, his already-firm mouth tightened. A bad sign. She'd have to ask Livy what was up.

❧❧❧

"Honey." Livy stood and faced Scott, hands on hips, and plastered on her most beguiling expression. "Don't be upset. This is between DeeDee and Dad. Nothing to do with us."

But Scott stiffened his back against the futon and crossed his arms. Blocking out her words. Her pleas. He regarded her with indignant green eyes. "Your father seems to believe he can solve any problem under the sun if he just throws enough money at it. Even if it's illegal. What kind of message will that send our future kids?"

Relieved that DeeDee was in the kitchen preparing a late dinner, Livy closed the sunroom door and resumed her position. "Why are you yelling at me? I have no control over how my father spends his money."

"Maybe not, but you can back me up if I ever have to refuse one of his generous gestures."

She blew out a breath, still eyeing his stony face. Until the honeymoon offer, she'd never refused any of her father's generous gestures, as Scott sarcastically referred to them. The trait she appreciated so much in her father, Scott considered a character flaw.

Gulping, she saw a long line of future arguments stretching before her. Conflicts over limited funds had proven destructive in Scott's first marriage. How ironic, then, if too much money proved the ruin of theirs.

"But what if it's something we need?"

"Then God will provide. Once we're married, God won't expect your dad to fill the provider role." His voice had softened, along with his eyes. "When I stand before God someday, I don't want to have to explain why I abdicated my role to your father." He patted the seat beside him, and she settled at his side.

He gathered her into his warm, comforting embrace and fingered a strand of her hair. "Make sense now?"

At her nod, he went on. "I'm not rich like your daddy. But God's blessed me with a decent livelihood, and you don't need to worry that I won't be able to provide."

"Of course, we'll have my trust fund." The dance school had grossed about seventy thousand the previous year, but her net share hadn't amounted to more than twenty grand. Which was why she relied on the trust fund Dad had set aside for her and DeeDee.

"We agreed it was for emergencies only."

He was asking her to adjust to a lower standard of living. For a moment, doubt reared inside her, like a spooked stallion. She'd always thought of her trust fund like a favorite childhood blanket—always there if she needed it, yet a shameful reminder of her ultimate dependence on Dad.

She searched Scott's hope-filled eyes. He flashed an uncertain smile. Expectation hummed between them as he waited for her response to his unasked question: Could she trust him with her future? And could she trust God?

⚜⚜⚜

"I think you're handling this really well," Livy told DeeDee after the dinner dishes were loaded and Scott had departed. DeeDee sipped Riesling from the Celtic-patterned goblet Nick had given her and reclined the corduroy sectional, hugging a geometric pillow to her chest. Maybe she should try something stronger like rum and Coke, something to fix the cracks in her heart.

But no, those remedies had never worked for long. She didn't want a replay of her meltdown at Quaking Aspen.

"I know it's in the past, and he regrets it." DeeDee took another sip, longer this time, relishing the warmth loosening her tense muscles from head to toe. "But can I trust him now?"

Beside her, Livy crossed her legs and shifted toward her. "The question is, do you sense he's sincere?"

DeeDee pondered this. "You know, I really do sense he means it."

"Then it's time to let it go."

A deep drink from the cast-iron goblet. "Easy for you to say. Scott isn't a cheater."

"Well, neither is Nick. One time doesn't a cheater make."

She held the goblet close to her heart as if to absorb Nick's essence. "What would you do if you found out Scott had done something like that?"

Livy winced. Ha. She'd find it hard to let it go, too. "Hmm…"

"See? Not so easy."

"I never said it was easy. Simple, yes. Easy, no."

"I suppose eventually the pain will fade.…"

"You could look at it this way. Is there anything in your past you wouldn't want Nick to know?"

Of course, there was. What a question. If anyone else dared ask her that, she'd need strength not to slap them.

But Livy didn't wait for an answer. "And if he ever found out, how would you want him to respond?"

Through the living room window, she watched a car creep along Laurel Court. DeeDee gripped the goblet tighter. "I see where you're going with this, but I…" She let her voice trail away.

"It's called grace. So many times, we hold others' wrong actions against them, but when it comes to our own, we minimize them, like they're no big deal. We shrug and say, 'Nobody's perfect.' Why can't we treat others' wrongs the same way?"

DeeDee clung to the goblet and pondered her sister's wisdom, her lips unable to form a reply. Nick knew he'd done wrong, yet she couldn't stop thinking about it. Livy was right. Nick wasn't perfect, but then neither was she.

And it wasn't like Livy spouted empty words. Last year she'd had to forgive twice: the person responsible for Mom's death and the person who injured her leg, robbing her of a future in dance. DeeDee wasn't sure she'd have the strength to forgive such major wrongs.

Livy reached over to squeeze DeeDee's shoulder. "Isn't that what relationships are all about? Two imperfect people doing their best to make it work?"

"Yes, but…" She took another sip to give herself a moment to work through her thoughts. "I know you're right. It'll just take time."

"It will. Remember how I wrestled with wanting to hate Mom's killer? And then God brought about that confrontation with him. After that, I just couldn't hate him."

"I still resent what he did to Mom. Not to mention the little girl who hit you. Although, come to think of it, you never hated on her at all." She gestured at Livy's scarred left leg. "I don't understand why. Look at you. Afraid you won't be able to dance at your own wedding. How can you be so non-bitter?"

"It has to be a God thing." Livy's eyes shrouded over with sad memories.

"If only there was a way you could accommodate your bad leg and still dance." DeeDee chuckled. "Too bad you can't dance on only one leg."

She stopped, a memory burrowing into her head. Of course! That was it.

"Hey, Livs. I have an idea."

"What?"

"Renee."

"What about her?"

"Maybe she's the answer to your problem. What do you think of this?"

Chapter Thirty-Four

By the time Nick's collect call came through Saturday evening, DeeDee had rehearsed her script for hours. "My love," she began. "I've been thinking about our conversation. About Sofie. And Pam."

"Sweetheart, that's all water under the ferry..."

"I know." She clung to the sofa pillow beside her. "Livy helped me come to terms with it."

"You talked to Livy?"

He should know by now she and her twin discussed everything. They harbored no secrets.

She breathed in courage, losing sight of the script for one scary moment. She grasped for the right words and knit her free fingers through the pillow's fringe. "I can accept that you screwed up. I've done things I regret, too."

"I promise it won't happen again. If you and I have a future, I give you my word I'll never stray."

His words warmed her thudding heart and stilled the wild roller coaster inside her. "Do we even have a future?"

"If we can..." He stopped, and DeeDee could picture him clamping his mouth shut. He had to censor his every word.

"If we can find the real murderer?" she finished for him. "Yes."

"I wonder if Pam's husband suspected the baby wasn't his. I think the authorities ought to look more closely at him."

"Yes," he repeated. "I'll talk to my attorney about it and

see what he can do."

"I don't like that man."

"You don't? Why not?"

She expressed her dislike with a string of expletives. She could almost see Nick nodding.

"I admit he's not the cuddliest guy in the world. But I trust he has my best interests at heart."

She snorted. "Best interests? No, I think he has your money at heart. Can't we bypass Adam Vernon and..." She released the corduroy cushion she'd been clutching and returned to the script. "Hire someone to find out?"

"Like a P.I., you mean?"

"I bet my dad will know someone. He knows so many people. Do you want me to ask him?"

"I suppose it wouldn't hurt to ask. But what if it turns out... I mean, can you handle the truth?"

"I can," she declared, infusing the assertion with more confidence than she felt. "Especially if it sets you free."

"Good girl. But who's going to pay for it?"

DeeDee punched her fist into the air, a grin splitting her face. "He'll probably front you the funds if I ask him nicely. He wants to prove your innocence almost as much as I do."

⋘⋙

On most Saturday evenings at Saffire, the tiniest of noises echoed through the empty studios. Tonight, Livy and Scott filled Studio A with Ed Sheeran music.

Renee directed from the bench. "Since you know it *is* possible to perform ice dance moves without skates and ice, let's see your basic one-foot spin. One, two, three, go!"

Livy laughed as Scott spun her around on her right foot, then maneuvered her into a horizontal landing in his arms. "Way to sweep me off my feet, honey."

Renee, watching from the bench, clapped. "You've got

the hang of the spin part." She laughed. "What was that at the end?"

Scott chuckled as he lifted Livy's face to his and planted a kiss, long and deep, on her parted lips. "Just a little embellishment on my part."

"Aw, you two. Getting mushy, are we?" Renee stood and demonstrated the next move. "Let me see the attitude spin again. Then we'll review lifts."

With her hands on his right arm, Livy fell back against Scott's anchoring left arm, her lame leg extended. Then he clasped her waist and sent her into a 360-degree spin as she folded her left leg behind her knee.

He kissed her again as the music stopped, but at once, another tune replaced it. Dad's hit song "White Cobra" sang from her bag. "Ah, snap." *Way to ruin our romantic moment, Dad.* She wiggled out of Scott's arms and limped to the bench to catch the phone before it disconnected.

"Hey, Dad."

Scott stood in the center of the room watching her, his arms still partly extended as if he forgot she was no longer in them.

"Hey, Punkin. Brittany wants to know if you and Scott could use a bar cabinet. She saw one at Neiman Marcus she wants to get you as a wedding present."

"What kind of bar cabinet?"

"Oh, I don't know. A big one, I assume."

"That's so generous, Dad."

"She also wants to know when you're going to register."

"Soon, I hope. Anyway, I can't talk. Scott and I were in the middle of something."

From his knowing chuckle, he'd jumped the wrong conclusion. Just like DeeDee. "Sorry, kiddo. I'll let you two resume what you were doing." He was still chuckling as he clicked off.

She needed to stop telling people she and Scott were in the middle of something. She returned the phone to her bag. "Sorry," she told Renee. Approaching Scott, she gave him her most flirtatious smile, hoping to wipe away the irritation in his eyes.

Her heart thudded when he spoke to Renee. "Can you excuse us a minute? We need to talk."

Scott gestured her into the empty, unlit corridor where the darkness cloaked the cheery lemon-yellow and vivid-crimson walls in varying shades of murky gray. There was no reason to fear, so why did she feel like she was being sent to the principal's office?

He faced her and pointed toward the studio door where the guilty phone hid. "See? That's what I mean. A bar cabinet? How much do those things cost, anyway?"

She refused to cower. "A Neiman Marcus one probably costs over a thousand dollars."

He gave an abrupt whistle. "That's a lot of money for an unnecessary extravagance."

"It's his money, and he can afford it."

Scott crossed his well-muscled arms across his chest, his feet firmly planted. "That's not the point."

"What is the point?"

His eyes were unreadable in the gloom. "The point is, I can see our kids someday running to Grandpa, begging him for something we said no to. And he would probably give in."

"I get it, Scott."

"Then why can't you just say no?"

"You don't just say no to Declan Decker."

"Why not? He's not Declan Decker to you. He's your father."

Distracted by the biceps flexing under his tee-shirt sleeve, she grasped his clasped arms and tugged on them. She needed to feel his comforting grip around her, needed reassurance that he still treasured her, despite their arguing. Finally, he gave in and allowed her to place his arms around her waist, pulling her close as she sensed, more than saw, the hardness in his eyes dissipating.

She reached up to stroke the bristle on his jaw. "Honey, let's not fight about this."

He nestled her head under his chin. "I don't want to fight about it, either. But we need to resolve it before our wedding. Not after."

She nodded against his chest. "I know."

"You just need to set some boundaries with him. If you don't want to do it, then I will."

৯৯৯

Once DeeDee gave Dad the go-ahead, time seemed to stand still. "How long is your computer guru going to take?" she asked after two days of waiting. She plopped sideways on her bed and put the phone on speaker.

"Well, first, he had to remotely search Pam's e-mail. It took him some time to find it."

She hugged the plush Yeti to her chest and stared unseeing at the conch-peach wall. "How can he possibly do that?"

"Once he broke into the main Moonstone server, it was easy to get into her e-mail. All he needed was a password breaker. He's still searching for any e-mails related to medical issues. Remember, we don't even know if she had a paternity test."

She stretched one knee to her chest and pointed her toes, imitating the pose of the dancer sculpture on her nightstand. "Let's say she did, and it proves Nick is her daughter's father. Then what? I've watched enough crime shows to know it'll be inadmissible as evidence in court."

"You call in an anonymous tip to the police."

"Oh, Dad, you rock. In more ways than one."

Dad chuckled. "Yep. For over twenty years."

⋘⋘⋘

"Any news, Dad?" Man, it was hard to wait. She'd hardly thought of anything except that blasted, possibly nonexistent paternity test. She'd run errands on autopilot, lost focus multiple times while teaching dance class, had to force food into her dry mouth. If she didn't eat, she wouldn't have the necessary energy to teach.

"He didn't find any medical-related messages in Pam's corporate e-mail. But he did find her personal e-mail address, so he searched it. Guess what? There was a whole e-mail chain about a DNA test."

DeeDee's breath caught as she froze beside the framed prints of dancers in the mystic-gray living room. "What did it say?"

"He looked for test results, but didn't find any. Normally test results are confidential and aren't sent by e-mail. But he did get the name of the lab."

"And?" Her shaky legs moved robotically past the built-in shelves and into the sunny kitchen.

"He'll send the fake e-mail tomorrow to about five lower-level staff at the lab. Then we just have to wait and see if anyone takes the bait."

"Oh, Dad. We have to wait another day?"

"Maybe even longer. Especially if none of the employees are stupid enough to click open the attachment."

Her sigh drew out. "If they don't, then what?"

"He'll try again. At least twice more. Don't worry, Punkin. People are careless. Someone will open that attachment and release the worm, especially if it looks legit. And he does whatever he has to do to make it look that way."

❧❧❧

Five days into the new year, DeeDee paced the kitchen as she waited for Dad's promised call, ignoring Livy, who enjoyed a dinner of Margherita pizza and Caesar salad in the breakfast nook. Since Scott disapproved of DeeDee and Dad's scheme, Livy didn't want to know about it. "The less I know, the less I have to put up with his protests," she'd said. DeeDee didn't get why straitlaced Scott was so opposed. He must not care that Nick was still rotting in jail, day after dreary day. In fact, she didn't get why free-spirited Livy put up with Scott's prudish ways.

Her phone went off in her hand, and she jumped. "Hello?"

Static greeted her, fizzled, and then cleared. "Hey, kiddo, I got news."

"Well, don't keep me in suspense. Tell me!"

From the corner of her eye, she saw Livy raise her head. Ha. She couldn't resist knowing, either.

"Mike was able to get into the lab's database. Didn't take long to find Pam's records. I've got his e-mail open in front of me." Dad paused, his breathing raspy. "Are you ready for this? Maybe you should sit down."

Her suddenly weak legs carried her to the bench across from Livy, where she plopped. "Ready," she said in a shaky voice.

"Okay. Here's what the lab determined. Sofie's paternity test: negative."

"What does that mean?"

"It means Bryan Campbell is not Sofie's father."

DeeDee gulped and clutched her thudding chest. An ache built around her heart, threatening to suffocate her.

"But there was another test result in there, too."

"Another one?" she gasped out.

"One for her son, Leon Jr."

"Why would she have Junior tested?"

Now Livy's narrow-eyed attention stayed riveted on DeeDee.

"She must have had doubts about his paternity, too," Dad said.

Words formed, but wouldn't emerge from her paralyzed mouth.

His voice pushed through the mist in her brain. "That test was negative also. Leon Brown Sr is not Junior's father."

Chapter Thirty-Five

"**V**ictoria Police Department. How may I direct your call?"

A patch of sunlight pierced the sunroom glass and bathed DeeDee in its glow, but couldn't stop a nervous tremor from knocking the prepaid phone against her ear. "Uh, hi. I have some information about Pamela Campbell, the woman who was murdered."

"Name, please?"

She fingered the gold heart on its new chain. "Um, I'd rather not say. But I know something that might help the investigation."

"Hold, please."

Outside, the toddler from across the cul-de-sac scampered along the sidewalk, his young mother's outstretched arm a few feet behind him. After what seemed like an eternity of necklace rubbing and hair tugging, a disembodied male voice spoke. "This is Officer Phillips. Can I help you?"

She repeated herself in a slightly more annoyed voice.

"We've closed the investigation," he informed her in a clipped tone.

Then reopen it. "Pam found out something about her daughter right before she died. I've been worried ever since that she was killed because of it."

"Oh?"

Now she had his attention. "Yes. She had a paternity test done and found out her husband is not the girl's father. Three days later, she was murdered."

Thick, wheel-humming silence on the other end. "And how do you know this?"

DeeDee crossed her fingers behind her back, the way she did in childhood whenever she told a fib. "She came into my shop for a manicure. I could tell she was upset about something, and finally, she confided in me." Angst edged her tone. "I've been mulling this over for two weeks, because she told me in confidence. And the more I've thought about it," she forced a sob, "the more afraid I am that maybe her husband found out and…" She gave a couple of convincing gasps and waited.

Papers rustled, thuds and male voices in the background bulleted into her ears. "Hold on a moment." A rude beep resounded, then silence. More nail biting, more hair tugging. Two minutes crept by, then Phillips's voice snapped into her ear. "Did she tell you the name of the medical facility where the test was done?"

"Yes." DeeDee drooped, her relief so sharp she collapsed like a rag doll to her knees. As she answered each question the officer threw at her, tears streamed down her cheeks, and she cradled the prepaid phone against her ear, a sudden precious lifeline bridging the gap between her man and his freedom.

సోంసోంసోం

"Help me." Pam's disembodied face hovered next to DeeDee's bed. At first, only her luminescent eyes were visible behind a black veil. Then a faint glow from somewhere beyond illuminated her studded leather jacket. On closer inspection, DeeDee shivered—at least ten studs stood where the buttons should be, each stud covering a blood-lined bullet hole.

"Help me." Pam's whisper rasped on DeeDee's already-frayed nerves.

"What do you want from me?"

Raven-black hair flew at DeeDee from behind Pam's veil, transforming into fiery red tendrils. DeeDee raised her arms in self-defense, but a strand of hair wrapped around her wrist like an angry snake, squeezing tighter with each passing second until DeeDee thought it surely would snap her hand right off. Feeling herself being dragged to the edge of the bed, she flailed, but found nothing to grip. The bed went on and on as Pam dragged her, kicking and screaming, along an ever-expanding mattress.

"Okay, I'll help you!"

The grip of the snakelike hair released, and...she was falling! She opened her mouth in a silent scream.

Then she lurched awake, blinking away visions of vicious snakes and black leather.

Black leather...Her mind seized on the image; memories rose to the surface.

"Ah." She clutched her racing heart, shifted to her side, and eased upright. The frightening images faded, but she could see a bright, lit path shining before her. And beyond it, the truth.

Chapter Thirty-Six

DeeDee awoke on Showcase Saturday with her plan swirling through her mind. Nothing had better go wrong today. She and Livy had gone over it a hundred times, step by step, until they could recite it in their sleep. Every variation, every possible glitch, they'd prepared for. Only Dad knew their intent. At his request, Livy hadn't even told Scott, knowing he'd strenuously object.

After showering, DeeDee donned the outfit she'd picked out last night. Bernardo jacket from Nordstrom in red leather. Matching pants. Over breakfast, Livy offered to pray for their plan's success. Grateful for Livy's steadying presence, DeeDee nodded, gripped Livy's hands, and closed her eyes.

DeeDee could picture her sister's words, simple and heartfelt, flying directly to God's throne. If only she could conjure up the same level of faith in her heart. She glanced at the stove clock as she chewed her last bite of hazelnut scone. "It's nearly time to go. Jazzy's going to meet us there at nine."

༄ ༄ ༄

By eleven a.m., chilly rain drenched the city, but inside Saffire, a festive mood prevailed. Parents, mouths lifted in proud expectation, filled Studio A's spectator benches. DeeDee smiled and waved at Scott, sitting next to his ex-wife, Shari, and her new husband. How Scott and Shari maintained such an amicable relationship, she didn't know. Maybe because they'd both found love again, there was no more need for conflict.

Her gaze skimmed the rows of parents, stopping at a couple of large men whom she didn't recognize. Both faces sported tight expressions, both sets of arms were crossed, as if they'd only showed up because their wives made them. But no wives flanked them. She moved in their direction, her hand out, poised to introduce herself. But when one of them glanced at her, and then looked quickly away, she stopped. Clearly, he wasn't in the mood for small talk. The other didn't once look her way.

She shrugged, hoping for an opportunity after the showcase to find out who they were.

She stepped out into the hallway, where the girls, plus one boy, lined up behind Miss Ella, awaiting their cue to make their grand entrance. She wandered to Studio C, where Jazzy put the finishing touches on Chloe's face—swipes of sparkly blush on her round cheeks, brighter-than-bright red on her puckered lips. DeeDee had to admire the way Jazzy could immediately grasp whatever tool or cosmetic she needed, without even looking, from her five trays filled with an assortment of makeup.

Livy waited nearby, phone in hand, to take Chloe's photo.

"We start in five minutes," DeeDee reminded them. "Chloe, you need to hustle. They're waiting for you."

Jazzy nudged the twelve-year-old toward Livy. "Go. You look fabulous."

Chloe posed and simpered for the camera, then darted from the room. Jazzy slumped in her chair, her hair lying limp around her face. "Wow, my first real, paying gig. I didn't know putting makeup on twenty-five whiny little girls would be so tiring."

DeeDee nodded. "Imagine how we feel after a day of demanding little divas who don't want to learn the steps we teach them. One girl told us she wanted to 'dance outside the box'. I finally had to tell her mother the girl was a free spirit and needed a non-structured dance environment."

Jazzy stood and stretched her thin arms high over her head. "I think I'll stick with adults."

DeeDee led the way across the hall, past the chattering, giggling students, into Studio A where several parents stood next to the full benches. She gave a go-ahead nod to Ella, then joined Livy and Jazzy in the standing-room-only section.

One of the two men she'd noticed earlier turned his head and watched them from hooded lids, as though he were trying to keep them from noticing him. DeeDee had been around enough bodyguards to know one when she saw one. She'd assumed the bodyguards Dad hired would arrive after the show. But these two had apparently decided to stay inconspicuous by blending in with the other parents. To hide in plain sight.

Hoping they didn't give themselves away with their suspicious, watchful stares, she lifted the sound system's remote control and flipped it on.

A mass of young-to-teen dancers ran to the center as the opening strains of Pharrell Williams's "Happy" buzzed through the room. They posed, hands on hips, sequins sparkling under the ceiling lights, and bounced on one knee for four counts until Pharrell started singing his familiar anthem, the song which had become as ubiquitous as Minions.

DeeDee hadn't expected perfection. Still, the girls' level of energy and spunk surprised and pleased her. Livy grinned, foot-tapping to the beat. Scott's face sported a matching grin as he and Livy eyed each other from across the room. Jazzy watched with pursed mouth and bemused expression, as if she were a judge on *America's Got Talent*.

After the group bowed and exited, each class filed in and showed off their best moves, then came the soloists. The showcase ended with enthusiastic applause. As everyone filed out to Studio B, where refreshments waited, Livy and Scott joined hands with Kinzie and Lacie, the four of them already looking like a real family. Shari and her husband, trailing behind and deep in conversation, didn't appear to notice. DeeDee fell into step beside lucky Livy, whose man didn't have to endure jail for a crime he didn't commit.

But if everything went down according to plan, today the injustice would be rectified.

⋘⋙

"Jazzy, you rocked the makeup artistry." DeeDee's leather jacket squeaked as she slid her laptop along the desk to her right and raised the black chair a few inches, the better to gaze down her nose at Jazzy in her most intimidating pose. Today, she was emulating Adam Vernon. She pointed to the green chair facing her, and Jazzy settled in, her back to the slightly-ajar door.

DeeDee's heart rate quickened over what was about to transpire. "Hasn't it been a great day?"

Jazzy gave a single nod. "When you told me about your dance studio, I didn't imagine such a classy operation."

"Our motto is, 'We teach your child to dance as if the whole world is watching. Because it is.'"

"Love it."

DeeDee leaned forward. "Since everyone's gone home, it's time to talk business."

Jazzy grasped one crossed knee in both hands. "Great."

"As I said before, we'll pay you for your hours worked plus travel costs. You have documentation for your hotel and mileage, right?"

Jazzy dug through her purse and produced receipts.

With the plan becoming reality rather than only in her mind, DeeDee's nerves sizzled, but she couldn't let Jazzy see her as anything but calm and controlled. She slowed her breathing and visualized a peaceful, sunny meadow, its green grass glowing, falling leaves acting out a subtle dance.

Maybe she should have asked Livy to join her, instead of having her wait in the supply closet with the bodyguards, where she'd hear everything. But the plan's success depended on Jazzy believing no one else was in the building.

"Also, as we agreed, I'll pay you via wire. Did you bring your banking info?"

Jazzy retrieved a printout from her purse, unfolded it, and held it out. "I did. Here's the routing number and the account number."

DeeDee kept talking, her voice smooth and level. "It's so much easier than writing checks, don't you think? I mean, how hard can it be to obtain people's banking data? I'm sure Leon would agree."

Jazzy narrowed her eyes, a sudden hardness there, then dropped her gaze to the bank statement still in her hand.

"Oh." DeeDee bit her lip. "Oh, I'm sorry. That was insensitive of me."

Her cheeks aflame, nostrils flared, Jazzy shoved the statement at DeeDee.

DeeDee set the paper next to the laptop. "I assume he's still…" A meaningful pause.

"Yeah, he's still in jail. His trial's coming up next week."

Softening her tone and folding her hands in her lap, DeeDee forced herself forward. "What a way to start a marriage. How are you holding up with your brand-new husband in jail?"

Jazzy shrugged, her bright eyes focused on the statement and the laptop. DeeDee smiled to herself. Jazzy was all, take the money and run.

Not if DeeDee had any say over it.

Jazzy squared her shoulders, her eyes shifting to DeeDee's four-hundred-dollar leather jacket. "I'm just trying to think positive and hope for the best. He could be acquitted, you know."

"I heard the authorities are reopening Pam's murder case, on the off-chance he was involved."

"He didn't kill his mother!"

"I know he didn't." DeeDee nodded, a slow, unhurried nod meant to drive Jazzy crazy.

"Nick did."

"On the contrary. I know for a fact Nick did not kill Pam."

Jazzy's eyes bugged. "Yes, he did."

"No, he didn't. Pam told me so."

DeeDee nearly laughed at Jazzy's jaw dropping like a bungee jumper off a bridge.

"How could she? She's dead!"

"She visited me in my dreams."

Another jaw drop, longer this time. "Wh–what did she tell you?"

"She told me who really killed her."

"No way."

"Way."

Jazzy's throat worked as she uncrossed her legs, then crossed them again, gripping her knee even tighter. "So, who killed Pam?"

The forced casual tone couldn't hide the tremble in her voice.

Leaning back, DeeDee folded her arms. "You did."

Jazzy's transformation startled even DeeDee's unflappable heart. She lunged and circled her hands around DeeDee's throat, and rings of light flashed, then faded, in DeeDee's vision. Choking, gasping, unable to pull air into her lungs. Then she was falling, falling, as though she were back in the dream. And now Jazzy loomed over her. DeeDee pushed upward with all her might, trying to dislodge Jazzy's grip. Pain seared through her head as she struggled to pull herself back to consciousness, but this time, she couldn't wake up.

Chapter Thirty-Seven

Livy, hearing DeeDee's declaration, then a thud from the office next door, gasped and ran out before the two bodyguards even moved. Out in the hall, the office door burst open, and a blur blew through. The blur smacked into Livy's chest and flung her backward.

"Whoa, there." A male voice spoke in her ear as her head flew back against something hard, yet yielding. A pair of arms steadied her. Somewhere nearby, curses flew through the air.

The front door chimed, signaling a visitor.

Her heart rate calmed and reality clarified. She twisted her head to the bodyguard still holding her upright. To her right, the other bodyguard had tight hold of a flailing Jazzy, whose curses would make Beyoncé blush.

"Livy?" came a familiar, oh-so-unwelcome voice. "What's going on?"

"Scott?" She scooted out of the bodyguard's grasp and faced her fiancé, whose feet were planted in his best Dirty Harry impression, his gaze boring a hole in her heart. Confusion, suspicion, curiosity waged war on his face as he looked between her and the bodyguard, who'd stepped away to help detain Jazzy, now being dragged toward the exit.

She rushed to him. Willing him not to be mad. Regretting leaving him out of the loop.

"Honey, we caught Pam's murderer."

His stunned expression froze for a moment, then softened to relief. "Really?"

She grabbed his hand and led him toward the office. "We need to hurry. DeeDee's in there. I don't know what Jazzy did to her, but it sounded..." She stopped at the doorway, her heart in her throat. DeeDee lay face-up on the floor, still and silent, the black leather chair upended next to her.

"Deeds!" Livy rushed to her sister's side and checked her pulse, then sagged in relief when a weak but genuine beat throbbed beneath her fingertips. She pulled out her phone and punched in 911.

While she and Scott waited for the ambulance, Livy knelt and dabbed her sister's face with wet cloths, hoping to rouse her, all the while recapping the events for Scott in a jagged, gasping narrative.

"Why didn't you tell me what you were up to?" From his squatting position beside her, he reached under her hair and rubbed the back of her neck.

Although his touch and voice stayed gentle, Livy couldn't meet his eyes. Surely, guilt shone from hers. "I wanted to, but Dad and DeeDee insisted..."

"Your dad knew about this?"

"Yes, he hired the bodyguards."

When Scott pressed his lips together, she reminded him, "If not for the bodyguard, I would've been flat on the floor. I could've reinjured myself."

"I should have been here for you."

He looked so hurt, she had to turn her attention from her sister on the floor. He drew her to him and forced her gaze to his. "This is the sort of thing a wife ought to tell her husband."

"I know. I promise I will."

The hurt in his eyes morphed to fear. "If anything happened to you, I don't know what I'd do."

She opened her mouth, apologetic words on her tongue,

when a wailing siren shattered the silence. She and Scott bounced up and hurried to the door just as an ambulance whirred to the curb. While Scott propped the door, two paramedics jumped out and hauled a stretcher inside.

Livy led them to DeeDee's side. DeeDee's eyes fluttered open and latched onto Livy's. "Jazzy…"

Livy took her sister's hand and squeezed. "Not to worry, Jazzy's been arrested. Are you hurt?"

DeeDee groaned. "My head. Sh–she tried to strangle me…."

Ironic how their roles had switched. When Livy got injured last year, DeeDee had knelt and held her hand while paramedics moved her into the ambulance. Now it was Livy's turn to pay it back. She could only watch, nestled under Scott's reassuring arm, as the pros examined DeeDee and lifted her onto the stretcher.

"She has a small gash on the back of her head," said the tall, sandy-haired young man. He bent and fingered the side of the desk. Scrutinizing something on his finger, he concluded, "Looks like she hit it on the side of the desk. I found some tiny hairs." He and the dark-haired paramedic hoisted the stretcher and carried her sister to the waiting ambulance. Scott and Livy wasted no time following them.

കൟകൟകൟ

A thin ray of sunlight shone through the hospital room window and hit DeeDee's eyes, intensifying her headache, at the same moment Scott walked in, carting a two-pack of Starbucks drinks.

"You are planning to tell me how you two figured this out, right?" he said.

Livy grabbed her cinnamon latte and took a deep, eager sip. "Yes, come sit down, and we'll tell you all about it." Holding out her hand to DeeDee, she smiled. "Deeds was the one who finally figured out the bad 'guy' was Jazzy."

DeeDee grinned. "It was that spendy leather jacket." The doctor had ordered her to lay as still as possible to minimize the swelling on the back of her head. But her eyes and mouth couldn't keep still. "The jacket Jazzy wore the day I met her was the same jacket Pam had on when I found her body. A Rebecca Taylor from Nordstrom with a missing button on the left cuff."

"And something about Pam's body kept bugging her."

"Nick told me Leon and Jazzy claimed they hadn't seen Pam. But they were lying. My subconscious noticed the missing button, figured out it was the same jacket, but I was in such shock, it didn't register in my conscious mind."

Scott frowned. "How did Pam end up with Jazzy's jacket?"

DeeDee shook her head side to side, then stopped when a pain twisted her mouth. "No, other way around. It was Pam's jacket. My gut was trying to tell me Pam had seen Jazzy and got her borrowed jacket back." She closed her eyes against another stab of pain. "About a week later, Nick told me Jazzy and Leon claimed not to have seen Pam. I sensed something was off, because that night, I had another dream about Pam."

Scott's frown deepened, accompanied by a scrunched forehead. "Jazzy killed Pam over a jacket?"

"No, no." Livy scooted forward. "Not because of the jacket. Because Pam was about to report her marriage to Leon as invalid, so it would be annulled. But Jazzy couldn't let that happen, because then she wouldn't have any legal right to all that lovely stolen money Leon stashed in the Caymans."

"Why was her marriage to Leon invalid? And what does the jacket have to do with all this?"

DeeDee raised her brows. "Oh, you're not going to

believe this. You see, Pam's biggest weakness was—she was a cheater at heart. She couldn't be satisfied with just one man. So her two children were actually fathered by someone other than her husband at the time."

She stopped for breath, wondering if Pam's first husband ever knew of her betrayal. "Unbeknownst to her first husband, Senior, she had a brief fling with someone else early in their relationship. So when she got pregnant with Leon, she and Senior both assumed the baby was his. But it wasn't."

DeeDee's words slowed, and Livy went to her. "Are you tired? Want me to tell about Leon and Erik?"

"I–I can do this." A feathery sigh emerged from her mouth, and she closed her eyes. "Yes, Leon and Erik. I should have guessed the truth. There were plenty of physical similarities between them. He even said to me, like father, like son."

"Who did?"

"Erik. He said most of the ex-cons he works with are sons of criminals. Erik admitted he'd robbed banks. And Leon, who was really his biological son, also robbed banks. But he did it virtually. I even noticed Leon's early-onset baldness. Like father, like son."

"Leon was Erik's biological son?"

"He was. The DNA test only told us Senior was not his father. But when I came across an old photo of Pam and Erik kissing, I began to wonder. Nick's attorney questioned Erik, and he admitted he and Pam had a fling about nine months before Leon was born. Once Pam knew the truth, she'd have known Jazzy and Leon couldn't legally marry."

"Ah, because they were actually half-siblings."

"Right, but nobody ever knew."

"Makes sense now. And the jacket?"

"Proves they lied. My subconscious made the

connection and asked, 'Where did Pam go after she left home that morning?' Obviously to her son's place."

"But he denied it."

"Yes. Not from guilt, but from fear. He was afraid they'd make him their top suspect if they knew Pam had been there. And Jazzy backed him. He truly thought Jazzy went shopping. He had no idea what she was really up to."

Livy nodded. "Pam must have confronted them about the test results. We think Jazzy followed Pam to the cabin to stop her from reporting their marriage as invalid, then went shopping afterward, as she claimed when the police interviewed her."

Scott could only shake his head.

"DeeDee told Jazzy that Pam revealed her murderer in a dream." Pride seeped into Livy's voice. "But the truth is, DeeDee put the pieces together all by herself."

"I only told her that to make her sweat."

Scott cast a wondering look at Livy. "How were you able to prove all this?"

Livy nudged him. "It helps to have a dad with friends in high places."

DeeDee chuckled. "After all the pieces came together in my mind, Dad asked his cyber genius friend to hack into Jazzy's computer. Guess what he found?"

"I can't imagine."

"Jazzy had been researching the price of homes in the Caymans. But she'd also been reading stories about women who'd killed their husbands. He found sites about various poisons in her search history. We think she planned to poison Leon then relocate to the Caymans."

DeeDee's heart throbbed at the thought of Leon as a murder victim. Sure, he might be a bad egg, but for Jazzy to cold-bloodedly plan to eliminate him…poor Leon. How tragic to go into a marriage with love and high hopes, only to discover you'd married a murderer.

"Still," Scott said, "none of that is admissible in court, since it was obtained illegally."

"True," Livy replied. "But DeeDee's attorney is pressing charges for assault, and we're hoping those things will be discovered in the investigation."

"Where is Jazzy now?"

"Locked up where she belongs. One of the bodyguards is an undercover cop. He arrested her for assault. Dad told him to make sure she doesn't get released."

෬෨෬෨෬෨

Livy searched Scott's eyes when DeeDee mentioned Dad. *There he goes again,* his expression said. His anti-Dad attitude was driving a wedge between them. And, in a flash of insight, she knew exactly what she needed to say.

But no opportunity to talk presented itself until DeeDee finished relating her conversations with Erik and Lisa, her frightening visit to Moonstone, her fruitless conversation with the arrogant Adam Vernon. "Dad has another attorney in mind who he thinks will do a far better job than Vernon." She rubbed her palms together, grinning. "I wish I could see that sonuva"—she cast a sideways glance at Livy—"that schmuck's face when Nick fires him."

Livy couldn't wait any longer. She shifted to face Scott and laid a hand on his arm, until he finally met her gaze. "Can we talk?" she mouthed, pointing her head toward the hallway.

A slow, questioning nod.

"Deeds, will you excuse us a minute?" Out in the sterile hall, she stood inches from him…close enough for his body heat to warm her. "I thought of something to help us work through this Dad issue."

He reached out one finger to stroke her hair. "What's

that?"

She placed her hands on his shoulders. "First of all, I want you to know I get where you're coming from. I really do. And I trust you, too."

He smiled and pulled her to him. "That's music to my ears, my love."

She leaned her head back, holding his gaze. "But there's another way to look at this. Imagine you were in jail for a crime you didn't commit." A cloud eclipsed the smile in his eyes. "If it were you, and not Nick, my dad would've done whatever he needed to get you free. Wouldn't you want that?" When his mouth opened to speak, but nothing came out, she went on, "It's sort of like what God did for us. He paid a huge price to set us free."

He shook her words away. "God wants us to obey our governments. We're not supposed to take the law into our own hands."

"Honey, I agree with you. I'm just clarifying where your future father-in-law is coming from. I want you to like him."

"I do like him. Always have. I'm just afraid after we're married he'll keep plying us with stuff we don't need. Like that bar cabinet. Where would we put it? We only have twenty-six hundred square feet of house."

"I'll talk to him. I promise."

"Why don't we talk to him together?" He lowered his lips to her forehead and brushed a light kiss across her skin. A delightful shiver coursed through her. "Let's Skype him tonight."

☙❧☙

Declan Decker's face filled the screen.

"Hi, Dad."

"Hey. What's on your mind?"

Livy kept her voice steady so Dad wouldn't sense how

difficult this was for her. "It's about that bar cabinet."

He merely raised his brows.

"Um, we just wanted you to know, we don't really need anything big or fancy for our wedding."

"I—"

"We appreciate the thought, sir." Scott gave her hand a reassuring squeeze. "And I promise you I'll take good care of your daughter and our future kids. But I'm just a simple man with simple tastes." He swept his free hand out in a gesture of appeal.

"As far as our honeymoon, Dad, we'd already decided on Hawaii. I'm sorry I didn't say anything sooner. It was sweet of you to offer the European tour, but we have to decline."

Livy exhaled and watched Dad. Not a trace of irritation marred his serene expression.

"Not a problem. I understand." His head bobbed robotically. "Sometimes I forget what life was like before I got my first hit record in 1991. Now, Brittany and I want to know. Have you two set a date?"

Chapter Thirty-Eight

DeeDee punched her fist in the air when the ferry carrying Nick home chugged to a stop at the Anacortes dock. "Yahoo!" In just minutes, her long-lost love would walk off that boat and back into her arms.

Actually, it could be closer to thirty minutes. She'd arrived when the queue of cars was already nearly a quarter-mile long, and he needed to clear customs first. She could picture him striding swiftly alongside the line, his searching eyes filled with hope, then frustration, when he didn't see her car. She couldn't focus with her mind jumping around to so many scenarios. He could still have his full beard that only partly hid his ashen complexion. He might be so scarred and broken, she'd have to dig six feet deep to find the Nick she loved. He might...

A knock on her window startled her. And there he was, a mile-wide smile stretched across his face, his gaze burning with love and anticipation. She jumped out and threw her arms around his slumping shoulders, kissed the stubble on his weary jaw. Words she hadn't planned on tumbled out of her mouth in no particular order.

"Nick! Oh, how I missed you." Another kiss, this one hard on the lips. "You look wonderful, babe." Not as wonderful as the pre-jail Nick, but no doubt, he'd be back to his old self in no time.

His lips nuzzled her ear. "Mmm, I forgot how good you smell."

They finally climbed into the car, and DeeDee headed

home. Their conversation proved jagged as they kept finishing each others' sentences, then laughing like teenagers after too many energy drinks, only to start a new thread of conversation. The further south they drove, the more color returned to Nick's face. Only his eyes, bloodshot from lack of sleep, betrayed his ordeal.

To the right, the Marysville casino appeared, marking the last leg of their journey. She glanced at his animated face. "I cleaned your house last week."

"Thanks, my love."

Best just to plunge in. "Can we talk about Sofie? And Gracie?"

She sensed, more than saw, his tension. "I have no moral right to the girl, if that's what you want to know."

"Does Bryan Campbell know?"

"He does now. My attorney said he flew into a rage."

"So he really didn't know Sofie wasn't his."

"More likely, he didn't want to know."

"True." She heaved a breath. "Did Gracie ever suspect?"

Nick wouldn't look at her, simply stared out the windshield. "She did. But not until Sofie was two. She and Pam were friends, you know."

A raindrop spattered on the windshield.

"No, I didn't know."

"Not super close, but they occasionally ran into each other." She sensed him studying her. "You really want to know this?"

"I do, Nick. I know it's history, but I don't want us to have secrets from each other anymore. I want transparency."

She reached her hand toward him, and he clasped it tightly. "I do, too, sweetheart. No more secrets. I promise."

She cast a smile at him.

As he spoke, rain fell in earnest. "Hindsight, as they say,

is twenty-twenty. I realize now if I'd told you what I was doing that day, maybe things wouldn't have turned out so poorly." He chuckled. "God has a way of reminding me of the consequences when I tend to take matters into my own hands."

Enough God talk. "Anyway, about Gracie?"

"Right. Well, Gracie ran into Pam one day at Baby Boutique and saw Sofie for the first time. She said something about not knowing Pam and I had had a child. Pam denied it, said the baby was Bryan's."

"Obviously planted a seed of doubt in Pam's mind. No wonder she decided to have the paternity test done."

"Gracie came home and told me about it, then asked point-blank if Pam was telling the truth. Asked me the same questions you did, in fact. I decided to be honest and told her it was certainly a possibility, told her about my post-split one-night stand with Pam." He cleared his throat, rested his fists on his knees. "She moved out the next day."

"Oh, Nick."

"But you see, I'm glad now she did. If she hadn't, I wouldn't have moved to Seattle and met you."

The smile stretched her face to almost-painful proportions. "You would've been just another spoken-for hottie on the stage that night."

He squeezed her hand. "And I would've missed out on the best woman I've ever known."

"Seriously, Nick? You really mean that?"

"I do." Another squeeze, firmer this time.

Her heart warmed. "I can stay with you tonight." She gestured with her head toward the back. "I brought some stuff." He probably missed their intimate nights as much as she did.

She stiffened as his face seemed to close in on itself. Without a word, he merely nodded and wouldn't meet her eye. What was up with him? He acted like he didn't want her with him. After a month's incarceration, how could he want to be alone on his first night of freedom?

By the time she pulled into his townhouse's ground-floor garage, Nick had turned pensive. The need to ask what was wrong grew like the molehills in her back yard. Miraculously remaining silent, she grabbed her overnight bag and followed him up the stairs.

Pine-Sol-scented air greeted them when they walked through the door. Nick breathed deep. "Nice. Thank you for keeping this place smelling like home." He turned then and took her in his arms. "You didn't have to, but I really appreciate it." He glanced around, his dancing eyes reminding her of the man she loved. "You don't know how good it feels to be home. This calls for a celebration. I believe I have some fine Zinfandel in the wine rack."

He retrieved the wine, filled two goblets, and carried them to the living room where he collapsed onto the brown leather sofa. "Come sit." He patted the cushion next to him. "We need to talk."

DeeDee's breath stuck in her throat. Those dreaded words *We need to talk…* No way could this be a breakup talk. Not after their intimate, transparent talk in the car. With growing apprehension, she sat and shifted to face him.

He kept her hand tucked into his, rubbing his thumb along her palm. She steeled herself against the pleasurable sensation, in case he planned to shatter her heart.

"I need to tell you what happened to me in that jail cell."

She couldn't look away from his piercing gaze. "What happened?"

"This may sound strange, but…" He glanced behind her for a moment. A memory flickered in the depths of his eyes. "I got right with God." Which would explain his babbling on about Jesus and the Godfather. At her flinch, he tightened his grip on her hands. "I know how you feel about religion. But that's not what this was."

"You sound like Erik."

"I'll take that as a compliment."

He'd never spoken to her in such a dry manner. He must be annoyed with her for not taking him seriously. Clenching her lips, she waited for him to go on.

"Anyway, I thought it only fair to warn you this is going to have some ramifications."

She swallowed. "What kind of ramifications?" *Not a breakup, please.*

"First of all, I'll be more involved in church. I plan to join a men's Bible Study. I won't be available on Sunday mornings or certain weekday evenings." He stared down at their clasped hands and his thumb tracing the soft spot between her thumb and index finger. Back and forth it went, like a windshield wiper. "Secondly…"

He looked up, locking gazes with her. "It also means we need to conduct our relationship Jesus' way. That is…" He cleared his throat.

She already knew what he was going to say.

"No more sleeping together," she finished for him.

He narrowed his eyes at her.

"Just like Scott and Livy," she went on. "After Livy got 'right with God' last year, she stopped sleeping with her boyfriend." And not long after, Will got disgusted and broke up with her.

For the first time since they arrived here, Nick's expression softened. He searched her eyes, and a tender look passed across his face. "There is a solution, you know."

"What's that?"

"A wedding. You and me." He scooted closer, reaching up his finger to stroke her cheek. "Then we can sleep together every night." He cast his devastating smile at her.

"Guilt-free."

DeeDee couldn't keep a laugh from bursting forth. She threw her arms around his neck. "Nick, that must be the corniest, most endearing marriage proposal I've ever heard of."

His fingers kneaded her spine, as expert as his head rubs. "Is that a yes?" His words tickled her ear.

"Yes. It's a yes." Still grinning, she lifted her head and met his penetrating blue eyes. Love shimmered in them, overlaid with joy, framed in those beloved crinkles.

He lowered his lips to hers, and her body responded as though they'd never been apart. But this time...the awareness floated in the back of her mind...this time, no culmination awaited her. Tonight, he wouldn't be tugging her into the bedroom as passion built.

This must be how Livy felt every day.

Nick pushed away. "Ah, sweetheart. It's hard to stop. But we must."

Why? she wanted to ask.

"I promise our wedding night will be extra special."

Her arms tingled as he ran his fingers along her skin, then grasped her hands, locking his eyes with hers. "I hope by then we're following God together."

Though she dreaded his answer, she couldn't stop the question. "What if I can't go there with you? Would that be a deal-breaker?"

Again, he tightened his grip on her hands. "Why wouldn't you want to follow a God who loves you enough to die for you?"

"Why would you follow a God who forbids you to have sex with your girlfriend?" At the spark of dismay in his eye, she bit her lip. She hadn't meant to turn this into an argument.

He pulled her head onto his shoulder and planted little

kisses on her hair. "Sweetheart, God isn't a killjoy. Once you get to know Him, you'll find out for yourself."

"I'm not even sure there is a God."

"If you just look around you—and keep an open mind—you can't help but see there has to be a Creator. Have you ever studied atoms?"

"Not since high school."

"Do you know how complex they are? More complex than the latest technological innovations. How can that not be evidence of a Creator?"

His arms around her shoulders prevented the shrug she attempted. "I've just always believed everything evolved into what we see today." She scooted away to show him she didn't want to have this conversation. First Erik, now Nick, trying to shove religion on her. "Erik kept at me about God, too. He kept telling me I was lost. But I don't think he meant it literally."

Erik's world had teetered off its foundation when he learned his daughter had committed murder. DeeDee's heart had twisted at his grief-ridden message to her last week, yet he still pushed God on her. "Lisa and I are praying you'll turn to God for comfort and peace," he'd written. "If not for God, I don't know how I would get through Jasmine's murder trial," he'd said. He apparently didn't hold it against her that she'd been responsible for bringing Jazzy to justice.

How could Erik's broken heart keep trusting a God who'd rock his world like that?

Nick placed his hands on her shoulders, then rose to his feet and hauled her up beside him. "My lost, beautiful sweetheart."

"Why do people keep saying I'm lost?"

He still held her at arm's length, as if afraid to venture too close. "You're lost because you're looking for God and can't find Him."

"I'm not looking for God!"

"You're not looking for peace, satisfaction, purpose?"

DeeDee, stumped, only stared at him. What did God have to do with self-actualization?

"Everyone I know who has true peace and purpose in their lives got that way because they're right with God."

"I have plenty of happy nonreligious friends."

He took a step back, but his gaze held her as intently as his arms. "Are you absolutely positive they're truly happy?"

"I could ask the same of you."

"I know people who used to drown their sorrows in alcohol." He pointed to the half-full goblet on the coffee table. "Or who escaped reality through drugs. Or porn. People who've been set free of these things. What about your friends? Can you say the same?"

Her mind scanned the names and faces of her numerous friends—many of them from the worlds of music or dance. The vast majority of them drank, sniffed, injected, or smoked some sort of substance.

Maybe that's why they came across as happy. It was all fake. Forced. Substance-induced happiness.

Hadn't she always striven for the next "high", anything to make her feel better? And when she didn't attain it, the letdown was almost enough to keep her locked in her room.

Nick studied her as thoughts roared through her mind. Livy gave credit to God for her newfound peace of mind. Sometimes DeeDee envied Livy's settled trust that God heard her prayers. Even though she'd always considered belief in God a crutch, she had to admit it brought stability to Livy's world after her life-changing accident last year.

And Erik—how drastically he'd turned his life around. A "God thing," according to him.

Nick himself seemed strangely calm. And not bitter at all over his ordeal. Whereas if she'd been jailed unjustly, she'd be seeking vengeance at the earliest opportunity. A trait she'd gotten from Dad.

She searched Nick's hopeful eyes and thought about him and Livy, the two people most dear to her. She trusted their judgment the way she trusted her car would get her where she needed to go. What if there was something to this God business? Could it really hurt to give it a try? After all, if nothing happened, she could at least claim she'd given it her best shot.

"So if I decide to try God and see what happens, what do I need to do?"

The undisguised joy on Nick's face surprised her, but he sat her down on the sofa and nestled his arm around her shoulders. "The Bible says if you confess Jesus is Lord and believe God raised Him from the dead, you will be saved. That's all you need to do."

"I don't understand what that means—Jesus is Lord."

Nick patiently explained and answered her questions, telling her things she'd heard many times from Livy, but paid no heed to. This time, the message was animated with a substance that hadn't been there before, as though Nick had taken a black-and-white photo and replaced it with colorful PowerPoint slides.

"Livy's been trying to convince me for months that Jesus was God in the flesh. But the way you explained it, it suddenly makes sense."

"It's God Himself who opens our eyes to see Him for who He is."

A strange sensation stole over DeeDee—a feeling unlike anything she'd ever experienced. A certainty that Nick spoke truth. How could she not have seen it before?

"I get it, Nick." She grasped onto his arms, hanging on as though he were her lifeboat. "I really do."

His smile radiated unearthly love as he embraced her.

"Sweetheart, you just gave me the best homecoming any man could ask for."

Chapter Thirty-Nine

The June sun came out from its hiding place and beamed into Ravenna Bible Chapel's high windows, burnishing the hair of Livy's bridesmaid, Paula, before it meandered across the stage to caress Brittany, then Renee, and finally DeeDee in their sapphire-blue dresses.

By the time the beam reached the groom and his groomsmen, Livy and Scott were husband and wife.

"You may kiss your bride!" Pastor White announced, and Livy flashed Scott the smile he loved as he lifted her veil and pressed his lips to hers. When he showed no sign of letting up after ten seconds, the cheers and applause turned to catcalls.

"Get a room!" someone shouted, and the place exploded. Livy and Scott, laughter bubbling over, pulled apart, grinning uncontrollably. Suddenly, the hooting crowd, the aromatic flowers, the church walls, all faded away, and it was just the two of them, husband and wife, sharing a chuckle.

"Ladies and gentlemen, may I introduce to you Mr. and Mrs. Scott Lorenzo!" Then they were half-running, half-limping, hand-in-hand off the stage, to Scott's car waiting to take them to Norse Hall for their reception and the big reveal.

They hopped into the back before the guests even knew they'd gone, and Scott's nephew Michael gunned it out of the parking lot. Between kisses, they whispered endearments all the way to the reception.

అఱఱఱ

After an hour of greeting guests and smiling until her jaw hurt, Livy longed to get up and dance. Even after DeeDee had removed the detachable train from her heavy Vera Wang gown, the pure white dress, dense with exquisite embroidery and layers of lace, weighed her down. Yet it couldn't touch her heart, as joyfully light as a happy-face balloon.

She forked the last bite of the chocolate-and-passion-fruit cake on her plate into her mouth and closed her eyes. Sweet chocolate cream glazed the zestiness the way Mom used to glaze their birthday cakes—oh, how Mom would have loved today. Sighing, Livy reopened her eyes. Only one of the five flowery tiers remained on the cake table. The two-layer, gluten-free carrot cake, not so popular. Only one-quarter gone.

Her handsome groom clutched her right hand; DeeDee clasped her left. Renee, on Scott's other side, patiently answered his nervous, last-minute questions about the choreography. What a trouper. He'd worked hard to master the unfamiliar moves, without the benefit of her years of experience. "You'll rock it," she whispered to him.

The rest of the bridal party had scattered throughout the ballroom. The roughly five-hundred guests had consumed the catered lunch and now Livy caught some of them edging expectant looks toward their table.

She turned to whisper in DeeDee's ear. "I think it's time for me to go change."

DeeDee grinned and nodded, then whispered something to Nick beside her. When Livy stood, Renee gave her a reassuring smile and pat on the back. She and DeeDee threaded through the curious crowd to the ladies' room, where Livy replaced the gown with a white skirt-and-leotard combo.

Back in the ballroom, DeeDee approached the sound booth at the rear, and within seconds, Ed Sheeran's voice resounded through the room—"Thinking Out Loud," the bride and groom's cue to meet on the dance floor.

Livy glided to the middle, where her groom waited, not once taking his eyes off her. Scott had removed his tuxedo jacket, and his crisp white shirt reflected in his smile. As the two of them stood facing each other, the lights dimmed, the room quieted, and Livy could almost hear the questions and whispers. How can she dance with that limp? So far, nobody had been rude enough to mention the elephant in the room, but judging by the skeptical silence, they were very much aware of it.

She curtsied, then smiled at her groom. Murmurs tried to distract her, but she closed her ears to them and focused on her husband, sending up a silent prayer. She hadn't performed publicly since her accident. Every eye in the room watched her. Despite their hours drilling with Renee, so much could go wrong. She could leap off-balance and come down crooked. Her leg could give out on her...

"Ready?" her husband whispered. You can do this, his expression said.

It was showtime.

Deep breath. Close eyes, center yourself. Dramatic pose, ballet hands extended, weight against Scott's arm.

When the vocalist sang about legs that no longer work like before, Scott, his eyes overflowing with love and understanding, embraced her around her waist and spun her on her right foot as if she were a jewelry-box ballerina.

When Sheeran sang that he couldn't sweep his love off her feet, Scott proved him wrong by swinging Livy around in a scissor lift. So far, so good. *Please, leg, don't give out on me. Scratch spin, plié, layback, extend, repeat.*

When the singer promised to love her until he was

seventy, she read the same promise in Scott's eyes and hoped he saw the same unspoken message in hers.

Someone whooped. Someone else started clapping. Soon the crowd's energy shot adrenaline into her veins, and she felt her face respond in sync as Scott effortlessly lifted her into the aerial move they'd practiced—the grand finale. He spun her round and round, as though they were an Olympic ice-dancing couple with the world's eyes on them, then slowly lowered her toes to the floor.

The standing ovation made all their hard work, all the long hours, worth it. They'd done it! She'd truly danced again for the first time since her accident. She couldn't squelch the uncontrollable grin if she tried. She and Scott bowed, over and over. Then he led her back to the table, accompanied by more shouts and applause.

She plopped in her chair, where Renee, DeeDee, and the other bridesmaids took turns hugging her and squealing out their congratulations. Livy, drained, could only smile. The adrenaline overdose had exhausted her.

Of course, Dad had to replace DeeDee at the sound booth so he could boom out his well wishes. "Attention, ladies and gentlemen!"

Murmuring voices died down as they all gave Declan Decker full attention.

He clutched a champagne goblet. "When I met my future son-in-law, the first thing I noticed was his high level of intelligence. The second thing I noticed was how much he loves my daughter. I thought to myself, 'Here's a man smart enough to know quality when he sees it.'" Chuckles echoed. "As I've gotten to know him, he's impressed me with his integrity. He was even man enough to stand up to yours truly. I admit I was getting a little too enthusiastic with the wedding gifts"—he glanced over at Livy, meeting her eyes in silent communication—"but he finally told me, 'Back off, buddy.'

Of course, those weren't his words. He was polite about it." His gaze still poured into Livy's. "I want to make a public promise to my daughter and son-in-law right here, right now. If I ever start interfering in your lives, all you have to do is say stop. And I will."

Scott hugged Livy closer as they grinned at each other. Dad held the goblet aloft. "Let's toast to the newlyweds!"

Livy and Scott linked arms and shared the traditional wedding toast. Cameras flashed all around her.

Dad cut a beeline in Brittany's direction, extended his hand, and escorted her to the dance floor.

"Want to cut out early?" Scott whispered in Livy's ear as other couples followed.

She nodded, as anxious as Scott to get a head start on their honeymoon. "We should probably stay a little longer, so they won't think we're rude."

Now that her big moment was past, half-hearted enthusiasm battled with exhaustion as the guests danced. DeeDee and Nick put on a show, dipping and spinning like they were on *Dancing With The Stars*. "Five more minutes," she whispered to Scott. "Then I'll throw the bouquet, and we can sneak out of here."

Five minutes elapsed at a maddeningly slow pace. DeeDee and Dad cleared the dance floor and beckoned Livy forward. Preparing to throw her bouquet into the bevy of single women, she winked at DeeDee, who moved into place. Livy turned her back and tossed it just the way they'd practiced. When she swiveled around, DeeDee brandished the bouquet, and Nick grinned and playfully ducked his head when everyone's eyes turned his way.

With DeeDee's and Michael's assistance, they encountered no obstacles when they headed outside to the waiting limo. They climbed in, and at last, they sped on their way to their honeymoon hideaway near SeaTac, where they'd board a plane to Hawaii tomorrow morning. Once the driver exited the lot, Scott snugged Livy tight against him, his eyes inches from hers. "I love you madly, Mrs. Lorenzo."

"I love you more, husband of mine."

"Aren't you glad we waited?"

"It was one of the hardest things I've ever done."

"But it's going to be worth it." His gaze burned with intent. "You'll see."

His mouth came down firm on hers, and they shared their first private kiss as husband and wife—long, intense, and deep. Livy never wanted to come up for air.

Chapter Forty

Sunbeams over Victoria cast multicolored rays through St. Paul's stained-glass windows and into the sanctuary. DeeDee, kneeling at the altar beside her soon-to-be husband, looked up into a rainbow. Livy, Renee, and Brittany clutched periwinkle-blue bouquets as they stood solemnly beside her. Her heart swelled. *Thank You, God.* No doubt, His way of shining a blessing over her and Nick's brand-new marriage.

She caught Livy's eye and smiled. Livy gave a knowing nod. To Livy, almost everything was a "God Thing". But DeeDee no longer minded her constant references. In fact, she didn't even begrudge Livy her newlywed glow after a month of happily wedded bliss. The same glow, enhanced by the rainbow from heaven, warmed her own face today.

The priest's words drew her back to the moment. Time to light the unity candle. As she and Nick took two tapers and united them as one, she nearly lost herself in his eyes, shining with pure love.

The long wait had been worth it.

"Ladies and gentlemen, I present to you Mr. and Mrs. Nicholas Rush!"

Down the aisle they dashed, hand-in-hand. DeeDee scanned the filled seats, trying to catch people's eyes, and nearly stumbled at an unexpected sight halfway back.

Leon. Sitting with Senior, Lisa, and his biological father, Erik. She hadn't dreamed Leon would actually show his face here, even though Nick insisted on inviting him. How could Leon attend Nick's wedding after what he did?

Lisa caught her eye and gave her that warm slanted smile, but DeeDee's had frozen into a stiff grimace. When they reached the lobby, DeeDee found Nick's arm and forced him to a stop, waves of alarm eroding her excitement. "Nick, did you see Leon? I can't believe he's here."

His startled face relaxed in a nod. "I suspected he'd show up after my long talk with him the other night." He steered her out the door and into the limo waiting to take them to the reception. "He knows I've forgiven him, and I trust he'll eventually repay me. We're on good terms now."

"Still." After the discoveries she'd made—the repercussions had tilted Leon's world one-hundred eighty degrees. What would she say to him? And Senior—surely, he must be hurt and angry over learning his only son was not really his. How could she face him?

"You know, I give him kudos. He returned a lot of the stolen goods, including all the band equipment he'd hidden in a storage unit behind his father's restaurant."

"Did Senior know?"

"I don't think so."

Thoughts and memories swirled through her head, and she hardly noticed when Nick cuddled her next to him in the back seat of the limo.

"Hey," he murmured in that smushy voice he got when he was feeling romantic.

"Hey, hubby." *Get a hold of yourself, girl. This is your wedding day!*

Focusing on her fine, tuxedo-clad husband pushed thoughts of Leon and Senior to the back of her mind. A girl couldn't ask for a better-looking life partner.

As for Junior and Senior…*God, give me the words to say to them.*

❧❧❧

DeeDee had to force her face muscles to keep smiling after the first fifty or so guests had greeted her. Her feet hurt in their spike heels, and she longed to be alone with Nick.

Still no Leon or Senior. She stifled a relieved sigh. Maybe they'd decided not to attend the reception, and she wouldn't have to face them after all.

A sixth sense, an intangible awareness, made her turn her head. There stood Leon at the entrance twenty feet away, eyeballing her as though she were the only person in the room.

His gaze darted away. She clung tighter to Nick's hand and spoke in an undertone. "Here they come."

"Who?"

"Junior and Senior."

About twenty bodies stood between her and Leon. Could she make an excuse to go sit at the wedding party's table? Everyone else was partaking of the catered luncheon—why couldn't she?

"Sweetheart, they aren't here to hurt you. I promise."

Then why was Leon giving her that hard stare?

Someone seized her around the shoulders. "Congratulations, girlie-girl!" When the person pulled back, DeeDee looked upon Devon, the waitress from Quaking Aspen. "You're the luckiest girl in the world. See? Look at Nick's face. He agrees with me." Devon laughed and gave Nick a playful slap on the arm, then moved on.

The reception line was moving much too quickly. If only she could slow it down, at least for a few minutes. People kept interrupting her thoughts, and she had no time to prepare what she'd say to Leon and Senior.

She kept the fake smile plastered on, received guests' hugs and well wishes, and before she knew it, Erik stepped in front of her.

She didn't even have time to think. He folded her into a

hug. "I'm so happy I can call you my sister in Christ now." He patted her shoulders. "God's blessings to both of you."

Lisa embraced her, then cupped DeeDee's face. "Such wonderful news. We're so happy for you."

DeeDee wasn't sure if she was referring to her new walk with Christ or her new marriage. Either way, it felt good, at least for the few seconds before Senior snagged her hand with one of his and her shoulder with the other.

"I wish you all the best," he said, his easy smile emphasizing his words. Not a trace of animosity darkened his eyes. Apparently, he wasn't blaming her for turning his and Leon's world topsy-turvy. Not to mention Erik's. He shifted to Nick, and then Leon was in her face, pumping her hand like he'd had one too many espresso shots.

"Hey, congratulations." He displayed shiny white teeth, his close proximity to Erik only emphasizing the resemblance—his bald spot, the identical gestures, the narrow features so similar to Jazzy's. How had everybody missed it?

Of course, Pam had seen it. And she'd been killed for it.

His jerky voice echoed through her head. "Hey, I owe you a big thanks for what you did."

Her jaw dropped. "Thanks for what?"

His already-narrow eyes slitted, and his face went hard. "For saving me from that bi—I mean, from my wife. I would be dead if you hadn't gone to bat for me."

She hadn't exactly gone to bat for Leon. It had all been for Nick. But if the belief made his life bearable, what could it hurt? Life couldn't be easy for him right now, being on probation and having lost his job. Not to mention losing his mother.

His voice dropped, and she leaned in to hear him over the din of voices, vaguely aware that a wedding reception wasn't the most appropriate context to discuss a crime, but unable to contain her curiosity. Clearly, Leon needed to unburden himself.

"When my mom told Jazzy and me about the DNA test, we didn't want to believe her. But the more I thought about it, the more I could see, you know, how it could be true. But Jazzy...I just thought she was in denial."

The truth had been far worse.

"Thank God, I was in jail where she couldn't get to me. Even though she's the one who put me there." Bitterness darkened his words.

DeeDee gasped. "Jazzy was the anonymous tipster?"

He nodded and wrung his hands. "She wanted me out of the way so she could transfer all our money to some account only she had access to. But once I got out, she was gonna make sure I was history."

"Oh, Leon." She blinked once, then twice, when tears prickled her eyes. "What Jazzy meant for evil, God meant for good." She cringed at the clichéd phrase, yet here was proof of its reality.

Her heart twisted. She'd pegged Leon as the bad guy. Yes, he'd made bad choices. But judging from his sincere expression, his eyes exerting hope, he'd made some much-needed changes.

On impulse, she threw her arms over his shoulders and patted his back. "Thank you, Leon. I needed to hear that."

The thirty-something couple behind Leon had been shooting daggers at his back with their eyes for two minutes, clearing their throats repeatedly. "Excuse us," the man said in a voice of strained civility. "We'd like a turn, if you please."

Leon jerked a glance at them, waved to DeeDee, and received Nick's bear hug. DeeDee stood stunned, not hearing the greetings, her face encased in plastic. She could hardly wait to talk this over with Nick. When would this day be over?

Nick seemed to sense her emotional state, for he pressed her hand twice, his way of saying, Hey, I'm here for you. She sought his eyes, and he winked.

She returned his wink. "Did you hear that?"

Ignoring the approaching guests, he grinned and nodded. "It was a God thing."

"Isn't God amazing?"

Epilogue

DeeDee clasped Livy's hand and glanced out Livy and Scott's kitchen window. The only sign of life on this dreary December day was the arborvitae Scott had planted alongside the redwood fence. The permanently green leaves reminded her of the eternal life God had graciously gifted her.

Livy swung their clasped hands. "Know what today is?"

"Of course. It's Monday."

Livy gave DeeDee's hand a playful tug. "No, silly. One year ago I was newly engaged. And you were in Victoria with Nick."

"Oh yeah, that."

"So it's the perfect day to do this."

"You're right. Let's get those husbands on the phone."

Phone in hand, DeeDee crossed the room and leaned against the living room entryway. Livy went to stand by the front door, her phone poised.

DeeDee put her phone on speaker and tapped Nick's number while Livy dialed Scott.

Nick answered first. "Hey, my love."

"Sweetheart?" Scott's voice echoed from across the room. DeeDee lifted her right hand like a conductor.

"Hi, honey," they both said.

"Hey."

"How's your day?"

DeeDee could hardly contain her smile. "I've got some news." She kept her voice low so Scott wouldn't hear. She couldn't hear Livy's reply.

"What news?"

Livy met her eyes from across the room, signaling DeeDee to raise her hand again.

On the downbeat, they spoke in unison.

"We're pregnant!"

THE END

Dear Reader

I hope you enjoyed revisiting the McCreary twins as much as I enjoyed writing about them. If this is your first time with Livy and DeeDee, you might enjoy the first book in the Seattle Trilogy, Sapphire Secrets. I also wrote a prequel featuring Declan Decker as a young man, and the day he met the twins' mom. It's a fun short story called When Lyric Met Limerick.

If you enjoy reading about controversial topics in Christian fiction (and, to my surprise, there's quite a lot of us), check out the first book in my Golden State Trilogy, Paint the Storm. I'm currently working on its sequel, Paint the Desert, and plan to publish it before the end of 2018.

You can keep up with my publishing journey by subscribing to my website. My subscribers are the first to know of new books to hit the market, and also get chances to win free books. Sign up today!

Blessings to you,

~DVC

Acknowledgements

Thank you, God, for seeking me out while I was still a sinner, and bestowing your amazing grace and love over me. May Your glorious attributes shine through every page of this story.

Thank you, Deirdre Lockhart of Brilliant Cut Editing, for bringing the city of Victoria, and this manuscript, alive. To beta readers Julia, Joy, and Marcy. Thank you for agreeing to read my less-than-perfect draft, and your honesty in pointing out what didn't work. Thank you, awesome critique partners of Scribes 211 – Gail, Nicole, Linda, and Jim. You helped polish this story more than you know!

Many other fellow authors from American Christian Fiction Writers (ACFW) and Christian Indie Authors lent their assistance in various ways. Thank you all for your roles in this exciting project.

About the Author

Dawn V. Cahill, an indie author from the land of hipsters and coffee snobs, published her first book in 2015, a short story called *When Lyric Met Limerick*. She blogs about puppies, substance abuse, and single parenting...sometimes all in the same day. She's going to finish that novel she started at age 11 called Mitch and the Martians...someday. She has written several newspaper articles and more limericks than she can count. *Moonstone Secrets* is her third full-length novel. Email her at dawn@dawnvcahill.com, or find her on Facebook, Twitter, and her website. She is a member of American Christian Fiction Writers (ACFW).

If you enjoyed this novel, would you be so kind as to hop over to Amazon or Goodreads and let the world know what you thought of it?

99367082R00167

Made in the USA
Lexington, KY
17 September 2018